Praise for *New York Times* bestselling author

Lori Foster

"Foster hits every note (or power chord) of the true alpha male hero…a compelling read from start to finish."
—*Publishers Weekly* on *Bare It All*

"A sexy, believable roller coaster of action and romance."
—*Kirkus Reviews* on *Run the Risk*

"Bestseller Foster…has an amazing ability to capture a man's emotions and lust with sizzling sex scenes and meld it with a strong woman's point of view."
—*Publishers Weekly* on *A Perfect Storm*

"Foster rounds out her searing trilogy with a story that tilts toward the sizzling and sexy side of the genre."
—*RT Book Reviews* on *Savor the Danger*

"The fast-paced thriller keeps these well-developed characters moving…. Foster's series will continue to garner fans with this exciting installment."
—*Publishers Weekly* on *Trace of Fever*

"Steamy, edgy, and taut."
—*Library Journal* on *When You Dare*

"Intense, edgy and hot. Lori Foster delivers everything you're looking for in a romance."
—*New York Times* bestselling author Jayne Ann Krentz on *Hard to Handle*

Dear Reader,

I'm so excited that Harlequin HQN is reissuing one of my favorite short stories. Readers often tell me that they laugh while reading my books. But when writing them, I'm never sure if the content is as funny as I intend it to be or not.

In *Uncovered,* I know it's funny—because *I* still laugh just thinking about it. Once you read it, you'll know what I mean—and I'm certain you'll sympathize with the heroine even while cheering her on.

In *Tailspin* you'll meet my little fur baby, Tootsie— renamed Tish for the purposes of the story. She's my adorable little Chihuahua—now my only doggie, since Brock passed away (you met Brock, aka Butch, in *Riley*)—and she rules the house with her very tiny paw. All the cats love her, and bow to her demands. When we first got Tootsie, she was *exactly* like the dog in this story...right down to her fascination with bugs.

An Honorable Man is unrelated to the other stories, but given my love, gratitude and respect for the military, it's also a favorite.

I very much hope you enjoy the stories as much as I enjoyed writing them.

To catch up on all my books, be sure to check my website, www.lorifoster.com!

All my best,

Lori Foster

LORI FOSTER

HOT IN HERE

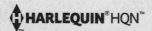

ISBN-13: 978-0-373-77816-4

HOT IN HERE

Copyright © 2013 by Harlequin Books S.A.

The publisher acknowledges the copyright holder of the individual works as follows:

UNCOVERED
Copyright © 2004 by Lori Foster

TAILSPIN
Copyright © 2004 by Lori Foster

AN HONORABLE MAN
Copyright © 2005 by Lori Foster

Recycling programs for this product may not exist in your area.

Printed in U.S.A.

www.Harlequin.com

CONTENTS

UNCOVERED

CHAPTER ONE

BECAUSE IT WAS DRIZZLING out, Harris Black pulled on a windbreaker before he headed outside to jog. Streetlamps left long slithery ribbons of light across the wet blacktop drive. After the heat of the mid-August day, the light rain had a sauna effect, making the air downright steamy.

He preferred jogging at night for two reasons: less human and automotive traffic, and Clair Caldwell.

Clair lived in the apartment building across the lot and always joined Harris in his evening run. For a dozen different reasons, Harris liked her a lot.

Unlike most women, Clair enjoyed the same things he enjoyed—televised sports, running, and junk food. Not once had she ever forced him to sit through a romantic comedy, thank God. But once, on a lazy Saturday afternoon, they'd watched the entire *Alien* series, back to back, without budging from the couch.

Clair's job fascinated him. When two well-respected private investigators relocated their offices close to Chester, Ohio, the town they lived in,

Clair had jumped at the chance to work for them as a receptionist. She was an adventurous sort and enjoyed the excitement of the job. But her duties went beyond secretarial. She was a computer guru, helping with online investigations, and an all-around know-it-all. She always had entertaining stories to share.

By the same token, she liked to hear about his work and his friends. Being a firefighter left him open to a lot of bawdy jokes, and Clair seemed to know them all. She teased him about the fires he put out, the length of his hose, and his specialized gear. But when he was serious, she was too, automatically picking up on his moods in a way no one else ever had. Even with his best friends, Buck, Ethan and Riley, he had to put on the occasional front. No one wanted a morose or moody friend, even if he'd just spent hours fighting a fire that sometimes didn't have the best conclusion. They always wanted to joke him into a better mood.

Not Clair. Once, after a really grueling car fire that resulted in two deaths, Clair had just sat beside him on the couch and held his hand. They'd stared at the television, but Harris knew neither of them was really paying any attention to the movie.

What mattered most about Clair, though, was the no-pressure tone of their relationship. He saw her when he wanted to, yet he never felt he had to call. Oddly enough, because of that, he called and hooked up with her often.

They hung out without any implied intimacy to muddy the waters. She didn't care if he shaved or if he ate Twinkies for lunch or if he stayed out all night with the guys. At first, her disinterest had bugged him, but after Ethan and Riley had up and married, Harris became leery of smiling women—and with good reason. The females had detected a nonexistent pattern of matrimony, and they pushed him constantly, to the point that he'd about given up dating.

Which meant he was celibate and that sucked, but it beat dodging topics of "happily ever after." Nothing messed up good sex like a woman grasping too far into the future.

With Clair, sex was never an issue. It just didn't come up. They were friends, totally at ease with each other, but neither of them ever crossed the line. It was such a relaxing relationship that he spent more time with Clair than with his buddies. Of course, Ethan and Riley now preferred the company of their wives, anyway.

As Harris stepped out from beneath the building's overhang, a fat raindrop landed on his nose. Given the heavy static in the air, he knew it'd be storming before they finished their run. He sprinted across the lot at the same time that Clair's doors opened and she strolled outside. Harris stared toward her with a smile.

Her personality put her somewhere between an egghead and a jock; she loved sports of all kinds, and was almost too smart for her own good. But no matter what the situation, and despite a lack of feminine flair, Clair always looked stylish. Granted, it was her own unique style, but her appearance was always deliberate, not one created out of lack of taste or time.

A few weeks ago she'd cut her glossy, dark brown hair shorter, and now she wore it in a stubby ponytail that looked real cute. She'd attached an elasticized band to her black-framed, oval glasses to hold them on her head while she ran. Somehow, on Clair, the look of an athletic librarian worked.

With her hair pulled back that way, Harris noticed for the first time that she didn't have pierced ears. In fact, he realized he'd never seen Clair with jewelry of any kind. Odd. In this day and age, he thought every grown woman had her ears, if not other body parts, adorned. But then he'd always known Clair was different from other women.

At five feet five inches tall, she would be considered medium height except that she was all legs. Very long, sexy legs that even in clunky running shoes looked great. Tonight she had those gams displayed in comfortably loose, short shorts. Like Harris, she'd made a concession to the rain and wore a nylon pullover.

Harris looked up at the black sky. There was no moon, no stars to be seen through the thick clouds. Branches on the trees bent beneath an angry wind.

Debris scuttled across the road. "Looks like we'll get one hell of a storm tonight."

"Backing out on me, sugar? Afraid you'll melt in the rain?" She swatted him on the ass. Hard. Then took off.

Grinning, Harris followed. "Paybacks are hell, sweetheart."

To tease him, she put a little extra sway in her backside for a few steps, then she got serious again. They ran side by side, silent except for the slapping of their sneakers on the damp ground and the soughing of their steady breaths. Within fifteen minutes, the drizzle changed into a light rain. Clair said nothing, so Harris didn't either. He could take it if she could.

After about a mile, Harris glanced toward her. She wore a concentrated expression, and her short ponytail, now darker with rain, bounced in time to her long stride. "Anything interesting happen at work today?" he asked.

She scrunched up her brow. "Dane caught a guy screwing around on his wife." Disgust dripped from her tone. "Dane was pissed when he came in to file it. Said the wife was real sweet and better off without the guy, but that she was bawling her eyes out."

"Shame." Harris didn't want to marry, but if he ever did, he knew he'd be a faithful hound. He thought spouses who cheated were lower than slugs. If you wanted to screw around still—as he did—then you shouldn't say the vows.

Clair pushed a little harder, her feet eating up the ground with a rhythmic slap, slap, slap. "I wouldn't cry." Her hands balled into fists and she picked up her pace even more until they were running instead of jogging.

"What would you do?"

The seconds ticked by and she slowed, gradually going loose and limber once again. With an evil, anticipatory grin, she said, "I'd take a ball bat to him. *Then* I'd leave him."

"Effective." Harris laughed. "But I think that's illegal."

"Yeah. Well, I'd find some way to make him pay—"

A slash of white lightning illuminated the entire area, followed by a crack of thunder that seemed to rip the night. They both pulled to a startled halt.

"Wow." Clair propped her hands on her knees, breathing hard, wide-eyed in awe of Mother Nature's display.

"This is nuts. Come on." Harris grabbed her arm and hauled her toward the main street. "Time to head back." Normally they'd take the long route to extend their jogging time, but now Harris just wanted to have Clair safely out of the storm.

She didn't protest, but then that was another of Clair's assets—sound common sense. He'd found it rare for people to have both book smarts and everyday logic. But Clair had both, which was another reason he liked her so much.

They were within minutes of their apartments when the rain turned into a deluge, soaking them through to the skin in a matter of seconds, making visibility nil. The sewers couldn't handle the flow and the streets filled like creek beds, washing icy water up past their ankles. With the help of the wind, the rain stung like tiny needles, making Harris curse. Trying to protect Clair with his body, he steered them toward a closed clothing shop and into a dark, recessed doorway. The opening was narrow, forcing them close together. Clair didn't seem to notice the intimate proximity.

Her hair was plastered to her skull, her entire body dripping. She shivered, but she didn't complain. "You think it'll let up soon?"

Another fat finger of lightning snaked across the ominous sky. The accompanying thunder shook the ground beneath them. "No. But we'll wait here a few minutes to see."

With a sigh, Clair pulled off her glasses, now beaded with rain. Lifting her pullover, she located a dry patch on her T-shirt beneath, and wiped them off. In the process, Harris got a peek at her belly. Not much of a peek, considering it was dark as Hades and she stood so close her elbows kept prodding him. He narrowed his eyes, straining to see her better.

She noticed him peeking—and flashed him,

yanking both her pullover and tee above her breasts for a single split second. Startled, Harris shot his gaze up to her face.

She grinned. "There, did that take care of your curiosity?"

He almost strangled on his tongue. "No." It took his brain a moment to assimilate what he'd seen, and then he asked, "Is that a sports bra?"

Laughing, Clair elbowed him, harder this time so that he grunted in discomfort. He crowded closer still, stealing some of her warmth and hindering her more violent tendencies.

"Yeah, as concealing as a bathing suit top, so put your eyeballs away. You didn't think I'd actually show you anything important, did you?" She tsked. "The rain must have made your brain soggy."

"I saw a flash of white," Harris argued, "and didn't know if it was boobs or cloth. Can't blame a guy for wanting clarification."

"I don't have enough boob to go around show-ing them off."

In the crowded confines, with icy rain blowing in against his back, there was no way to get comfort-able. Harris flattened one hand on the wall behind her and leaned in a bit, inching farther away from the storm—and closer to Clair. With his gaze zeroed in on her chest, he murmured, "You have enough," and he meant it.

"Spoken like a loyal friend. Thanks." And before

Harris could say more on that topic, she went on tip-toe to look over his shoulder. "Hey, the rain's letting up a little. Looks like the worst of the storm is moving away from us. Let's get home before we freeze."

The rain *was* cold, and with it, the temperature had dropped by at least ten degrees. Not that Harris was especially chilled. Discussing a woman's upper works with her, even a woman he wasn't intimate with, had a decisive effect on his libido. Given that the woman was also pressed up against him—well, he was having some surprisingly lascivious thoughts. But then, he'd been on a month-long, self-imposed dry spell. Under those circumstances, just about anything could turn him on.

Maybe on his next day off he'd have to break down and take his chances with a little one-on-one comfort of the female kind.

Together, he and Clair continued on their way, not jogging now, but not exactly taking their time either. Since Clair stayed silent, Harris had too much time to think. About her boobs.

He gave her body a surreptitious look without turning his head. The cold had tightened her nipples, and with her clothes wet and clinging, there was no way to miss it. His pulse sped up a bit, doing more to warm him than their jaunt.

The snug sports bra didn't allow for much jiggling, but he judged her to be a B cup. Plenty enough there to fill his hands. Well, not *his* hands, but some other guy's... No, he didn't like that thought either. Not that he had any claim on Clair other than friendship. But the idea of her snuggled up and intimate with some faceless, nameless bozo didn't sit right. Harris shoved the disturbing image away and concentrated on her comment.

Why did women assume men were only drawn to pinup models? A woman was a woman was a woman. Each different, each sweet and soft in her own way.

"Hurry up, slowpoke. I swear, my granny could move faster than you."

Maybe not so sweet, Harris admitted to himself with a grin. But definitely soft. He fell behind another step and took in the sight of Clair's full bottom. No lack of curves there. Yep, even egghead jocks were soft when you looked in the right place.

Clair turned to face him, walking backward. "Want a cup of hot chocolate? I'm going to make me some."

Her glasses were beginning to fog over, her ponytail was more out of its band than in, and water dripped from her ears.

Harris shook his head. "Can't. I'm on first shift this week. I need to get home, shower, and hit the sack." As a firefighter, Harris had a rotating schedule. The good part was that every third week he got extra days off, and the third week was rolling around.

"Okay." They were only feet away from his apartment building. Clair turned back around to head across the street. "I'll see you tomorrow then."

Harris took swift advantage. The moment she presented him with the opportunity, he landed a stinging swat on her behind. Given that her shorts were wet, it had a little more impact than he'd intended.

Her hands slapped over her butt in shock. Before her gasp of outrage had a chance to fade away, Harris darted to his side of the street, barely muffling his chuckles. "Good night, Clair!"

He bounded up the steps to his apartment, but waited at the door, watching as he always did until Clair had time to get inside. She rubbed her bottom as she climbed her own steps, muttering and casting him dirty looks. Moments later, a light came on in her living room, then Clair was at the window, waving to him. Harris waved back.

At first, Clair had objected to his protectiveness. But he'd worn her down until now she did the routine by rote. While he waited, she went in and checked out her place, then waved to let him know she was safely inside. Alone.

One of these days she'd have a boyfriend to look after her. But until then, Harris didn't mind keeping watch. In fact, he insisted on it.

Within half an hour he was showered and stretched out in bed, his hands folded behind his head. He should have been relaxed, but instead his naked body hummed with tension. He listened to the drubbing of rain on the windows, the continual rumble of thunder, and he watched the strobe effect of the lightning on his ceiling.

Storms always made him horny.

Touching women's butts made him horny.

Was Clair making him... No. He scoffed at himself, even laughed out loud in the silence of his dark room. That was just nuts. He wouldn't think about her that way.

Determined to get to sleep, he closed his eyes, metered his breathing—and saw again that flash peek of Clair's belly and sports bra. He groaned, and gave up the fight, allowing himself to ease into a very vivid dream where he stripped Clair naked, kissed her from head to toe, and loved every minute of it. The dream was both disturbing in its intensity and comforting in the rightness of it.

Sometime during the night, the storm knocked out the electricity. His internal clock woke him to a dark house and street, and the continuation of the storm. Without being able to make coffee or catch the morning news, he headed into work early. And good thing, too, because not five minutes after he dashed through the pouring rain into the station, the fire alarm went off. Lightning had struck the back of an abandoned building and someone saw smoke.

When Harris caught the address of the building, his heart shot into his throat. It was his block—*right next door to Clair*. Not since his first year as a firefighter had he suffered the debilitating effects of fear, but damn it, he felt them now. Even with the drizzling rain, the high wind could spread a fire quickly. Without electricity, Clair might sleep late, unaware of the danger. Worry plagued Harris all the way to the location.

But the moment the fire engine blared onto the street, Harris saw the crowd. Umbrellas formed a large canopy around the area, as if everyone had crawled from their beds and braved the weather for a show. Clair still looked sleep-rumpled under her cheery red umbrella, but she was fully dressed and in charge of things. In typical Clair mode, she urged curious onlookers farther away from possible harm. Harris was so relieved to see her he nearly fell off the truck. But knowing she was safe, he put her from his mind to do the job he'd been trained to do.

The storm was a real bother. Even through his Bunker Gear of fire-retardant jacket and trousers, helmet, and pull-on boots, he got soaked. The fire hadn't done too much damage yet, mostly to the exterior rear wall where the lightning had hit.

The abandoned structure had been up for lease for over six weeks and wasn't in the best of shape anyway. There were already broken windows in back and debris everywhere. In the process of putting out the blaze, a forgotten metal Dumpster in the back alley got knocked over. It was packed full, but luckily, not with the type of trash that got more disgusting

with time. Mostly papers, probably from the previous businessman. In less than an hour, they had everything taken care of. The rain had let up and the
sun even struggled to shine through the gray clouds.

Harris pulled off his helmet, wiping soot and rain
and sweat off his face. He was contemplating all the
mess, both from the spilled trash and the damage of
the fire, when Ethan, a fellow firefighter and one of
his best friends, let out a whistle. Harris turned, saw
Ethan riffling through a shoebox from the Dumpster,
and raised a brow. Usually that absorbed expression
on Ethan's face was reserved for his wife, Rosie. Harris went to investigate.

"Whatcha got?"

Without looking up, Ethan said, "Pictures of a
naked woman."

"No shit?" Harris forgot his fatigue for the moment and muscled his way next to Ethan. Yep, sure
enough, that was an unclothed female. A very sexy,
naked female. "Wow."

Harris picked up one photo of her reclining facedown on a twin bed. Her mussed hair was long
enough to hide her face, but who cared when she
had a beautifully bare backside on display? Harris
tried, but he couldn't look away.

"Check out this one." Ethan handed him another.

The same woman, judging by the shape of her
body, was stepping into the tub. Again, she had
her face averted as she moved the shower curtain

aside, but this shot showed her entire body in profile. Breasts, belly, long sleek thighs. Harris let out
a slow breath. "*Hello* sweetheart."

"Wonder if she lives around here," Ethan com-
mented. "Or maybe she was the last one to lease
the building."

"The last person here was a guy. I never met him,
but I saw him occasionally." Harris peered toward the
shoebox Ethan held. "Any more pictures in there?"

"One more—of her pulling on her panties." Ethan
laughed. "You still can't see her face, but it's a damn
fine rear shot."

Feeling strangely territorial, though he didn't
know why, Harris snatched the photo away from
Ethan. "Let me have that."

"Hey, I was going to keep it."

"No way. You'd just show it to Buck and Riley."

Ethan raised both brows. "So? How come you get
to look and we don't?"

"You must've forgotten, but you and Riley are
married now."

"I'm still swimming in marital bliss, so how could
I forget?" He grinned as he said that.

"Then think what Rosie will do," Harris murmured while studying the photo with rising heat, "if
she catches you ogling some strange naked woman."

Looking much struck, Ethan said, "She'd probably kill me. Here." He shoved the entire shoebox
into Harris's arms. "There are notes and such, too.

Maybe an address, since you're so interested. And so single."

Wincing, Harris said, "Don't tell me you've taken up the campaign to get me hitched, too?"

"No, I like women too much for that."

"Ha ha."

"But Rosie wants you and Buck both married so I can't be around any of your single female friends." With a lot of satisfaction, Ethan added, "She's a jealous little thing."

"She trusts you."

"Yeah, but she doesn't trust the women you two date." Ethan strode away, giving orders as he went.

Harris didn't bother to reply to that jab. Buck might still be going strong, but Harris hadn't dated *anyone* lately. Rosie could rest easy on that score.

Now the woman in the picture... If he could look her up he just might be interested. Strolling over to lounge against the back wall of the alley, Harris held his helmet under his arm and rummaged through the shoebox. Unfortunately, he didn't find any addresses, but he pulled out one folded sheet of paper. Confusion reigned around him, but he gave all his attention to the feminine script on the note.

I'm sorry for just leaving a note. I know you wanted me to call, but there's no point. You'd just try to convince me to go with you, but it's

over. It's not you, so please don't think of this
as an insult. You knew how I felt all along.

I'm hung up on Harris.

Harris's eyes widened. Talk about coincidences.
How many guys could there be with that name? It
wasn't like a Tom, Dick or Harry.

It'd be tough for any other guy to measure
up to him. If being a firefighter isn't heroic
enough...

Harris nearly dropped the shoebox. Coincidence,
hell! She was talking about *him*. Suddenly feeling on
display, he glanced around the surrounding area, but
no one paid him any attention. The crowd had dis-
persed. Those who'd stopped to watch the firefighters work were now scuffling back into their homes.
The other firefighters were chatting, bitching about
the weather, generally just hanging around.

Harris swallowed hard and went back to reading.

...he's also funny. He makes me laugh all the
time. And he's so generous. You don't notice it
at first, because Harris likes to clown around,
but he's really very sensitive to other people.

No shit? Harris blinked in disbelief. She thought
he was sensitive?

He works hard and he's proud and I love him.
Again, I'm sorry.

She loved him. Wow. Harris looked, but there
was no signature, damn it. He turned the note over,
but no, it was blank. Who had written it? The idea
of a secret admirer tantalized him, made him feel
warm and full and anxious. He lifted another photo,
the one of her stepping into her panties, and smiled.
Sweet. Very sweet.

"Slug. Shouldn't you be helping out instead of
snooping through the garbage?"

Startled by the verbal intrusion, Harris glanced up
and got snared in Clair's disapproving green gaze.
Her hair was loose, parted on the side and hanging
in blunt lines to just skim the tops of her shoulders.
She had her head tipped forward a bit to look at him
over the rim of her glasses. Her eyes were twinkling
at the pleasure of insulting him. Obviously, *she* didn't
consider him sensitive.

"It's not garbage," he grumbled.

"No?" She went on tiptoe to peer over his shoulder.

Harris held the photo out of reach. "You don't
want to see this, Clair."

"I do too."

"I doubt that." He grinned, imagining her reaction if he showed her. "They're photos."

"That's private. You shouldn't be looking either."

"Someone threw them away." He shrugged. "Free for the pickings."

Hands on her hips, she demanded, "Let me see, Harris."

Prodded by the devil in him, Harris decided *why not?* With a flourish, he handed her the photo.

Her face went beet-red and she gasped so hard she nearly strangled. "Harris!"

"Hey, I'm not the photographer." He winked. "I just found it."

"That's…that's obscene."

"You really think so?" He took it back from her and stared some more before murmuring with great sincerity, "Nice ass."

"Pig."

Laughing, Harris searched through the box. "Here's another." He handed her the one of the woman getting into the shower. In that pose, she had one shapely leg bent, one arm raised. Gorgeous.

Clair narrowed her eyes and accepted the photo. After several moments scrutinizing it, a small frown pulled down her brows. But at least this time she didn't choke.

"And one more." Harris gave her his favorite, the one of the woman reclined in bed. He thought she might be sleeping, she looked so boneless and re-laxed. Her back was smooth and graceful, rising up to a plump rump, then tapering down again to long thighs and shapely calves.

Clair stared so long that Harris cleared his throat. "Anytime you're done with it…"

"Oh, sorry." She looked bothered about something, then glared. "I can dispose of those for you if you want."

"Not on your life." Harris held the photos protectively out of her reach. "I'm keeping them."

Clair's mouth fell open. "Keeping them? But that's…lecherous! You don't even know that woman." And then in a smaller voice: "Do you?"

"Nope. But I know she has a major case for me." He tapped the letter. "Says so right here."

Clair went white. She tried to grab the note. "You just said you don't know her."

"I don't. Yet. But she obviously knows me." Harris opened the paper and pointed out his name. "Harris the firefighter. Gotta be me, right?" He folded it and put it back in the shoebox for safekeeping. "So actually, this pertains to me. I have a right to this stuff."

"You're sick."

"I'm in lust." Harris touched her nose. "But then, you wouldn't know about that, would you, Clair?"

Her back snapped straight. "What the hell is that supposed to mean?"

"I'm just saying that you don't date much. Now if you'll excuse me, I gotta get to work."

Smiling sweetly, Clair said, "Want me to hold that shoebox for you?"

"No." Harris laughed at her fallen expression.

"I'm going to run it over to my place and lock it inside, safe and sound."

The way her jaw worked, Harris thought she might be grinding her teeth. "So you can stare at the photos and fantasize tonight?"

"Don't sneer, Clair. It makes you look like a prude." As he walked away, Harris heard Clair call him a choice name. He glanced around in time to witness her stomping toward her apartment. Too bad Clair didn't understand about lust. If she ever turned all that emotion loose in the sack, she just might be magnificent.

Harris caught his train of thought and growled. He'd better find his mystery lady soon, because lack of nookie was making him crazed.

He needed a woman—his mystery woman. Sexy. Provocative. And she thought he was sensitive. What more could a guy ask for?

CHAPTER TWO

THANKS TO THE DUAL effects of worry and mortification, Clair suffered through an endlessly long, sleepless night and was dragging as she headed into work the next day.

Thank God Harris hadn't recognized her.

Just thinking about his expression as he'd stared at her—Clair shuddered in agonizing horror. This was too unbelievable. If she ever found Kyle, the jerk she'd dated, the jerk who'd taken those pictures without her knowing, she'd strangle him.

During the darkest hours of the night, memories had flooded back on Clair, memories of Kyle begging her to let him photograph her, and the distinct recollection of her saying a firm, unequivocal *no*.

But she also recalled him showing off a teeny tiny camera, one he used to take photos without anyone knowing. At the time, he'd claimed it was to get candid, rather than posed shots of people for his gallery. And he had taken some, but to her knowledge, he'd never shown one without a signed permission slip and financial compensation.

At least he hadn't put hers in the gallery. But to throw them away behind the building…had the idiot never heard of a paper shredder? And to include her notes with them! Clair pulled into the lot where she worked and took a moment to cover her face with her hands. The only saving grace was that she hadn't signed any of the notes. If Harris had seen her signature at the end… Well, she honestly didn't know what he'd do.

It had taken Clair a moment to realize she was the subject of the photos. Her hair had been longer then, and her face hidden. But she had recognized herself. Harris, however, had been utterly oblivious to that fact. He plain and simply didn't see her as a sexual woman, which emphasized how little attention he paid to her femaleness.

That had been really frustrating over the past few months, but now she was more than a little grateful. She only hoped he never showed the photos to anyone. Even if no one ever guessed her identity, she couldn't bear the thought of people seeing her in the raw.

Because moping wasn't something she enjoyed, she shoved her car door open and stepped out into the blistering day. If the humidity had been bad before the storm, it was ten times worse now. Immediately her shirt stuck to her back, and even through her dressy, flat-heeled sandals, she could feel the scorching heat of the blacktop. As a concession to the weather, she wore a sleeveless cotton shirt and loose, flowing skirt. She slung a canvas bag over her arm and started in.

She'd use the day at work as a distraction to get her mind off nude photos, thickheaded men, and her jackass ex-boyfriend. At the moment, there wasn't anything she could do about any of them, so it was best not to dwell on it.

Cool air-conditioning rolled over her the moment she entered the building. Though she was early, Dane and Alec, the P.I.s she worked for, already had a client in the inner office with them. They'd relocated from the city so they'd have more free time for their wives and kids. But it seemed their small town was rife with drama, and they often stayed busy. At least here, though, the cases were seldom all that threatening.

Clair could hear their quiet conversation, see the movement of male bodies through opaque glass. She put her purse away and turned her computer on, then went straight to the coffeepot.

She already had things underway when Dane stuck his head out the door. "Clair, would you mind bringing in some coffee?"

"Not at all. It'll be done in two more minutes."

"Thanks." He ducked back inside.

Making coffee wasn't in her job description, but small requests never offended Clair. It helped that Dane and Alec were consummate gentlemen and didn't take her, or her talents, for granted. As often as not, they carried coffee to her.

A few minutes later, with sugar, powdered creamer and three mugs of steaming coffee on a tray, Clair used her foot to tap at the door. Alec opened it. He looked darker and more intense than usual, but then Alec could be a poster model for tall, dark and dangerous.

He gave her a nod. "Nothing like caffeine to kick off the day."

Clair smiled. "Tough case?"

"Different, that's for sure." He took the tray from her and she started to exit the office.

"Hey, Clair."

At the sound of Harris's voice, Clair froze in mid-step. *Oh no. Please, no.* Slowly, wincing with dread, she pivoted stiffly to face him.

He was at Dane's workstation—the cursed photos spread out on the surface.

Oh. Dear. God.

Heat rolled from her chest right up to her hairline, making her dizzy with the shock of it. For a single moment, Clair thought she might faint, especially when Dane picked up the shower shot for a closer look.

Alec rejoined the men, staring at *her* naked body with a frown. "Do you see any distinguishing marks? Moles or scars or anything?"

Clair's knees trembled, threatening to buckle.

"No. No jewelry either."

Did she have time to run out and get her ears pierced?

Dane shook his head. "Just lots of smooth skin. Maybe we should have these photos blown up."

Clair staggered back against the door. Blow them up? *Blow them up!* As in, make them…bigger? Her throat closed and she couldn't draw breath, couldn't say a single word. She tried to get out a denial, to dissuade them from that horrendous plan, but all that emerged was an appalled squeak.

Harris glanced her way, did a double take, then rushed toward her. "Damn, Clair, you okay?" He caught her arms and physically forced her into a chair. Good thing too, because she was about ready to sink to the floor. Maybe *through* the floor if she got lucky.

Over his shoulder, Harris said to Alec, "I think she's been in the heat too long this morning. You got a cold cloth or something?"

Alec was a man of action. Within seconds, he had a pad of paper towels, dripping with icy water from the rest room.

All three big men loomed around her, Harris trying to slap the wet towels against her face, Dane fanning her with a stack of papers, and Alec taking her pulse.

They'd seen her naked.

It wasn't to be borne. Never in her life had

she known such bone-deep humiliation, and it numbed her.

Harris reached for the top button of her blouse. "I'm going to loosen her clothes. She still looks too pale."

That brought Clair around. She shot to her feet, staggered, got steadied by six big hands, and shoved away from them all. She waved a fist with credible intent. "Touch my clothes and I'll brain you."

Harris straightened. He still looked concerned. "You're all right now?"

She wanted to die. "I, uh…you were right. It was just the heat. I'm fine."

Dane cocked a brow. "You're not pregnant, are you?"

Clair stared at him, aghast that he'd come to such a conclusion.

Alec nodded. "Celia stayed light-headed when she was pregnant. Especially when she got too warm."

Laughing, Harris said, "Clair's not even dating, so unless you can get pregnant from a toilet seat, I don't think that's the problem." He again tried to reach for her top button.

Clair swatted at him. "I'm not preg—"

"She dates," Dane argued. "Okay, not much, but I know a few months back she was seeing some guy."

Harris scowled. "She was?" He turned to Clair. "When were you dating? Who was he?"

Ohmigod. No way in hell was Clair going to talk

about Kyle. Not with his photographic efforts spread out in all their lack of glory on Dane's desk. She swallowed, found her voice, and rasped, "Enough. From all of you."

They stared at her. Three pairs of discriminating, curious eyes. Eyes that had just been looking at her in the most revealing poses.

"My personal business is none of your concern." And before Harris could object, Clair added, "We *jog* together, Harris. In no way does that entitle you to pry." *Even if you have seen me in the nude.*

Harris's eyes narrowed and he crossed his arms over his chest. "Keeping secrets?" His hot stare threatened to bring on a swoon. "I'll find out, you know."

Over her dead body! She tucked in her chin and summoned her most serious, meanest voice. "You'll leave me alone."

Dane cleared his throat. "So you two are good friends? I thought you were just neighbors."

Harris kept his gaze trained on Clair. "I told Dane and Alec that I learned about them through you."

Alec gave her a fierce, speculative glance. "You make me sound fearsome, Clair. I'm not sure if I should thank you or not."

She rolled her eyes. Alec Sharpe lived up to his reputation and he knew it. Marriage and kids hadn't softened him. He was still dark as the devil and so strong and imposing that even in his mid-forties, he intimidated men with a mere glance. Dane wasn't much better. Both men were walking icons of masculinity. Not that Harris seemed intimidated. No, if anything, he'd bonded. But then, in her opinion, Harris fit right in.

Dane put an arm around her. "Harris is right, Clair. You still look a little shaky. You want to take the day off?"

So they could get back to perusing her photos? Not a chance. "Of course not." Inspiration struck and she said, "You want me to take something to the developers for you? You mentioned enlarging some photos."

"I can do it on the scanner," Alec said, ruining her chances to steal the photos. "You just rest up and regain your breath. You sound wheezy."

Dane steered her toward her desk. "If you really want to help, you can do a search and find out who leased the building where the pictures and notes were found."

Alec picked up the photo of her putting on her panties, making her go pale, then red-hot again. "Assuming the last guy who lived there took them, we can hunt him up and ask him about the...model."

All three men grinned, and their humor in light of her disgrace rubbed Clair the wrong way.

"You know damn good and well that woman wasn't modeling."

"Probably not," Dane agreed. "But neither was she objecting."

Ready to blast him for his misassumption, Clair opened her mouth, but snapped it shut again. How could she explain without giving herself away? No, she hadn't objected because she hadn't even known the pervert was looking at her, much less that he had a camera. She'd only slept with Kyle twice, and both times were disastrous.

She hadn't realized how disastrous until she saw the sneaky photos.

Clair closed her eyes. "All right. Sure." She'd hunt from now till the end of time without giving them Kyle's name. If they had a name, Alec and Dane would find Kyle. And then the jig would be up.

In fact, if she forced herself to face reality, she knew they'd eventually find him even without her help. They were good. Better than good, they were the best. They were, as she'd often bragged to Harris, awesome. If enough opportunities arose for her to sabotage their efforts, she maybe had a month. Less, if they did some of the computer work themselves, as they occasionally did.

Harris paced to a window overlooking the back lot. "I hope you can find him. It's driving me nuts not knowing who she is."

If Dane and Alec hadn't been in the room, Clair would have kicked Harris in his sexy backside for that remark.

"We'll find him," Alec assured Harris. "Even if we don't, we'll figure out who she is. She had to be local, someone you come into contact with, maybe on a daily basis. Eventually someone will recognize her."

Spots danced in front of Clair's eyes. She gasped, drawing a lot of male attention. In a raw whisper, she pleaded, "Don't tell me you intend to show those photos to people?"

"No." Dane's statement allowed her heart to slow to a more normal pace, until he added, "At least not yet. We'll try other routes first."

"What other routes?"

He shrugged. "We'll hunt for the owner."

And with any luck, she'd find Kyle before they did and rip his heart out—or at least his tongue, so he couldn't tell them about her.

"We'll talk to photography shops to see if anyone remembers developing any photos like those."

A dead end for sure, since Kyle did his own developing. Not that it mattered, because by then her photos would have made the rounds of the neighborhood.

"But eventually it might come down to going door-to-door and asking about him or her or both."

"That's an invasion of her privacy," Alec explained, "so a last resort. But if all else fails…"

Clair knew that if she didn't get out of there right then, she was going to be sick. She plastered on a very false smile. "Well then, by all means, let me do my best to find him on the computer first." She went to her desk.

Unfortunately, Harris followed on her heels. "You feeling better?"

No, never. "I keep telling you, I'm fine."

"You're sure?"

She stared at him, adjusted her glasses, and said with succinct finality, "I'm. Fine."

Harris held up both hands. "All right, all right. Don't get in a temper. I have to get to work and I wanted to make sure you're up to jogging tonight, that's all. If you're not, then I don't want you to push it."

She didn't want to. She wanted to hide. But any variance in their routine right now might tip him off. She forced another fake smile. "I wouldn't miss it."

He nodded, still watching her curiously. "Great." He started backing toward the door. "I'll see you then."

Once the door closed behind him, Clair started to relax, but Alec didn't give her time. He came out of the office with the pictures in hand.

Straightening in her chair, Clair said, "He left them with you?" Maybe she could swipe them after all. Or spill coffee on them. Or...

"Not a chance. These are copies we ran off when he first got here. Your friend Harris is carrying the originals in his front pocket like a lovesick swain." Alec smiled. "Funny guy."

"He's an idiot."

"He has a secret admirer and he's hooked. It's understandable. Not only is the woman attractive and sexy as hell—"

"Being naked does not necessarily make her sexy."

Alec's slow smile looked positively wicked. "Yeah, it does."

Well, hell. Clair slumped under another wave of embarrassment. So all it took was a little nudity for a guy to find a woman sexy? How stupid was that? What about her personality? What about her interests?

Alec seemed to read her mind. "She said some pretty profound things about him in her notes, too. Any guy would be intrigued."

Profound? She'd only spoken the truth.

"I'm going to enlarge and enhance these," Alec said, tapping the copies against his thigh, "to see if I can pick up any details."

Details—like her identity? He disappeared into the backroom. Heart in her throat, her stomach in knots, Clair kept her eyes on that door for a full five minutes until Alec returned—carrying a stack of 8 x 10 photos.

The one on top was of her right shoulder, boob, and ribs.

Clair gulped. He'd taken each photo and divided

it into fours, then enlarged each piece. When put together, her buck-naked body would be poster size.

Worse and worse and worse. But Alec didn't so much as glance at her on his way back to talk to Dane, so he still hadn't recognized her.

It took her a few more minutes of slowly dying inside before she realized Dane must not have recognized her either. No one budged from the office. There were no outbursts of hilarity, no accusing stares. They were probably too engrossed with ogling the oversize photos.

And here she'd always considered Dane and Alec astute. What was she, invisible? Clair pulled off her tortoiseshell glasses and looked at them. Like Clark Kent's specs, were her glasses an ingenious disguise that instantly afforded her anonymity?

The door opened and Clair hastened to shove her glasses back on, almost poking herself in the eye. Her face burned. Much more blushing and she'd be permanently scalded.

Both men looked at her with expectant expressions. Clair shriveled inside, until Dane prompted, "Make any headway?"

She hadn't even started. "Oh. Um, no. Not yet. I'll keep looking."

"Thanks." Dane and Alec headed for the door.

"Where are you two going?" In a panic, Clair left her seat and rushed after them. Surely, they weren't going to show those pictures around *now*.

Alec barely slowed. "I have to appear in court, remember?"

"Oh yeah."

Dane paused. "I'm working on a missing person." He stopped and faced her with concern. "Are you sure you're okay, Clair?"

Did they have to keep asking her that? "Of course. I just forgot, that's all." Reluctantly, she asked, "What about the photos?"

"Harris is impatient, but we'll spend a week or two exploring alternatives before we show them to anyone."

Thank you, thank you, thank you. "I think that's best." She couldn't help adding, "Can you imagine how embarrassed she'll be if she finds out that you showed them?"

On his way out the door, Dane laughed and pointed at her. "A good reason to never pose nude, huh?"

Or date photographers with sneaky streaks and lack of moral fiber. Clair groaned. With everyone gone, she ran into Dane's office—and stumbled to a horrified halt. She pressed a fist to her mouth. They had the photos up on a pegboard. Pieced together.

Adrenaline carried her to the board in a flash. It took Clair all of thirty seconds to snatch them down and hide them under a stack of files, but she didn't dare destroy them. That'd look too suspicious, and what was the point? They'd only make more.

She dragged herself back to her desk and collapsed in her chair, her face in her hands, her stomach roiling. Sooner or later, they'd know it was her—and then she'd have to quit and move to Outer Mongolia.

Unless… She swallowed hard and tried to think beyond her embarrassment. It wasn't easy, but she tried to take an objective view of the situation.

First, Alec claimed Harris was smitten. And Harris had acted obsessed with the "mystery woman." Heaven knew she'd been obsessed with him forever. But he hadn't shown any sexual interest, and she was too proud to throw herself at him. So they were friends. Clair knew he liked her as a person, but she'd assumed he didn't find her attractive in "that" way.

But judging by his rapt expression when he'd looked at the photos, he definitely liked what he saw.

So, secondly, what did she have to lose now? Not her modesty. After today, she had no modesty to protect.

And as to her pride…well, pride didn't help much when you saw your own behind in an 8 x 10 glossy, held on a presentation board with a thumbtack.

Maybe, just maybe, if she worked this right, she could use her newfound knowledge of Harris's interest to make him fall in love with her—before he found out she was his secret admirer.

It was either that or tell him straight up that he'd seen her naked and that she'd written those notes.

He'd know all of her secrets then, leaving her soul as bare as her body. But if he felt the same, it wouldn't be nearly as embarrassing.

She'd probably have to seduce him, and that wouldn't be easy because she couldn't take off her glasses and she definitely couldn't take off her clothes. If she did, he might make the connection too soon. It'd be a tricky bit of business, but she'd figure something out. Maybe she'd just ensure they only got romantic in the dark. That might work.

Given Alec and Dane's expertise, there wouldn't be any time to waste. She'd jump-start Harris on their new relationship tonight. If she was good enough, maybe he'd even give up on the mystery woman and she'd never have to tell him anything at all.

HARRIS WAITED IMPATIENTLY for Clair to present herself. The storms had left the night air fresh and clean. It felt good, but it was warm. Deciding against a shirt, he wore only black jogging shorts with socks and running shoes. The shorts had a single back pocket to hold his apartment key—and the photo of his secret admirer reclining on the bed. He hadn't wanted to leave her behind.

Not that he intended to show it to anyone. He appreciated Dane and Alec's efforts to uncover the woman's identity, but already he felt protective and possessive of her. He didn't want anyone else, especially anyone male, to see her.

Something about her, some vague intangible thing, seemed familiar to Harris. He wished he could pin it down. Maybe she reminded him of someone. But who? While he stretched, preparing to run, his mind churned.

Work had been uneventful, which was a relief after the fire the day before. Unfortunately, that had given Harris too much time to think—about the notes, the sexy photos. And about Clair's old boyfriend.

Neither Dane nor Alec would give him any details on the guy. They claimed not to have any. They said they knew Clair had dated, because she'd gotten a few calls at work. Period. Nothing more. They didn't understand why he cared. Hell, he didn't understand either.

But why hadn't she told him? They were friends. Close friends. Didn't friends share that kind of info?

Harris's internal grumbling got interrupted when the entrance door to Clair's building pushed open and she stepped out. The streetlight reflected off the lenses of her glasses. She, too, had trimmed down to the barest covering. Dressed in snowy white cotton shorts and a tank top, she looked…good. Real good.

She smiled at him, adjusted the white band holding her glasses in place and joined him at the street. "Ready?"

Harris studied her. He figured it was the combined effects of sleeping alone, his mystery woman, and hearing about Clair's boyfriend that had him seeing her with a new perspective. "How come you've never gotten contacts?"

Bending this way and that, stretching her arms high, Clair asked, "Why? You don't like my glasses?"

"I didn't say that." Watching her flex was getting to Harris. She was a supple little thing. Funny how he'd never noticed that before.

Clair straightened, then stared up at him with her big green eyes, magnified behind the lenses of her glasses. "I tried contacts once, but they bugged me. I think my eyes are just too sensitive. Besides, I like wearing different frames."

"I noticed that." Tonight her frames were red, a stark contrast to the white shorts and tank. What she lacked in jewelry she made up for in eyewear.

"I have as many pairs of glasses as I do bras."

Harris did a double take. Bras? Why the hell did she have to mention her unmentionables? His besieged brain launched into a series of visuals: Clair in something white and lacy. Clair in something black and slinky. Clair in something barely there.

Clair in his bed.

She said again, "Ready?"

Oh yeah, he was ready all right. For all kinds of things. His gaze dipped to her breasts, but he didn't see any telltale signs of lace through her tee. "How many bras do you have?"

Laughing, Clair shook her head and started walking at a pre-run clip, leaving him two paces behind her. "What is this? Twenty questions?"

"It just occurs to me that I don't know you that well." He tried, but he couldn't seem to get his gaze off her ass. Was she sashaying just a bit? Putting a little extra swing in the swing and sway?

Turning to walk backward, depriving him of his preoccupation with her behind, Clair frowned. "You know me better than most people."

"I didn't know you had a boyfriend." Harris took satisfaction in pointing that out.

She turned her back again and started moving a little faster. "What'd you think, Harris? That I was a virgin? A nun? A misanthrope?"

"A misan-what?" Harris trotted to keep up.

"Misanthrope. You know, a hater of men."

"No." He was sure of one thing. "You like me and I'm a man."

Over her shoulder, she smiled at him, a smile unlike any he'd ever seen from Clair before. "That you are."

Harris's eyes widened. Was she flirting? Did Clair even know how to flirt? But her voice was different, too, sort of soft and playful. He caught up to her. "So who was the boyfriend?"

"No one important." They began jogging in earnest, gliding along smoothly. "Just a guy I knew who seemed nice enough and interesting enough to pass the time."

"You weren't serious about him?"

She snorted, giving Harris all the answer he needed—though why he needed an answer, he couldn't say.

They loped on in silence, past the dark, quiet park, along deserted streets where older homes sat back in majestic splendor, along the levy where a concrete path had been poured.

Their movements were fluid, well timed to match. They had a great rhythm together. Harris groaned. He could just imagine setting the pace in bed, and how easily Clair could keep up.

"So how many bras do you have?"

Her laugh got carried away on the evening wind. "At least one for every day of the week."

He thought about that. "A special one for each day?"

"No, just variety. Different colors, different fabrics."

Like French lace or slinky nylon or maybe... "What are you wearing tonight?"

"We're jogging, sweating. So it's plain old comfortable white cotton."

Somehow, when he pictured it on Clair, cotton didn't seem the least plain. He was wondering about her panties, whether they matched the bra or not, when Clair slowed, veered off the pavement to mosey into the grass, then leaned her shoulders against a thick maple tree.

That far from the street, the light of lampposts barely penetrated.

Immediately, Harris was beside her. "Hey, you okay?"

"Mmm-hmm." She tipped her head back and closed her eyes. "Just a little tired today."

She'd been pale earlier, unsteady on her feet, and now she was tired? Clair never got tired. Hell, usually he was the first to get winded when they ran, and he knew he was in extremely good shape. All firefighters were.

Come to that, so was Clair, and he didn't mean healthwise, although that applied too. Her white shirt and shorts reflected the scant moonlight, emphasizing certain swells and hollows, making her body look more feminine than ever.

She bent one knee, stuck the other leg out straight. The pose showed off the length of her long legs, causing Harris's mouth to go dry. Her dark brown hair, hanging loose tonight, lifted a bit with a gentle breeze. His fingers twitched with the need to smooth it back into place. He resisted.

Still with her eyes closed, Clair smiled.

"Why," Harris asked, full of suspicion now, "are you smiling like that?"

Her eyes opened, her head tilted. "Like what?"

"Like you have a secret."

For a single moment there, Harris thought he saw alarm flicker in her gaze. Then she straightened away from the tree. "Don't be absurd. Can't a woman smile?"

"Sure." He propped his hands on his hips. "When she's got a reason."

"I'm happy," Clair snapped, in a very unhappy tone. "I feel good. The air's fresh, your company, before just now, wasn't too heinous, and so I smiled." She shoved past him. "I won't make that mistake again."

Harris caught her arm and pulled her around. She slammed into his chest, but quickly back-stepped. "You get mad too easy, too fast."

She relented just a bit, tugging free of his hold and folding her arms around her middle. Sounding mulish, she said, "I'm not mad."

"No? Then what?"

She stared up at him, one expression after another crossing her features before she stalked in a circle around him. Harris turned, keeping her in his sights.

"You told me I wouldn't understand about lust."

Oh hell. First bras and now this. Except for the racing of his heart and a twitch of male interest, Harris went very still. "Yeah." *Shut up, Harris. Let it go....* "And?"

"You were wrong."

He shouldn't have pushed for an explanation. "I am, huh?"

She nodded. "I'm...antsy. The guy you were asking about? We broke up two months ago." She peeked up at Harris, all innocent temptation. "I haven't been out with a guy since."

No way could he have this conversation. Not with a platonic girlfriend. Not without a bed around. He took a step back. "Right. Gotcha. Maybe a, uh, run will help."

"No. I need to find a new guy." As if she hadn't just dropped a verbal bombshell, Clair turned away and headed back to the sidewalk. "In the meantime, running just exhausts me so I can sleep at night instead of fantasizing."

Fantasizing! Well, yeah, so all women probably fantasized, same as men. But Clair? Harris stomped after her. "What the hell does that mean, you have to find a new guy? You make it sound like shoe shopping."

She ignored his furious blustering to say, "Come on. Let's finish our run." Rather than wait for him, she took off, forcing Harris to catch up.

Because he was annoyed now, it took him only two long strides to reach her side. "So where do you intend to look for this new guy?"

"I dunno." She glanced at him over her glasses. "You got any suggestions?"

Of all the nerve. "You can't tell me you're horny, then expect me to help you find a guy."

She whipped around so fast he nearly plowed over her. They bumped. Hard. Harris had to catch her arms to keep them both on their feet.

Giving her a small shake, he groused, "What the hell is the matter with you?"

"Me!" She pushed him away, almost landing him on his butt. "I didn't say anything about being *horny*—how crass is that?"

"You think antsy sounds prettier? It means the same thing."

Clair gasped. "It does not."

Disgusted, Harris stared into her sexy green eyes and taunted, "Then I was right. You don't know anything about lust."

Her pupils flared. The seconds passed with the impact of a ticking bomb. He could feel the tension building, stretching almost to the breaking point— and she attacked.

One second Harris was standing there, smirking at her, and then he was flat on his back in the cold dank grass, little rocks prodding his spine, mosquitoes buzzing with delight at the feast thrown to them.

And Clair, well, Clair had an unshakable grip on his skull and her mouth was plastered to his, hot and wet and demanding. Somehow, with the prodding of her tongue, he opened and she plundered, licking and tasting, stealing his objections and melting them with her heat.

Astounded, instantly aroused, Harris cupped her head, felt the silkiness of her hair, the warmth of her skin. He tipped his head for a better angle and let her deepen the kiss more. *Clair,* he thought. This was Clair straddling him, Clair kissing him with so much passion. Her breasts flattened on his chest, her thighs shifted against his, wrenching a deep groan from him.

Then she was gone.

Moon and stars filled Harris's vision. His lungs labored to draw in more cool night air. His body burned. Confused, he pushed up to his elbows. Clair stood over him, hands on her hips, her glasses askew, her white shorts now dirty.

"That," she said, "is lust."

Harris nodded in complete and total agreement. "I'll say."

She offered him a hand, and when he took it, she helped haul him to his feet. Looking down into her earnest face, Harris scrambled for something to say, some way to get back into that full-body contact. But before a single idea could form, Clair touched his chin, his jaw, gently, softly.

Harris went mute with anticipation.

She stepped up against him, cuddling into him, wrapping her arms around him. After a long, meaningful stare into his eyes that scorched him clean through to his bones, she went on tiptoe and kissed him again. This kiss was as different as night and day from the first. It was purposeful, sweet, and it consumed him.

Like a slow burn, she involved his entire body, her small hands touching up and down his bare back, over his shoulders, as if in awe of his muscles and strength. Her feet moved between his, which aligned her soft belly with his groin. She pressed, proving she was aware of his erection.

Her breasts brushed against him, teasing, taunting, until he felt her stiffened nipples and growled.

She made small sounds of pleasure and hunger too, her tongue now shy, loving.

Loving?

With a pat to his rear, Clair pulled away. He watched as she slowly licked her lips. "And that," she whispered, "is antsy."

Breathless, hot, more than a little ready, Harris reached for her. "I don't think I quite understand yet. You better do a little more explaining."

CHAPTER THREE

CLAIR'S QUICK BACK STEP kept her out of reach. "If that explanation didn't suffice, then nothing will. You're hopeless." She turned away.

Did women always have to be so confusing?

Neither of them jogged this time. Hell, just walking was tough for Harris. He had a major Jones and she just didn't seem all that affected. Except for the wobbly way she walked. And the way she breathed too deeply.

He couldn't just let it go, so after half a dozen steps, he cleared his throat and ventured into murky water. "So...that was just a lesson, huh?"

"Think what you will."

She sounded all prickly again. Clair never got prickly with him. He wasn't used to it and didn't have a clue how to deal with her in this mood. "How about you just explain it?"

One shoulder lifted in a halfhearted shrug. "Men get horny and want to get laid. Women get antsy and want to touch and be touched, to cuddle and be affectionate." She cast him a quick look. "And then make love."

He raised his hand. "I'll take either one."

"I wasn't offering."

"Yeah, you were." When she turned to face him, Harris chastised her with a look. "I'm a little slow on the uptake sometimes, but I'm not a complete dolt. You're coming on to me."

She didn't reply to that one way or the other.

He needed verification, damn it. "I'm willing, Clair."

The incredulous look she gave him didn't bode well. "Willing? Oh great, bring out the band. Harris is *willing*." Her laugh reeked with sarcasm. "How did I get so lucky?"

Figuring her out wasn't going to be easy. "Bad word choice? Should I have said happy to oblige? Anxious? Maybe desperate?"

Her eyes narrowed behind the lenses of her glasses. "Are you?"

"After those killer kisses, what do you think?"

She reached around him to pat his ass again—right over the pocket that held the photo and his key. The woman sure had a thing for his rear.

"I think you're desperate to find your stupid mystery woman and I'd just be a way to pass the time." She crossed her arms over her chest, going all stiff and angry.

Uh-oh.

He took too long trying to figure out what to say, because she demanded, "Isn't that right?"

Harris held out his hands. "C'mon, Clair. I can't just forget about her. But hell, I don't even know her."

"You told me you didn't know me that well either."

They were a good mile from home, which ensured no matter what he said she couldn't just stalk off in a temper. That gave Harris small comfort, though, when he didn't know what the hell to say. "Up until a few minutes ago, I didn't know you were interested in…that."

"That?" she asked meanly, curling her lip, being deliberately derisive.

"Sex. Me."

"The two combined?"

"Exactly." He wrapped his fingers around her upper arm, slowing her furious stomp to a more sedate pace. When she didn't object, he decided to just hang on to her. Touching her was nice. At least now it was. Before she'd kissed him, he hadn't really noticed how it felt to touch her. Realizing that, he said, "I need a few minutes to adjust, that's all. Neither of us has thought that much about sleeping together."

"Speak for yourself."

Was that a confession? His interest sharpened to an ache. "You've thought about me?"

"You're not an ogre, Harris. Most of the time, you're not too moronic. I'm not with anyone else. Do the math."

Harris chewed over those critical and question-
able compliments, and didn't like the conclusion he
came to. "So like your ex-boyfriend, I'd be filler until
something better came along?"

She laughed. "Harris, honey, do try to remember
your own credos, okay?"

Honey?

"You don't want to be anything more than filler.
You don't want a woman getting ideas of forever
after. You're totally against marriage." She waited
two heartbeats, then prodded him. "Right?"

"Uh, yeah." But somehow that didn't seem to be
the point right now. "So you thought about, what? A
quick fling?" He could start with that, maybe work
up to more….

"You weren't listening to my instructions a minute ago, were you?" Typically Clair, she turned to
walk backward so she could see his face. "I thought
I was more than clear that men want it quick. I want
it slow and easy. I want to—"

He swallowed hard.

"—take my time." She continued pacing backward. "But there's that mystery lady occupying you
right now." Her sigh was absurdly long. "So we can
just go on being sexless buds. No problem."

No problem? What about his boner? That was a
definite problem. And his curiosity, which was so
keen he suddenly felt obsessed with knowing Clair
intimately. And there was a strange excitement he'd

never felt with any other woman, too. Maybe it was the way she insulted him so energetically. "I may never meet that woman, Clair. I mean, I know Alec and Dane are good, but that doesn't guarantee they'll find her."

"And if they did?"

How should he answer that? The mystery alone made him want to approach the woman, to talk to her, to find out how she knew him and why she hadn't ever told him how she felt. There was her sex appeal, and the notes, her sincerity and admiration...

"Yeah, that's what I thought." Clair reached out and clasped his hand, lacing her fingers with his. "Come on. No more lagging. Time to run."

"I don't think I can." He'd never run with a hard-on before. It didn't seem all that comfortable.

"You can," Clair assured him, "or you'll be heading home alone, because I'm not walking. I'm tired and I want to get to bed."

"So you can *fantasize,*" Harris accused. Possibly about him. The way her hand tightened shored up that belief.

"Maybe."

He did not need to hear this. She dragged him along, never once releasing her hold on him, and in a few minutes, they were jogging again. At the pace she set, it didn't take them long before they were on their own street. This close to the burned building, the lingering scent of smoke still hung in the air. It reminded Harris of his reaction when he'd feared Clair might be involved in the fire. His reaction had been extreme, and that was before she'd been flirting with him.

He also thought of the shoebox he'd found, and the tantalizing prospects it had presented. Harris was strangely aware of the photo in his back pocket, and Clair's hand in his.

Two women, both of them making him nuts.

What the hell was a guy supposed to do?

CLAIR STOPPED in front of her steps. So far, Harris seemed more than a little interested in sex, but she wanted more than that. She wanted him to want her, in and out of bed. She felt manipulative, teasing him and then pulling back. Making comments that she knew would get him thinking about sex. But she didn't know what else to do.

And already it was working with Harris. He wanted her now—but he still wanted her alter ego, the Naked Lady, too. Somehow, she had to get him to give up the fantasy prompted by those stupid photos.

Feeling awkward, Clair said, "It's early yet."

A light sheen of sweat dampened Harris's bare shoulders and chest. He had his hands on his hips, breathing deeply, watching her. "You pulled our run short."

Clair shrugged, adjusted her glasses nervously. "Want to come up?"

His gaze sharpened. Like a blue laser, his gaze pinned her in place. Slowly his hands dropped from his hips and he took a step closer. "Are you playing with me again?"

Man, he was still primed, ready to jump the gun—apparently ready to jump her. "I've had you up to my place a dozen times, Harris. For drinks, a snack."

His hands came to settle on her waist. "For more?"

Despite her urge to say *yes,* Clair laughed. "We're both sweaty and you have to be up early."

"I'm never too tired for—"

"Will you send me in alone if I say I just want to talk?"

For a brief moment, his hands tightened, then the heat left his eyes and he released her with a sigh. "What the hell. I always enjoy talking to you." His smile didn't quite reach his eyes. "Lead the way."

Her apartment was dark when they first went in. Clair turned on lamps as she headed to the kitchen. "You want something to eat or drink?"

"Just some water." He trailed behind her, far too close, in Clair's opinion.

She filled two glasses with ice, then got the spring water from the fridge. "So tell me what the attraction is."

"To you?"

He looked perplexed enough that Clair wanted

to hit him. "No, not to me. Far as I know, you're *not* attracted to me."

He cocked one brow, then looked pointedly at her body. "I'd be more than happy to prove you wrong on that."

Clair groaned. "So then why do you want the woman in the photos so bad? She gets naked and that makes you so interested you can't let it go?"

He immediately shook his head. "She does look hot, no way around that. I mean, any woman who's comfortable being naked is okay in my book."

"Really?"

He grinned. "Hell yeah. If it was up to me, all women would stay naked. At least when we were alone together."

That had Clair blushing a bit, especially as Harris let his gaze roam over her, no doubt imagining her in such a state. Not that he had to imagine, if he only realized....

"But the woman in the photo also said some nice things in her notes."

"So?"

Harris rubbed the back of his neck and paced away. He had a gorgeous back, strong and broad, sleek and hard with muscle. His shorts rode low on his hips, hugging a narrow behind and strong thighs. "This is kind of embarrassing."

She knew all about embarrassing. "Why? We're friends."

He nodded, turned to face her. "She said I'm generous." Harris looked uncomfortable. "And funny and heroic."

Men could be such dolts. "Well, of course she did. Because you *are*." Clair handed him his water. "You're one of the greatest guys I know."

The water never made it to his mouth. "You think so?"

"Absolutely."

"But I didn't know...."

"Harris," she said with aggrieved sigh. "Do you think I'd hang out with a guy who was an idiot?"

His mouth tipped in a crooked grin. "You call me an idiot all the time."

Too true. It had always been her way of making sure she kept her feelings to herself. A self-protection mechanism of sorts that reminded her she wasn't to get too romantic with Harris.

Clair moved back to the living room and dropped onto her overstuffed, oversize couch. She stretched out her legs, caught Harris staring at them, and smiled. "Yeah, well, I insult you with affection. I don't mean it." She sent him a quick grin, just to keep her comments from getting too dramatic. "If I didn't like, respect and admire you, I wouldn't want your company."

His brows came down, his expression arrested. Clair stared at him over her glasses. "Now what's wrong?"

With a small shake of his head, Harris muttered, "I need to think. You've sort of thrown a bunch of stuff at me all at once."

"Thinking is good." Clair waited while he, too, plopped onto the sofa. Because of their conversation, sitting so close to him felt different this time. "You should decide what you'll do once you find this woman. I mean, have you considered that?"

He propped his big feet on her coffee table and let his head fall back. "At least a hundred times."

Clair stared at his abdomen. It, too, was hard, lean and ridged with muscle. A dark, silky line of hair led from his navel to beneath the waistband of his shorts.

She held herself in check, when what she wanted to do was attack him again. "So," she said, sounding a little strained, "what if she's a witch? What if she has an ogre's personality? She could be like a fatal attraction or something. A nut. A slasher even."

Harris rolled his head toward her. "You made your point early on, hon. Now you're just stretching it."

Clair shrugged. "But the point is valid."

"Maybe." Harris stared at her, surveying her face as if trying to read her thoughts. "She didn't sound like a slasher in her notes. She sounded like a nice lady."

Here we go again. "You don't *want* a nice lady, Harris, remember? You want someone who's out for kicks. Nice women tend to get serious thoughts when they're having sex with a guy."

His blue eyes filled with speculative interest. Still lounging back lazily, he said, "You're nice."

Nervousness fluttered through her. Was there a point to that? Maybe something she was missing? She took a big gulp of her water, then agreed, "I'm very nice."

Harris warmed to his topic, leaning toward her a bit, resting his arm along the back of the sofa. His fingers just touched her nape, teasing her a bit. "So if we slept together," he asked in a slow drawl, "you'd want to settle down with me?"

Lord yes. She wanted to claim him as her own, and have babies and make love every night.... "I dunno." Her feigned indifference was laudable. "See, even if we did sleep together..."

"Yes?"

"I have an advantage."

"Do tell. I'm on the edge of my seat here."

Smugly, Clair stated, "Unlike other women you know, I have no illusions. I've watched you revel in your bachelor ways."

"I don't revel." His mouth flattened in distaste. "You make it sound like I go around dancing and singing about it. I just enjoy my life, that's all."

"Thing is," Clair continued, ignoring his protests, "I'm not sure you really know what you want or feel."

"So I can't figure out you or me, huh? What a dope I must be."

"I didn't say that, Harris. Don't put words in

my mouth." He grinned at her, seeming far from insulted. "Look at the way you're panting over a photo. That proves you're anxious for a serious relationship."

"You think so? I thought it just meant I was curious."

So curious, he'd hired two very expensive detectives to find the woman. Clair made a face at him. "What if," she said, determined to get her theory out in the open, "what you really want is to be loved?"

For a suspended moment in time, Harris froze. Then he jeered. "Do I look that needy to you?"

"No." Given the perfect opening, Clair spoke from her heart. "You look like a guy who's a great catch. Earnest when you need to be. Reliable. Dedicated." Melancholy got a stranglehold on her. Helplessly, she said, "You're a hero, Harris. A gorgeous, sexy, funny, bona fide hero."

He slowly straightened in his seat. "Don't overdo it, Clair."

"I'm serious." She scooted closer to him on the couch. "You're an incredible guy."

His gaze zeroed in on her mouth. "Clair, you do realize you're turning me on again, right?" His big warm hand came up to cup her cheek. "I hope that's your intent and not part of this new sadistic streak you've developed."

Clair chewed her lower lip. She did want to arouse him, but she didn't want to push him too far.

She wanted them to talk more before they took the plunge.

"Listen. I've told you what I really think of you." She drew a deep breath for courage—and inhaled his scent. After their jog, he was a little sweaty, but he smelled delicious. The way a man should, the way Harris always did. "Now why don't you tell me what you think of me?"

His thumb brushed her jaw. "Sure." The left side of his mouth kicked up. "You're cute, in a funky egghead, jock sort of way."

The romantic haze cleared from around her. "Be still my heart."

The teasing glimmer in his blue eyes clued her in. "Now Clair, what did you want me to say? You keep changing on me, so I don't know your personality anymore."

He knew her better than anyone, including her family. He just didn't realize it yet.

"I can't even tell what you're thinking most of the time because you always hide behind your glasses." The seductive way he caressed her neck mesmerized her. "Do you shower in them? Sleep in them?" His voice dropped. "Make love in them?"

Clair tried to rear back, but Harris kept her in place with the gentle hold on the back of her neck, and his compelling stare. "I'm not telling," she whispered.

"Then I think I'll find out on my own." He reached for her frames.

Clair couldn't let him take her glasses off! He might recognize her. She shoved him hard, but Harris being Harris—a big, sturdy, physically fit firefighter—he didn't budge.

"You want to wrestle?" he said with a laugh, and he caught her flying hands while somehow managing to tickle her. The next thing Clair knew they were rolling off the couch and onto the floor. She landed on Harris with a grunt, but only had a split second to enjoy that position before he flipped her beneath him. The coffee table got shoved away, and Harris settled himself between her thighs.

Uh-oh. "Harris…"

He caught both her hands in one of his, pinning them in place, keeping her still. And then, with her squawking and protesting, he slid her glasses off and placed them gingerly on the table.

Clair went mute in fear, sure that he'd recognize her.

Instead, he leaned down until his mouth just touched hers. "Can I show you my ideas on the differences between horny and antsy?"

He wasn't wearing a shirt, and all that sleek bare skin was against her. He smelled like a man should, like something that could be bottled and sold to make a fortune. And she could feel his hard, hair-roughened thighs on the tender insides of her legs. "Yes."

Her heart threatened to punch out of her chest. "You can show me."

"I love a good sport."

Her breath caught at the word *love,* and then Harris murmured, "Here's horny."

His mouth settled over hers, moving hotly, urging her lips to part so his tongue could sink inside. At the same time, he gently rocked his pelvis against hers, teased her nipples with the pressure of his chest. His breath was hot on her cheek, fast and low.

Wow. When he lifted away, Clair had to struggle to get her eyes open. "Lust," she whispered in complete agreement.

"Right. And here's antsy." He released her hands to cup her face, holding her still as he kissed her deeply again. Clair groaned. Kissing Harris was a revelation. She now realized that among his other accolades, she'd have to add "awesome kisser."

He eased away. "So what do you think?"

Her head was spinning, her heart beating too fast. "They were the same."

"Right, because there isn't a difference." He dropped a kiss on her nose. "It's just preference, Clair. Sometimes I like it hard and fast."

She groaned again.

"But sometimes," he said, drawing it out and searing her with a look, "I like to make it last all night."

Clair wasn't sure she could take an all-nighter.

But then he kissed her temple, and when he spoke, his voice was a rough whisper.

"For you, I'd make it last."

Okay, so maybe she could take it. Clair started to wrap her arms around him, but Harris held her off. His smile looked pained, and his muscles were taut with restraint. He kissed her nose again—and sat up.

"But since you're playing some strange game here and I can't quite figure out the rules yet, I think I better call it a night."

She didn't want him to go now, darn it. She wanted…

Harris touched her cheek, smoothed her hair. "When we sleep together, Clair—and we will, so don't deny it—I don't want any miscommunication or regrets. We'll both be in agreement, and we'll both enjoy it. Okay?"

A little numb, Clair nodded.

When Harris pushed to his feet, she sat up and quickly located her glasses. She felt more self-assured with the visual barrier in place. "Harris?"

He smiled down at her, giving her a sense of déjà vu, but with her in the wrong position. In the park, she'd done this to him—led him on, then walked away.

He tipped his head toward her.

"Thank you."

A smile warmed his expression. "For waiting?"

"And for understanding. I…I guess I'm not a hundred percent sure what I want yet."

"Between us?"

"Yes." She bit her lip. "I don't think you are either."

"Now there's where you're wrong. I know what I want—and I know I'll get it. That's the only reason I can be so patient now."

Clair blinked hard. Had she finally made some serious progress?

"Good night, Clair," Harris said, and his expression was warm, intimate. "Sweet dreams."

CHAPTER FOUR

EVEN WHILE HE HOVERED next to Dane, waiting to see the results from the information he'd supplied, Harris kept listening for Clair to get to work. He was curious about the mystery woman still, no two ways about that. When he'd seen a dark-haired woman flirting with him, all his senses had gone on alert. He'd made note of her license plates, and now he waited to see if she could be the one. He hoped so. The suspense was killing him.

But even while he waited in tense silence, more than half his attention was on the door, anticipating Clair's arrival. The way that girl kissed… Hell, she was so hot, he probably should stay in uniform when with her. He needed the fireproof protection.

She was the same Clair he enjoyed so much, but she acted different with him now. He liked the changes, the feminine layers to her personality. The teasing. Like refined foreplay, Clair's advance and retreat kept his excitement very close to the surface, ready to explode with little provocation.

"Her name is Melody Miles." Dane, with his hand

over the receiver of the phone, glanced up at Harris. "*Miss* Melody Miles—so she's single."

Somehow, that didn't thrill Harris as much as he'd thought it might.

"Alec says up close, she doesn't look the same to him."

"None of the photos show her face."

"He didn't mention her face." Dane shrugged. "He was talking about her body. She's a little heavier than she seemed in the snapshots, but that could be due to a time difference between when the pictures were taken and now."

The door opened and Clair strolled in. She was smiling—until she saw Harris. Then she snapped to a standstill; her back slowly straightened.

Harris barely heard Dane still talking. Today Clair wore narrow, rectangular glasses that added an air of supreme intelligence to her appearance. Her dark glossy hair was a little windblown, proving she'd ridden to work with her car window down. Beneath the short hem of a navy-blue jumper, her long legs were bare. White sandals matched her white T-shirt. She looked adorable.

He was so glad to see her again. "Clair."

Her mouth flattened. "What are you doing here, Harris?"

Dane hung up and stepped out from behind her desk. "He thought he might have found the mystery lady."

Clair crossed her arms and thrust out a hip in an arrogant pose. "Do tell."

Clearing his throat, very unsure of her mood, Harris said, "Yeah, well. She was flirting with me at this coffee shop where I stopped this morning. I realized I stop there a lot, and that could be the connection. You know, where she knew me from and everything."

"Have you ever met her?"

"No." Clair sounded so...accusatory. "But she could have heard my name from someone. I've been in there with the guys a few times too. Occasionally in uniform, so she'd know I was a firefighter."

"Assuming she hangs out there as well."

"Yeah. Assuming that." Harris wished Dane would offer a little help. He'd acted enthusiastic about the possibility of the woman being "the one," yet now he just stood there and grinned, enjoying Harris's plight.

"Ever notice her before?" Clair asked.

Feeling harassed, Harris said, "No. But that doesn't mean she hasn't noticed me."

"Obviously she has if she's flirting with you." Her eyes narrowed in thought. "Did you ask her if she's the one?"

"No, of course not." Sheepishly, Harris admitted, "I followed her so I could get her license plate number."

"Oh gawd." Clair flounced the rest of the way

into the room and dropped her purse on the desk. "A stalker, that's what you've become."

Dane laughed. "No one saw him, Clair, and the plates paid off." Then he turned to Harris. "But as I said, Alec doesn't think it's her."

At the moment, with Clair glaring at him, Harris didn't really care. "All right."

Though he hadn't asked, Dane explained. "Body shape isn't the same." He pulled out the larger photos they'd created. He put the one of the woman's derriere on top of the stack.

Clair made a choking sound, but when Harris glanced at her, she didn't seem to be paying them any mind. In fact, she was busily arranging and rearranging things on her desk.

"Your woman—"

"*His* woman?" Clair repeated with mocking disbelief, her desk and its clutter forgotten.

"—has a heart-shaped behind." Dane shrugged. "The woman you saw in the coffee shop is rounder. Or so Alec tells me."

"Then it must not be her," Harris agreed.

"He's not positive," Dane said, "so he's going to check her out a little more. But he said not to get your hopes up."

Clair started laughing. Loudly. When Harris frowned at her, she put her face on the desk and covered her head with her arms. She roared with hilarity until her shoulders were shaking.

"What," he demanded over the awful noise she made, "is so damn funny?"

Gasping, wheezing with her humor, Clair straightened. She had tears of mirth rolling down her cheeks. "You three," she gasped, apparently including Alec, though he wasn't present. "Tracking a woman by... the shape of...*her ass.*" She burst out laughing again.

Dane cocked a brow. "I guess it does sound funny. Not that we have much else to go on." And then louder, to make his point to Clair, he said, "Since *somebody* hasn't found us the address of the previous owner yet."

Her amusement dried up real quick. "Oh." Her frown was fierce. "I'm working on that."

"Work harder," Dane suggested. "Or better yet, I can do it."

"No! I mean, I've got it covered. I'll have something for you in a few hours." Disgruntled, she seemed to sink in her chair. "Will that be good enough?"

"That'd be great." Dane picked up a file and headed for the door. "I'll be staking out the Westbrook Motel today if anyone needs me."

"A stakeout?" Dane and Alec handled a lot of mundane, annoying cases—like cheating spouses and stolen lawn ornaments. But they also got involved in some really cool situations that Harris loved hearing about.

"Yeah. The owners of a small motel suspect one

of their employees of spying on guests in the pool changing rooms. I'm going to hang out back in the bushes and catch him in the act, then we can call in the cops." Dane winked. "You kids be good. I'll see ya later."

Finally. The second Dane was out the door, Harris headed for Clair. Anticipation hummed inside him. He couldn't wait to taste her again.

As he advanced, her eyes widened and she hastily pushed her chair back, but Harris didn't give her time to retreat. He braced his hands on the arms of her chair, caging her in, and leaned down to take her mouth. She made a small sound of surprise—and then the sound got muffled.

Oh hell yeah, he'd missed her mouth.

Clair stayed stiff for about three seconds, then melted with a small moan. He liked that. He liked her. Maybe a lot more than he'd ever realized. When her lips parted, Harris accepted the invitation and slipped his tongue in for a deep, hot, wet kiss that lasted just long enough to get him semihard.

"I missed you," he growled against her mouth.

Speaking must have broken the spell, because she blinked and shoved him back. She was breathing fast and her lips were slightly swollen and very pink. She readjusted her crooked glasses, then scowled. "Yeah right. You missed me so much that you're following strange women around, desperate to meet your secret admirer."

"Not desperate." Harris wasn't all that steady on his feet at the moment. The idea of laying her out on the desk, pushing up her sensible jumper and indulging in a little office sex tempted him. But she didn't look too receptive to that idea. "Just curious. If some guy was in love with you, wouldn't you be curious?"

A myriad of expressions—anger, frustration, hopelessness—crossed her face before she sighed and flopped back in her seat. "Maybe." Her chin lifted. "But not if I was interested in someone else."

Harris propped his hip on the desk. He needed the support. "I'm more than interested, Clair."

Eyes flaring, she caught her bottom lip in her teeth. "Really?"

Was she in love with him? As to that, was he in love with her? Harris had always figured that when he fell in love, the realization would hit him over the head. He wouldn't have to wonder about it, he'd just know. But Clair was so different, he couldn't figure her out. And that meant he couldn't really figure himself out either.

Choosing his words carefully, Harris hoped to talk her around to his way of thinking, without looking too pushy or, God forbid, desperate. "I like being with you, Clair. Even before all this sexual teasing started between us." That brought another thought, and he asked, "You won't go changing on me if we get involved, will you?"

Clair was as still as a statue. "What do you mean?"

"You tell me what you think and what you feel. But you don't get hung up on little stuff. You're always honest with me."

She'd closed her eyes and Harris wasn't sure if she was listening. "Clair?"

Leaving her chair to pace, she said, "We're already involved. We just haven't slept together. If you like me how I am now, well, I can't see why sex should change anything."

"Sex changes *some* stuff."

She turned to face him, one brow raised in an attitude of skepticism. "How?"

How? Harris shook his head and rethought his words. "I should say that sex between *us* will change things. If you were a different woman—"

"Your secret admirer?"

"Don't sneer, Clair." He liked her show of jealousy. It sort of tickled him, because he'd never thought of Clair as a jealous woman. "All I'm saying is that with another woman, I might not care. But if *we* do this, I'll expect some rights."

She crossed her arms over her chest. "What rights?"

Somehow, this was backward, Harris thought, almost laughing at himself. Here he was, a man who avoided commitments, now trying to pin her down. But what had seemed so appealing just days before, now felt too open-ended. Clair never pressured him, never wanted to know where he was or when he'd be back or if he'd call. He was a firefighter, yet, to his knowledge, she never worried. And that had been cool—till now.

If she cared, shouldn't she show a little concern every now and then? Shouldn't she want to know if he was with another woman? Damn right, because if she didn't demand that special consideration, how could he demand it of her? And he wanted to. All this talk about her past boyfriend had him feeling his own dose of jealousy. He didn't want her with anyone else.

Harris pushed away from the desk. "I won't want you to ever jog at night without me." He warmed to his topic, moving closer to her. "Hell, I don't want you to do that now. If I can't make it, you'll skip it."

Her mouth fell open, then snapped shut and she declared with feeling, "I will not."

"Now Clair." He closed the space between them, forcing her to back up. "It's dangerous."

"You never cared before."

He was a dumb ass before. "We didn't have that kind of relationship. Now we will."

"Ha. What if you find your mystery lady? Then I'll be put on hold. So until you resolve your feelings for her, I'll just continue to do as I damn well please."

Harris loomed over her. The thought of her alone at night infuriated him. "Then I guess I'll just have to make sure I jog every damn night until we've got this settled."

Her back touched the wall and stopped her retreat. "You do anyway," she grumbled. And then, a little defeated, she added, "Besides, I don't enjoy jogging without you. Odds are, if you couldn't go, I'd skip it too."

Harris cupped her face. Logical, honest Clair. "Thank you." He kissed her again, but kept it light because he was running late. "I'll be over tonight as soon as I get off work."

"Why?" Thanks to the kiss, her eyes looked soft behind her glasses. "We don't run until it's dark."

"We've got a lot to talk about. Me, you, sex." He grinned at her. "We'll hash it all out, because I don't think I can wait too much longer."

He started to turn away, and she said, "Harris?"

"Yeah?"

"I don't want to wait either."

Oh hell. A statement like that guaranteed he'd be semihard for most of the day. Not a comfortable circumstance while working with a group of men who lived to harass each other. And no doubt Ethan would be the worst, but then Ethan still prodded him about the shoebox. If he found out how much Harris cared about Clair, there'd never be an end to it. Without another word, Harris made his escape.

But just as he'd suspected, Clair stayed on his mind, distracting him, filling his thoughts and making him edgy. That is, until a truck driver swerved off the road, striking a gas line and sparking an apartment fire on the north side of the town.

The collision smashed a natural gas manifold, and intense, gas-fed flames shot up into the building's roof, turning the four-unit apartment into a gigantic blaze. Harris temporarily plugged the gas lines so the fire was no longer fed, but flames were already licking a large portion of the building. Harris's unit was forced to fight the flames on two fronts, one group using a fog stream to keep the fire contained in the rear, while Harris and several other men engaged in fire attack and an internal overhaul.

Not long after that, gas workers arrived to shut off underground pipes, diminishing the danger. It was still another two hours before the fire was completely out and only smoke remained. Cleanup would take a while, but thank God, other than a few minor injuries, no one was seriously hurt. The renters, including several small children, all made it out safely. One older woman suffered smoke inhalation, but she'd be okay. A young man had some minor burns and the paramedics were already working on him.

Harris was exhausted, dirty, and reeking of smoke. Muscles in his neck and shoulders cramped. His eyes burned. He shoved aside a pile of embers, making sure they were cold before moving on. Ethan stepped up beside him. He looked as bad as Harris felt, but he was smiling.

Harris said, "There has to be about fifty-thou

worth of damage. Three of those apartments are no longer habitable, and a bunch of people are going to be hunting for a place to stay." He pulled off his helmet to swipe black soot from his face. "So why the grin?"

Ethan followed suit, removing his helmet and running one gloved hand through his sweat-soaked hair. "Rosie."

"What about her?"

"Whenever there's a fire, she dotes on me." Ethan elbowed him. "And I don't mean she brings me chicken soup, either."

Reminded of the love between Rosie and Ethan, Harris felt a little melancholy. He forced a smile. "I might be too young to hear this."

"You're definitely too young for details. Let's just say that I'm sorry for the damage, I hate it that people will be displaced, but I'm anxious to get home to my loving wife." Ethan winked, replaced his helmet, and sauntered away.

Harris grumbled to himself. It'd be nice to have a loving woman waiting for him...whoa. He stopped in his tracks, his gaze unseeing. A woman waiting? The same women, *every day?* That sounded a lot like...marriage. Was he ready for that? He knew he wanted Clair, definitely more than he'd ever wanted any other woman. And it wasn't just sexual.

Hell, he'd given up sex with other women, but not

once had he considered giving up jogging with her. He felt more alive when he was around her.

As he worked, removing the burned remains of an old lawn chair, tearing down the precariously hanging door on one unit, Harris considered all the different things he felt for Clair. He wanted to be with her, damn near all the time. He never tired of her company. Clair seemed to read his moods, sitting quietly with him when that was what he wanted, or teasing him when he felt like clowning around. Her company never felt intrusive. Being with her just felt…good.

He knew her moods, too. But maybe that was because Clair didn't play games like most women did. If he said something that pissed her off, she told him so. Other than the sexual teasing of late, which he knew they both enjoyed, she was open and honest.

For sure, she didn't like his attention veering to the mystery woman. Harris didn't really like it either. Not anymore. Who needed a woman who left secretive notes and naked pictures rather than confronting him face-to-face? He'd much rather concentrate on Clair and all the new ways she bedeviled his libido and his dreams.

His mind made up, Harris decided that he'd thank Dane and Alec for their help, pay them what he owed them, and pull them off the case. Tomorrow.

Because tonight, he wanted Clair.

He shook off his distraction and got to work. The

sooner they had the site cleared, the sooner his shift would end. And the sooner he could see Clair.

CLAIR HEARD about the fire on the news and she was so worried, she couldn't stop pacing. Loving a firefighter had never been easy, but now, as Harris had claimed, things were different. She didn't have to hide her feelings behind friendly camaraderie.

The second she saw Harris's car pull up, she grabbed her keys and dashed out the door. She didn't think about her shoes, or Harris's reaction, she only thought about reaching him, making sure he'd escaped once again without harm.

Harris was already inside the building, but only just opening his apartment door when Clair arrived. She stopped when she saw him, catching her breath, absorbing the sight of him. He looked...wonderful. Exhausted and red-eyed, but still strong and tall, still the man she adored with all her heart.

Seeing him now, with the evidence of his work weighing heavy on his shoulders, Clair didn't know what to say. Emotion closed her throat, love burned her eyes. She twisted her fingers together. "Harris."

He'd just shoved his door open and he turned to her with a smile. "Hey. I was going to change and come over in a few minutes."

Clair swallowed hard, fighting the urge to leap on him. "Change into what?" Dunce. What did it matter?

He turned his nose against his shoulder, sniffed, and made a face. "Something that doesn't still reek of smoke. I showered at the station, but the damn smell clings to my hair and my—"

Clair gave up. She couldn't stand it, couldn't wait a second more, couldn't patiently stand there while he went through cordial chitchat. Launching herself at Harris, she grabbed his neck, kissed his mouth, his chin, his throat, then rested her cheek on his chest and squeezed him tight.

Slowly, Harris brought his arms around her. "Hey? What's wrong?"

Almost too overwhelmed to speak, Clair shook her head, then confessed, "I was…worried."

"I'm sorry." He smoothed her back, returned her bear hug, then caught her arm and urged her inside.

He was sorry? Agog, Clair tried to acclimate herself to Harris's new persona, to his easy acceptance. What did it mean?

His voice low and somber, he said, "Let me shower again and change, then we'll talk."

Clair watched him walk away, and he was whistling. The exhaustion remained, in the set of his shoulders, the dark smudges beneath his eyes. But he seemed more lighthearted, as if she'd pleased him in some way.

Clair looked around herself with dawning realization. Harris was in a mellow, receptive mood. His apartment, other than a small kitchen light, was dark.

She had the perfect setting and probably wouldn't get another chance like this anytime soon.

Her heart in her throat, her pulse humming in anticipation, she trailed silently after him. She pushed open his bedroom door to see Harris standing in the middle of the floor, his shirt off, his shoes and socks gone, and his hands at the snap of his jeans.

Almost there, she thought.

Harris looked up, their gazes locked for long moments, and his expression heated. "Clair?"

Not giving herself a chance to back out, she flipped the wall switch, stealing the scant light and filling the room with obscure moon shadows.

Harris, now a vague shadowy blur, asked, "What's this?"

Cautiously moving forward, Clair found his chest, firm and sleek and very hot. She moved her hands up to his broad shoulders, then to the back of his neck. She pulled his head down to hers. "I was afraid for you."

His hands looped around her waist. "I'm good at what I do, honey. You don't have to worry."

"You said sex would change things." Clair tunneled her fingers into the cool softness of his thick hair, such a dramatic contrast to his hard, hot body. "Well, get used to me being concerned. I know you don't like it. God knows you bitch enough any time a woman starts to worry, but if we have sex—"

His hands widened, sliding down to her hips. "We are," he murmured. "Right now in fact."

Clair drew in a breath. "Great. Then I have rights."

She could hear the smile in his voice when he asked, "The right to worry?"

"You betcha. And I also—" He kissed her, cutting off her demands in midsentence. "Harris?"

"I'm open to the new rules, honey. But let's talk about them all in the morning."

Morning? The sun would be out, light flooding through the windows. "Do you expect me to stay the night?"

"Damn right. Next to me. In my bed."

"Oh." Maybe by then it wouldn't matter. Maybe by then he'd realize that he wanted her and only her. Or maybe he'd even figure out that she and the mystery woman were one and the same.

"You followed me into my bedroom, Clair. You're claiming the right to worry. That gives me a few rights too. Like the right to make love to you all night long, whenever the mood strikes me." His hands kept moving on her, caressing her back, her hips, her waist, stroking her, learning her in a way that had been forbidden before now. "In case you get antsy or horny," he teased. He turned, took two steps and lowered them both to the bed, half covering her. In a near growl, he added, "Or if you just plain want me."

"I always want you." Clair closed her eyes as his

fingers found her inner thighs. Her heart pounded. "Harris?"

"I smell like smoke," he complained. With his mouth open and damp, he kissed her neck, her shoulder, leaving her skin tinging. "No matter how long I shower or how hard I scrub…"

"I don't mind." Clair pressed her nose to his throat and inhaled. She wondered if the fires affected him that way, made him feel like he couldn't get away from the smoke, the damage. She nuzzled against him. "All I smell is you, Harris, and you smell delicious."

"Yeah?" He chuckled, rising up to smooth her hair. With a smile barely perceptible in the dim room, he removed her glasses, stretching to put them on the nightstand. When he leaned back to her, he caught the hem of her shirt and tugged it up and over her head. His hand found her breast, gently shaped her, then he stilled. "Damn, Clair, I need a light."

"No, not yet." If he turned on the light, he might recognize her. She wanted the intimacy between them before she told him the truth. In the morning, she'd confess. But not yet, not before she had that special bond to cushion her admission.

Harris continued to caress her breast, toying with her nipple, making speech impossible. "Why not?"

Why not? Why not? She forced herself to concentrate, then murmured, "I'm shy?"

Slowly, with delicious precision, he tugged at her nipple. "You don't sound certain, Clair."

Oh Lord, how could he expect her to talk while he did that? "I just…I'd rather leave the lights off."

Harris sat up beside her. "*I'd* rather see you. All of you." Clair tried to protest, but before she'd even raised herself up on her elbows, a lamp came on, spilling light across the bed. Clair hurriedly turned her face away, her breath catching in dread.

The seconds ticked by in agonizing silence. Slowly, because she couldn't bear it any longer, she turned back to Harris. He didn't look the least bit exhausted now. His blue eyes were bright, his gaze piercing while he stared at her breasts. His dark hair fell across his brow; his muscles were tight, delineated. He got to his feet beside the mattress, his gaze still unwavering, and began stripping off his jeans. "Can you see me without your glasses?"

Clair bit her lip. "You're a little fuzzy, but yes, I can see you."

Slowly, he nodded. "Good." His jeans got shoved down and off his hips, and he stepped out of them. Her eyes widened. She could see him, but she wished she still had her glasses on so she wouldn't miss a single detail.

She started to sit up, to get closer to him, and he said, "Now you."

Not yet! If he saw her tush, would he recognize her as the woman in the photo?

Clair tried to scuttle away, but that only amused Harris. He caught the hem of her shorts, and since they had a loose elastic waist, they came right off. Unfortunately, he took her panties with them, leaving her naked. "Harris!"

"Clair." His voice was dark, intense. "You're beautiful."

He still didn't recognize her? Clair couldn't believe it. She should have been only relieved, but damn it, she was nettled too. The man had fawned all over those photos, studied them in detail, had them enhanced. But he didn't see her as a sexy mystery woman, so he didn't make the connection.

When Harris stretched out beside her, she flattened both hands against his chest, holding him away. He tried to kiss her, but Clair wasn't having that. Not yet.

With dark menace, she demanded, "What about your mystery lady?"

CHAPTER FIVE

"WHAT MYSTERY LADY?" Harris murmured with deliberate lack of concern. At this particular moment, he didn't care about anyone else, not with Clair in his bed, ready for him, looking sweet and soft and as perfect as a woman could look. Ready to take the next step in binding their relationship, he pulled her hands away, leaned down and licked her tightened nipple.

Her back arched and her breath caught. "You know who I mean," she panted. Her hands clenched on his shoulders, stinging in force. But still she persisted, saying hesitantly, "I, um, found the name of the guy who leased the place."

With a long, exaggerated sigh, Harris dropped his forehead to her chest. "I don't care, Clair." He cupped her breast, thumbed her now wet nipple. "Can't you see that I'm busy here?"

Clair tried to hold him back again. "You don't care?"

She sounded so stunned, Harris grinned. "Honey,

if you don't shut up, how the hell can I make love to you?"

"But you said—" He sucked her nipple into his mouth, drawing on her, teasing with the tip of his tongue. *"Harris."*

Her hips pressed up against his, seeking. He could feel the wild rapping of her heart. In a rough growl, Harris said, "I know I promised slow and easy, but honey, I'm not sure I can manage that this first time."

"No." She panted too, sounding every bit as affected. "I don't want you to."

Clair wasn't a weak woman, and the way she gripped him now told Harris that she meant it, that she was as anxious as he felt. Unwilling to cheat her, to rush her too much, he switched to her other nipple at the same time his hand moved down her body, tickling her skin into a fever, over her ribs, her waist, her hip. She had a lush, full bottom, and her skin was silky soft, warm. He trailed his fingers over her sleek runner's thighs, and smiled at the way she clenched them together.

Knowing how his words would affect her, he said, "Open your thighs for me, Clair. Let me touch you."

Another moan bubbled up from deep in her throat. She squeezed her eyes shut, trembling from the anticipation, and slowly parted her legs.

Teasing her a bit, Harris traced around her pubic curls.

"Harris…"

He loved the way she said his name. Cupping her mound, he carefully stroked, opening her, then slid one finger in deep. She was hot, wet, and immediately her hips lifted, deepening his penetration.

Clair gasped—and opened her legs more.

Such an honest response, so typical of Clair. With his free arm, he pulled her closer to his chest, to his heart, while still stroking her, bringing her closer and closer to the edge.

"You're the one who smells good, Clair," he couldn't help but tell her. "Sweet and soft. I love how you smell." To emphasize that, he pressed his nose into her neck. He thought about what Ethan had said, about having a woman coddle him when he got home from a hard day fighting a fire. He wanted that woman to be Clair. He wanted her scent to cloak his body, instead of the scent of smoke. He wanted her to hold him, not any other woman. He wanted to come home to her every day and know that she was his, and only his.

The acknowledgment of his emotions pushed him over the edge. He needed to be inside her, soon. She was gasping, moving rhythmically against his hand, her skin radiating heat. But it wasn't enough. Harris wanted her pleasure to be a foregone conclusion, because God knew once he got inside her, he wouldn't last.

"You'll like this," he told her, and kissed her

breasts again, sucking hard, nipping a little with his teeth.

She gasped, then gasped again when he kissed her ribs, gently bit her soft belly, and settled between her legs.

"Harris?"

"God, you smell good, Clair." He pressed closer, inhaling the scent of her excitement, her femaleness. Using his thumbs, he parted her, sought her out with his tongue, and then closed his mouth hotly over her.

Her groan was long and satisfying, accompanied by a stiffening of her legs, the spontaneous lifting of her hips, a surge of new warmth. She whimpered, and in a breathless whisper, said, "Oh God."

Harris pressed himself hard against the mattress, trying to curb the ache her pleasure created. He felt her straining, getting closer and closer, and he worked two fingers into her even as he continued to suckle her clitoris, working her with his tongue—and she came.

Her shout took him by surprise, and thrilled him. He locked one arm around her, holding her still as she shuddered and trembled and cried out. He could feel her squeezing his fingers, feel the surge of wetness and heat. He loved eating Clair, and if he hadn't wanted her for so long, he could have started all over again.

But he had wanted her, whether he realized it or not. His feelings for her had made it easy to give up other women. Celibacy was much simpler when he wanted only Clair. But no more. He needed her. Now.

Harris realized his hands were shaking when he sat up and fumbled with the bedside drawer, seeking a condom. Clair didn't move. But he could hear her uneven, still-labored breathing, and he smiled.

He had the condom on in record time and then he turned, hooked her legs in his elbows, spread her wide—and surged into her.

She arched hard against him, crying out, sinking her nails into his shoulders. "Yeah," Harris panted, blind with lust and love, shaken with the fury of his feelings for her. "Come for me again, Clair."

She did, almost too soon, because hearing her moan, feeling her inner muscles grip his cock, forced him to the finish line. She was wet and hot, open to him, letting him in deep, and he lost the battle. He closed his eyes and arched his neck and growled out his release, pumping hard, heaving.

Minutes later, when his heart slowed its frantic beat and he could think coherently again, Harris thought to tell her how he felt, to admit he loved her. He pushed back to see her face, smiled at the sight of her sound asleep, and carefully separated from her.

She mumbled, rolled to her side, and snuggled into his pillow. Harris looked her over again, smiling, but his vision still felt blurry and his heart felt too soft. He removed the condom, turned out the light, and spooned Clair. As he'd already known, she fit him perfectly.

His life, with Clair in it, was good. He hoped like hell she wanted to marry him, because no way would he give her up.

HARRIS MADE LOVE to her once again in the middle of the night, when she rolled to face him, and somehow her leg ended up over his waist and her breast was right there, close to his mouth—too tempting to resist. Though he was half-asleep and just going with the moment, he remembered to protect her—just barely. In the future, he'd have to keep a box of condoms on top of the nightstand, for easy access. Having Clair around and accessible would sorely test him, not that he'd complain.

The second time was slower, gentler, and they rocked together for a long time, kissing softly, cuddling, until Clair started to moan. The sound of her pleasure seemed to ignite him, and once again, he lost the battle with control.

After that, Harris didn't wake up again until he felt Clair leaving the bed. He'd seldom slept the whole night with a woman, but having Clair close was comfortable and comforting. As she slipped away, he protested with a groan and tried to pull her back.

She mumbled and swatted at him. "I have to go get ready for work, Harris."

He got one heavy eyelid open and found the clock. "It's early yet." *With plenty of time for some morning hanky-panky.* He glanced up at Clair, and got both eyes opened.

She was naked, with rumpled hair and sleep-soft eyes, but she'd already put on her glasses. She looked like a fetish come to life. His fetish. He wanted her. Again. Always.

But when he tried to reach for her, she laughed and stepped out of reach. "Down boy. I need a long hot shower."

Harris looked at her soft, sweet belly and murmured, "Shower with me."

"Oh no, not on your life. I know where that'd end up."

"Yeah," he agreed, more awake by the moment.

"Harris, I can't."

"Why?"

Her mouth went crooked in a silly grimace. "I'm a little sore."

Harris shoved into a sitting position. He couldn't help it; he smiled like a conquering warrior. "I was too energetic?" He tried to look at her face, but her body held all his attention. Clair naked was a surprise. A wonderful surprise. She was so damned sexy...

"It's just been a long time, that's all."

Harris looked at her hips, and frowned in thought. He'd never seen her nude body before, yet it all

seemed somehow familiar. "I'll be more consider-
ate in the future." *In the future.* He liked saying that.

Clair drew a long, steadying breath. "For the record, you can be as energetic as you want." And
then, with a small smile, she added, "In the future."

Damn, he loved her. He patted the side of the bed.
"We need to talk."

Worry darkened her eyes and she fretted, looking
away from him. "I know."

Why did the idea of talking make her so solemn?
Harris didn't like it that her smile had disappeared.
He much preferred her teasing, so he decided to put
off the talk until later. "It'll wait." And because he
couldn't be with her and not want her, he agreed to
let her head home. "Go get your shower before I forget I'm a gentleman and drag you back into my bed."

"I'll…see you later?"

Did she have doubts about his intentions? Was
that why she looked so burdened? He reached for her
hand and laced his fingers with hers. "You'd have
one hell of a time getting rid of me."

Her grin returned, filling him with warmth.
"Soon?"

Sooner than she expected, most likely. He'd head
to her office first to remove Dane and Alec from
the case. Mystery women no longer interested him.

"Absolutely." But she'd hesitated too long. Harris
left the bed to stand in front of her, pulled her close
so he could feel her skin against him, and kissed her.

He'd meant it to be a perfunctory goodbye kiss, but her mouth was soft and warm and she smelled so good, he went a little out of control. Only the worry of causing her more discomfort kept him from making love to her again. Against her lips, he whispered, "Damn woman, I can only take so much provocation and you naked is pretty darn provoking. You better go now while I'm still willing to let you."

Laughing, Clair snatched up her shorts and T-shirt and pulled them on. Harris watched, enjoying the easy familiarity. If he had his way—and he would—he'd be able to watch her dress every morning from now on.

Because he was ready to jump in the shower too, Harris didn't bother to dress when he walked her to his front door. "After today, I'll be off for a week. Will you stay with me?"

"For the whole week?"

Forever. But he'd get to that later. For now, he just wanted the immediate future confirmed. "Yeah. With me, in my apartment." And in a lower, suggestive voice, he added, "In my bed."

She went a little breathless on him, nodding in mute agreement. But two seconds later, she frowned. "I will—if you want me to."

"I want you to." But she didn't look quite convinced. Was she afraid he'd get sidetracked with the woman in the photos again? Not a chance. Harris wanted to tell her that he loved her and only her, but it'd be better to show her first. He could wait until he saw her at her work, when she'd witness him tearing up the photos.

Anticipating her reaction, Harris kissed her one last time, then gently urged her out the door. As soon as she left, he went to his window to keep watch. Moments after she entered her building, her lights came on, and right after that, he saw her wave. He smiled and dropped his curtain.

Soon she'd be living with him, and he wouldn't need to watch her go safely into her own place.

In less than an hour Harris had showered and was at her office. He'd pulled into the parking lot in time to see Dane and Alec entering the front doors. They had their wives with them. Both were blondes, both were attractive. *Well hell,* Harris thought. The presence of wives would make it difficult to discuss photos of a naked woman. He could have put it off till the women left, but he wanted everything taken care of before Clair arrived.

They were all in Dane's inner office when Harris got there. He went in, lighthearted and eager to get things underway. Maybe he'd even ask Clair to marry him after he tore up the pictures. He grinned, envisioning how that'd play out, what she might say.

Harris raised his fist to tap on the door frame, announcing himself. Almost at the same time, one of the women said, "Dane Carter! Why in the world do you have naked pictures of Clair on the wall?"

Naked pictures of *Clair?* Harris raised a brow, confused, mentally scoffing.

Dane choked. "It's not."

And the other woman said, "Well, of course it is." And then with some confusion, "You didn't know?"

Together, Dane and Alec barked, *"No."*

"How could you not know?" one of them asked. "It looks like her."

"It's her shape," the other added. "Her long legs, her posture, her—"

The woman continued, but Harris wasn't listening. He shook his head in denial, even as the pieces began to click painfully into place. His heart pounded and his head throbbed.

The mystery woman wore no jewelry—because Clair didn't wear any. The mystery woman had longer hair—because Clair had recently cut hers.

The mystery woman had a lush derriere—*just like Clair's.*

He remembered Clair's near hysterical reaction to seeing the photos enlarged, how she'd hidden her head on the desk when he and Dane discussed the mystery woman's posterior.

And he remembered those notes, so full of emotion and love, which meant the woman had to know him, and *not* from afar.

The wives had seen what he hadn't. Until now.

Dane's office was eerily silent as Harris stepped

inside. Numb, a little unsteady on his feet, he barked, "Get them down. Now."

Alec, not one to take orders, was already doing just that. He moved faster than Harris could have, given his present state of mind.

Harris drew a slow breath, but it didn't help. He was aware of Dane watching him in appalled consternation, Alec grumbling and scowling. Hell, it almost looked as if Alec was blushing. The wives were silent.

And behind them all, Clair strolled in whistling.

Everyone turned to face the doorway in various stages of disbelief and anxiety.

Clair saw them all congregated together, watching her—and her whistling died a quick death. She took in all the expressions of shock, alarm and dismay, and she stalled. "Um…what's going on?"

Dane and Alec began to sputter and cough, and now they were both red-faced. The wives looked worried, casting Clair looks of sympathy. Dane's wife even scooted closer to him. "Dane?"

Dane said, "Shh," then bent to whisper in her ear, most likely explaining the inexplicable. His wife's eyes widened and she darted a fascinated glance between Harris and Clair.

Harris just stared at Clair, trying to take it all in, trying to accept that he'd passed around naked pictures of the woman he loved. Dane and Alec had seen her. Ethan had seen her.

Not once had she let on.

Alec, his hands full of photos, shoved them against Harris's chest, saying, "Here." Then he grabbed his wife and fled the office. Dane quickly followed, stopping to clap Harris on the shoulder in commiseration while avoiding Clair's gaze.

Dane pulled the door shut behind him with a finality that hung in the air like nuclear fallout.

They stared at each other until Clair, her face white, groped for a chair. "You know, don't you?"

The photos got wadded in his fist. His stomach cramped. Through his teeth, Harris snarled, "Why the hell didn't you tell me?"

Without answering, she dropped her head and shrugged.

Feeling savage, Harris paced a circle around her. "Jesus." Then, leaning close to her nose, he said, *"I let Dane, Alec, and Ethan see."*

Her mouth firmed. "And you carried one photo in your pocket. I know." Curling her lip, she added, "You were smitten, Dane said. And Alec claimed you were totally obsessed."

"With *you,* Clair, if you'd only have admitted it before I…" He shuddered with the awfulness of it. "Before I showed them to other men."

Outrage brought Clair to her feet, to her very tiptoes. "How was I supposed to know you'd do that? But once you did, what would be the point in confessing? It was too late to take it back."

He waved a shot of her behind in her face. "It wasn't too late to keep from having them enlarged!"

She slapped the photo aside. "So you're a pervert! I didn't know that either."

Dane tapped on the door before pushing it open. He stared fixedly at Harris. "Um, we can hear you, and in fact, with the way you're both roaring, most of the people in the building probably can. If you want to tone it down just a little, that'd be good." He cleared his throat, dared a flash peek at Clair. "Uh, Clair? You can have the day off." He snapped the door shut again.

Harris strangled on his anger.

Clair didn't seem to even hear Dane. Somehow, she managed to get her nose even with Harris's. Her hot, angry breath pelted his face with each word. "Why didn't you know it was me, Harris? How could you *not* know? We see each other every damn night." Harris backed up—and Clair followed. "We've been friends a long time, close friends, and yet you never once considered it might be me. So tell me, why would I confess to you when you were never inter-ested in me?"

The shock was slowly wearing off, and Harris began to see things clearly again. Clair wasn't em-barrassed—at least, not that he could tell. And she wasn't exactly apologizing for duping him, either. No, she was royally pissed off.

And she accused him of not being interested?

Now that was just plain wrong. He stopped retreating and leaned into her anger. "Since when am I not interested?"

She slugged him. Her small fist thumped hard against his pec and, damn it, it hurt. "I don't mean to jog, you moron. I mean for more. For *everything*."

Harris narrowed his eyes. "I was interested enough last night. Twice, as I recall. You could have told me then."

Alec's loud whistling could be heard.

"I was going to tell you today." And then, in a smaller voice, she murmured, "After I got those stupid pictures off the wall."

"They're off now." Harris slapped the crumpled photos onto the desk behind him—facedown so no one could see them. He tried to get himself under control. Most of his reaction was due to jealousy. He couldn't believe he'd studied her naked ass, in detail, with Dane and Alec. "You told me your boyfriend was nobody. If that's so, why'd you let him take naked pictures—"

She slugged him again, aghast and appalled and wide-eyed. "I didn't *let* him." She swallowed and her eyes looked a little glassy, her bottom lip trembling. "Do you know me at all, Harris?"

She sounded so forlorn, it about ripped him apart. "If you didn't let him, then how did he...get..." Fury erupted, black and mean and sharp-edged. His jaw set, his teeth locked. "That son of a bitch."

Clair looked resigned. "He has a tiny little spy camera. I didn't even know he was looking at me, much less that he was photographing me. I never would have allowed that. I was only with him for a little while, because..." She stared up at him, solemn and sad. "He wasn't you."

Harris's eye twitched. His lips felt stiff. "I'll kill him."

Clair held her breath, then said, "Why?"

"Why?" Harris caught her shoulders and brought her to eye level. "I love you, damn it. No way in hell am I going to let some bastard—"

"You love me?"

He gave her shoulders a gentle shake. "What the hell did you think?"

"I don't know." Her eyes were round behind her glasses, filled with hope. "You didn't recognize me. Even after last night, you didn't recognize me."

Harris couldn't believe she was hung up on that. "I looked at those pictures with totally detached lust. It was a naked woman, period. How I looked at them is entirely different from how I looked at you."

"How'd you look at me?"

He pulled her closer. Took a deep breath. "With lust, for sure. God knows, Clair, you make me hot. But with so many other feelings, too—love, tenderness." He hesitated and then added, "Need."

"You need me?"

Harris hauled her into his arms. "I love you so

damn much I almost can't think straight, so of course I need you. You make me laugh, and you make me feel easy, sort of rested. Like I've found the perfect place to be. With you."

She smiled up at him, laughing a little, weeping a little. "I love you too."

Finally hearing her say it relaxed something inside him, something he hadn't realized was tense until she fully accepted him. "That's a relief." He released her and rubbed his hands together. "Now if we can just figure out where this ex-boyfriend of yours is, I'll go have a talk with him. Then everything will be perfect."

Dane again tapped on the door before opening it. Alec was beside him. "Give us his name, Clair. We'll handle it."

Clair bit her lip. "I don't know...."

"He could have negatives still," Alec pointed out.

"Or more shots," Dane added.

Harris watched her face flush with anger, saw her hands curl into tight fists. "*I'll* go talk to him—"

Harris pulled her around in a bear hug. "Forget that idea. I don't want you anywhere near the creep."

Dane's eyes narrowed. "You shouldn't go near him either, Harris. You just want to take him apart."

"Damn right."

Alec raised a brow. "Hitting him would only get you in trouble. Whereas we can likely prove what an unscrupulous jerk he is."

"How?" Harris demanded.

"If he did this to Clair," Dane explained, "then he's likely done it to other women, too. All we need is the evidence, and hey, gathering evidence is what we do."

"Then we can have criminal charges filed against him—and neither Clair nor her photos will have to be involved."

It didn't feel right to Harris, letting Dane and Alec take care of the matter. Clair was his, and he felt so damn protective. He needed to punch the guy at least once. Hell, he wanted to break his nose. But he definitely didn't want Clair involved.

"Think of it as a wedding present," Alec urged him.

At the mention of a wedding, Clair pushed away from Harris with a gasp. He hauled her right back again. "We are getting married, Clair."

Her brows snapped down and she looked at him over her glasses. "Since when?"

"Since I just told you I love you and you told me you love me too."

Angel Carter, Dane's wife, grinned. "Sounds reasonable to me, Clair."

Celia Sharpe nodded. "Let Alec go get this awful man, and you and Harris just concentrate on wedding plans."

Clair still looked mutinous. "I expected a proper wedding proposal."

"Everyone in this room has seen you in the buff, Clair. Hell, Dane and Alec were looking at your photos with a magnifying glass, trying to spot details. They were—"

"I'll marry you."

Harris grinned at her burning face and the rushed way she'd interrupted him. But now the wives were scowling at their husbands too, and the husbands looked ready to hang him. Harris laughed. "Sorry. All's fair in love and war."

Dane caught his wife's hand. "Let's go before Clair starts shedding blood and gets my office all messy."

Alec threw his arm around Celia. "Wait for us."

They were gone in moments, leaving Clair and Harris alone. With everything in place, Harris relaxed. "Ethan and Riley are going to be damned pleased, but Buck will have a fit."

"Buck is one of your friends, right?"

"Yeah, soon to be my only single close friend. He won't like it that I've jumped ship too."

"So he should get married."

"He claims he's married to his lumberyard."

Clair rolled her eyes. "Some guys just like the bachelor life, I guess."

"No." Harris tipped up her chin. "Some guys just haven't met the right woman yet. Which is why I have to get you tied to me. I may not have recognized you in the photos, but I definitely recognize you as the perfect woman—for me."

"CAN WE ESCAPE, NOW, do you think?"

Clair smiled at Harris. Because they'd both wanted a small, simple wedding with only close friends and family, they'd been able to organize it all in just under three weeks.

Harris had been very impatient the entire time. The rehearsal dinner had lasted hours, filled with good food and a lot of laughter. Her family loved Harris, and vice versa. Ethan and Riley were beyond pleased, and Buck wasn't too disgruntled. In fact, he seemed to be wallowing in the fact that he was the only single one in the bunch.

Dane and Alec were finally able to look at Clair again without turning red, but they were still more hesitant with her. For her part, she doubted she'd ever be able to face them again without blushing.

"I think we can leave now." Clair scooted closer to him. "You have big plans?"

"Yeah." Harris nuzzled her neck. "Plans to have my way with my soon-to-be-bride."

She sighed, now as anxious as he was to be alone. They made an announcement, put up with a few more toasts, and finally headed out the door.

In the parking lot, however, Celia Sharpe and Angel Carter chased them down. Celia carried a large package and Angel had a manila envelope.

"We've been elected to do the honors," Celia explained when they reached them.

"The men are still shy about that whole photograph thing," Angel added with a shrug. "They say you're too valuable to the office to replace you, but no way can they discuss this with you."

Harris put his arm around Clair and smiled. "Discuss what?"

Angel presented the envelope with a flourish. "They located that ex-boyfriend of yours. They found these."

Clair went blank. "Ohmigod."

Beside her, Harris stiffened in anger. "Damn it. I should have—"

"Dane did that for you. Punched him right in the nose." Angel seemed to relish the retelling. "And he did it in such a way that he wasn't the one who started it. If I know Dane, he goaded the guy into taking a swing first."

Celia nodded. "Then *pow,* Dane laid him out." She laughed. "Alec thought it was great."

Clair bit her lip. "If they found more photos…"

"Not to worry," Celia rushed out. "They went over his place with a fine-tooth comb. There wasn't much that pertained to you. Just a few souvenirs, apparently."

Clair closed her eyes in mortification, then felt Harris hug her to his side.

"It's all right now, Clair."

"It really is," Angel assured her. "He'd done the same with two other women, one that he was still dating. Dane and Alec clued them in, and they confronted the jerk, even ransacked his place until they found some of the photos themselves. They both agreed to prosecute, so he'll be taken care of for sure."

Clair pulled herself together. It was over and she had her whole life ahead of her—a life with Harris. "Please, tell Dane and Alec how much I appreciate it."

"You also get this," Celia said with a grin. "It's a paper shredder. Alec said the photos belonged to you, and you could do whatever you wanted with them. But he said he figured you'd want to shred them."

"He figured right!"

Harris snatched the envelope out of her hand. "We'll definitely do that." He leaned toward Angel for a hug, then to Celia for the same. He held the bulky box under one arm, the envelope in his free hand. "Thank you, ladies. Knowing that situation is settled is the very best wedding present."

Celia and Angel left them with smiles. The moment they were gone, Harris opened the envelope and started to peek inside.

Clair snatched it away and held it behind her back. "Oh no you don't."

Trying to look innocent, and failing, Harris said, "I just wanted to see—"

"I know what you wanted to see. But these are getting destroyed the moment we get home. You've seen all the nude photos of me that you're ever going to see."

Harris grinned, and the grin spread into a laugh. "All right, babe," he soothed. "Don't get all bristly on me." He turned her toward the car.

Clair didn't understand his new mood and thought to soften her denial. "I'm sorry, Harris. I hope you can understand how I feel."

"Yeah, I do." After she was seated, he leaned in the door and kissed her. "I was just teasing you. It doesn't matter to me at all."

"You're sure?"

He took her mouth in a long, satisfying kiss. "Positive. After all, what do I need with photos when I've got the real thing?"

* * * * *

TAILSPIN

CHAPTER ONE

IT WAS BARELY SIX O'CLOCK on a cloudy Saturday morning in Chester, Ohio. The sun struggled to shine without much success as Buck Boswell finished brushing his teeth, then splashed his unshaven face with cold water. Saturday mornings were meant for sleeping in, preferably with a soft, warm female. But for the next couple of weekends, that was out.

Butch, the little Chihuahua he'd been roped into babysitting for two weeks, was causing a ruckus. For a four-pound dog, he made a lot of noise.

Butch had already been out to do his business—the reason Buck was up so early on a vacation day—so he should have been curled up on his blankets, back to dreaming blissful doggie dreams. For the two days Buck had minded Butch so far, that'd been his routine: up at dawn, out for his morning constitutional, back to bed.

Unfortunately, Buck couldn't do the same. Once Butch woke him, getting back to sleep proved impossible. He was starting his vacation by keeping the hours of his grandpa instead of those of a thriving bachelor.

It sucked.

Riley, one of his best friends, had asked Buck to sit the dog so he and his wife, Regina, could take a cruise. But Riley hadn't mentioned that Butch rose with the roosters, only to nap again afterward.

Owning his own lumberyard and working sixty-hour weeks as a result hadn't allowed Buck much time to bond with pets. Free time was spent with his friends, his family and a selection of very nice females. Not animals.

But since he was the only bachelor left in their close circle of friends, the duty fell on him. And despite his lack of familiarity with furry creatures, he and Butch got along well enough.

So what had upset Butch enough to cause that mournful sound?

Concerned, Buck dried his face and dropped his towel. Because he slept in the nude, he'd had to pull on underwear when Butch had first awoken him. In the dark, he'd chosen monkey-print boxers given to him as a joke by Ethan's wife, Rosie. He hadn't bothered to put anything more on yet, so he cautiously poked his head around the corner to see what had Butch riled.

The dog sat at the French doors at the back of Buck's apartment, staring out at the shadowy yard.

"Hey, bud, what's the deal?"

Butch cast him a quick worried look, then went back to staring. Buck strode forward, leaned close for his own peek and narrowed his eyes to see through the hazy morning shadows. A trim figure moved across the high grass.

Sadie Harte.

Figured it had to be a woman who'd get the dog baying like a crazed wolf. Occasionally Sadie had the same effect on Buck. He didn't understand her. She was unlike other women he knew. And she made him nuts.

Sadie was the most buttoned-down, prudish, spinsterish twenty-something woman he had ever seen. To call her plain would be an understatement. But did that stop Buck from being nice to her? No. He even teased her a little, tried flirting some. He was friendly, cordial.

It got him nowhere.

In fact, despite her cold politeness, he thought she actually disliked him. In the three months that she'd been his neighbor, not once had she invited him to her apartment. And when he'd invited her to join a small get-together with his close friends, she'd refused. She'd chat with him in the yard, or give a passing greeting, but anything remotely indicative of a relationship seemed to scare her off, even one as casual as friendship.

The only time she'd been to his apartment was to ask him not to make so much noise.

It nettled him that he couldn't get her to warm up to him. Women liked him, damn it. He wasn't an ogre, he had his own business, his mother had taught him manners and he loved to laugh. Not bad qualities, right?

So, why did Sadie keep him at arm's length?

Curiosity was getting to him. Not once had he ever seen her with a boyfriend. She never had company, either. No one. Not family, not friends.

But she did take in rescue animals. Pitiful creatures with their tails between their legs, their ears down. They'd cower whenever anyone got near. Sadie was patience personified, tender and careful and caring. Too many times, Buck had stood at his door and watched her with a dog or two in the small backyard. He'd open his window so he could hear her soft voice as she cajoled an animal into trusting her.

Broke his heart, it really did. The worst part of it all was that Sadie didn't keep the pets. She helped them, and then found them good homes where they could have the love of a family, a big fenced yard, maybe kids to play with.

Today, however, wasn't the same. Normally when he saw Sadie, she had on her schoolteacher duds, as Buck liked to think of them. Even while working with the animals in the yard, she wore long shapeless skirts, flat shoes, loose blouses better suited to a maiden aunt than a young woman. Far as Buck knew, she didn't own a pair of jeans. Or shorts. Or, God forbid, a bathing suit.

She always looked prim and standoffish—and it drove him crazy wondering what she'd look like in something more revealing.... That was the way with men. They always wanted what they couldn't have. He wanted a peek at proper Ms. Sadie Harte.

Today was his day to have his wish come true.

Mesmerized, intrigued and a little amused, Buck leaned against the wall and took in the sight before him. For reasons he couldn't fathom, Sadie was in the yard, running from his lot to her own and back again.

In a thin nightgown.

Now he knew what she slept in. It wasn't the nudity he'd imagined many times over, but the long white gown made of thin cotton would do for future fantasies. The gown was innocent, romantic and hinted at the body beneath.

As Sadie dashed past, his gaze tracked her from the top of her head to her dew-wet feet and back up again. Sleepiness got replaced with sharpened awareness. If Sadie dressed like that more often, her social calendar would be full.

Had she just woken, too? Maybe had a nightmare? They'd talked enough for him to know that Sadie was the sensible sort, not a woman prone to theatrics. Given her wardrobe, she was really modest, too. But this morning she hadn't even donned a housecoat.

At that precise moment, early morning sunbeams

burst through the clouds, making Sadie's gown slightly transparent. Breath caught, Buck took in the sight of the few subtle shadows that hinted at female curves.

The new view was damn interesting. He made note of her narrow waist, her small, high breasts and long thighs. The image of her curled in bed, half-asleep, soft and warm, crowded into his brain.

Butch howled again and scratched at the door, forcing Buck back into the moment.

"Sorry, buddy. I don't want you running after her. No reason for you both to look wacko."

Sadie's light brown, baby-fine hair danced around her head as she whipped this way and that in a crazed fashion. He'd always wanted to see her with her hair down. Because she usually had it twisted up, Buck hadn't known it was bone straight, shoulder-length, or that it had glints of red and gold when the sunlight hit it just right. Now that he did know, he wondered why she always kept it up. It looked real pretty around her shoulders.

Suddenly her small bare feet slid in the tall, dewy grass, almost landing her on her tush. Her arms did cartwheels in the air. She looked panicked before catching her balance and taking off again.

Damn it.

Buck slid the door open a little so she could hear him, but not wide enough for Butch to get out.

"Sadie," he called, hoping to gain her attention without startling her. "Is something wrong?"

Her head jerked in his direction, her chocolate-brown gaze locked on his, and to Buck's surprise, she came barreling toward him. Except for her nose, which had turned pink with the morning chill, her face was pale.

"What the—?" Buck braced himself for the unexpected attack.

Screaming, Sadie jerked the door right out of his hand and nearly knocked him over in her haste to get inside. Her wet feet shot out from under her again when she stepped on his tile floor. Buck caught her under the arms before she hit the ground, aware of her slight weight and fragile bones. She was such a delicate woman—

Sadie paid him no mind. Immediately she slammed the door shut again, using enough force to rattle the panes of glass. Panting, nose glued to the glass, she watched the yard as if expecting something momentous.

Crossing his arms over his chest, Buck leaned against the wall and stared down at Sadie. At six-three, he stood taller than a lot of people. He was used to looking down. But Sadie was more petite than most, damn near a foot shorter than him.

And she was in her nightgown. With pretty, sleep-rumpled hair. And small feminine feet, now wet and dirty with grass stains.

He was still ogling her feet when Sadie jumped. "Ohmigod, there it is! There *she* is!"

Buck looked over her shoulder—and saw another Chihuahua, way fatter than Butch but not much bigger otherwise. The poor thing was soaked from running in the grass. It was also missing some fur. It had a bald forehead with other bare patches on its belly and behind. It was about the ugliest little dog Buck had ever seen, and it charged right up to his door, then put both front paws to the glass.

Sadie screamed. The shocking sound caused Buck to nearly jump out of his underwear. Bewildered, he caught Sadie's upper arm and turned her toward him.

"What in the world is wrong with you?"

"Cicada! Cicada!"

"No," Buck said reasonably, "*Chihuahua*. Probably the homeliest Chihuahua I've ever seen, but you apparently agreed to take it in...."

Sadie turned on him, stretched on her tiptoes to glare and said, "In. Her. Mouth."

Her snarling tone startled him. Buck glanced down at the female dog and...*ewww.*

Right there between the dog's teeth was a chubby, still screeching, red-eyed cicada. He shuddered in honest, horrified revulsion. No wonder the dog was losing fur if she kept things like that in her mouth.

"Good God, is she going to eat it?"

"I don't know," Sadie wailed while doing a little dance and flapping her hands. "She keeps getting...

things, and bringing them home to me. A dead frog, a slimy night crawler, and now *this*."

The little dog whined around the pulsating bug.

"She wants in," Sadie gasped.

"Over my dead body," Buck said.

Her expression earnest, Sadie turned to Buck. She even flattened a hand on his chest, which nearly stopped his heart.

"Go out there and take it away from her," she said, her tone commanding.

Buck stiffened. Of all the things to ask, why did it have to be *that?* And she had asked it while touching his naked chest with her soft little hand, he in his underwear and she in her nightgown, leaving room for all sorts of possibilities.

He hated to disappoint her, but some things were too much. "Sorry, no can do."

Her lips trembled. "Why?"

"I hate cicadas."

Her doelike eyes widened. "But you're a man!"

"Last time I checked, yeah." At least he knew she'd noticed that much. "And stop yelling. You're upsetting the dogs."

Only Butch didn't look upset. He looked...lovestruck. From the moment the other Chihuahua appeared, Butch had gone stock-still, his head tilted, his bulgy little eyes wide. Deep in his throat, a low, husky rumble escaped. Close to a whimper, but

Butch was all male dog, so no way would Buck accuse him of whimpering.

Maybe Butch had bad eyesight and didn't realize the other dog was balding. Maybe—

Sadie's hand, still on his chest, curled into a fist, grasping a handful of hair. "She's *leaving*. You have to go get her."

When Buck just winced, she changed tactics. "Oh please. I can't lose her, but I can't go out there, either. I just can't. Not while she has that awful thing in her mouth."

Buck watched the dog trot around the corner. He shook his head, denying the inevitable. "I hate cicadas. If it were a spider, no problem at all. A snake, I'm there. But cicadas—"

Sadie jerked, nearly removing his chest hair. "She's going to get lost!"

Yeah, she probably would. Disgusted and feeling very put out, Buck gently untangled Sadie's fingers from his chest hair. He leaned down till his nose almost touched hers.

"All right. But you owe me."

Her lashes fluttered in incomprehension.

"Agreed?"

She swallowed, then gave a small nod. "All right."

Satisfied, Buck picked up Butch and handed him to her. "Hold him. I'll be right back."

"Her name is Tish," Sadie yelled in a belated effort to be helpful.

Buck crept out, his eyes darting this way and that, his ears alert to the scream of the cicada. No sign of the dog. No sign of other neighbors, either, thank God, since he wore only boxers.

In a ridiculously high voice for a man who weighed two-twenty-five, all of it muscle, he called, "Tish? Come on, sweetie pie. Heeeere, Tish…"

He rounded the corner of the building and there she sat, her round butt almost hidden in the tall grass. She'd put down the cicada, but it wasn't moving. It just…lay there, looking gruesome and wicked with its fiery eyes exposed. Ick. Why wouldn't the damn thing fly away?

Buck drew a fortifying breath. "Come here, baby," he cajoled.

Tish tipped her head and stared. Her ears perked up, forming a wrinkle in her bald forehead. Buck could see her belly and what looked like a scar. He frowned—until Tish put one paw on the vibrating bug.

Buck's stomach lurched. How could she bare to touch it? "Come on, Tish. Be a good girl, now. No reason to be afraid, baby, I promise. I just want to hold you. That's all."

Behind him, Sadie whispered, "I bet you say that to a lot of girls."

Buck's eyes narrowed. Slowly, so he wouldn't startle the dog, he pivoted to face her. "I thought you were too chicken to come out."

The hem of Sadie's gown was soaked and clung to her ankles. She was shivering in the brisk morning air, with Butch hugged up to her chest, shielding her breasts from view. Butch didn't seem to mind. In fact, he looked real cozy.

"You're between me and the bug." Her expression was taut. "That helps."

A thought occurred to Buck and his eyes rounded. "You didn't close my door, did you?"

Sensing his alarm, Sadie hesitated before admitting, "Um… Yes. Why?"

Just what he didn't need this morning. Letting his gaze settle on hers, he growled, "Because now it's locked. And in case you didn't notice, I'm in my boxers."

She cleared her throat. "I, uh, noticed."

She had? *Of course she had,* he told himself. *They're bright yellow and have monkeys all over them.* His eyes narrowed more. "All right, brainiac, so how am I supposed to—"

Sadie started backpedaling. "Here she comes!"

Buck jerked around, prepared for the worst, but thank God, Tish had left the cicada behind. "That's a good girl, Tish. Come here, baby." He knelt down, held out his arms, and the dog…dodged around him.

Buck tried to grab her, lost his balance and landed butt-first in the wet grass. Dew instantly soaked through his boxers.

Sadie dropped Butch into his lap and took up the

pursuit. After more wild scrambling and a few near spills of her own, she caught Tish. Wild-eyed with alarm, the pudgy little dog wiggled, getting the front of Sadie's gown wet before settling against her and tucking her head into Sadie's underarm.

"There you go, Tish," she crooned softly. "It's okay now. I've got you. I'd never hurt you."

Cradling the fat little dog securely, Sadie came back to Buck. She kissed the dog's ear, which thankfully had fur on it. "Thank you, Buck." She kissed the dog again, and her voice went soft and sweet. "She's more trouble than three Great Danes, but I already love her."

Watching Sadie, Buck felt a funny melting sensation in his chest. Sadie the spinster really did seem to adore the animals she took in. How hard it must be to get attached to a pet, and then let it go to someone else.

Yet that's what she did. Because even though she cared, she couldn't possibly keep them all. She rehabilitated animals, found them good homes and then said goodbye.

What an incredible woman.

Behind him, the cicada began screeching and took flight. Buck ducked, Sadie squealed. Luckily, for all concerned, it flew in the opposite direction before they had time to get too excited.

"No problem." Unwilling to wait around to see if the bug returned, Buck shoved to his feet, reached

back to pluck the clinging wet material of his boxers off his ass, and nodded. "Now how am I going
to get back into my place?"

A blush stained Sadie's cheeks, making her pink
nose less noticeable. Her shoulders slumped and she
bit her lower lip.

It was a nice, full lip, Buck realized. He watched
her teeth worry it and his heartbeat sped up. She was
such an intriguing mix of contradictions. Rigid and
formal in some ways, but overtly sensual in others.

He shook his head and concentrated on her eyes.
They were a soft brown, almost the color of milk
chocolate, framed by darker lashes, and at the moment, filled with guilt.

"I, uh, suppose you could come into my place and
call the manager."

"At six in the morning?" He tucked Butch under
one arm and shifted. Everyone in the complex knew
better than to bother Henry before a respectable hour.
"Respectable" to Henry was around noon, but Buck
wasn't going to sit around in his boxers that long.

Sadie continued to chew on that soft, full bottom
lip, agonizing in indecision until Buck took pity on
her. "How about you pour me a coffee, maybe even
throw some breakfast together, and at eight I'll call
him?"

Her eyes rounded. "Coffee?"

"Yeah. It's a morning drink. Hot, loaded with caffeine. I didn't get a single cup yet, and right about now, I need it."

"I know what it *is*." She struggled again, then gave up and cradled the dog a little lower in her arms. "I have some made already."

"Great." The damp front of her gown clung to her breasts. "I'm freezing my ass off. My nipples are so hard, I could cut glass."

Her mouth fell open, and she looked at his chest.

Buck, feeling provoked by that hot, nearly tactile stare, pointed out gently, "Yours too, for that matter."

Her stunned gaze clashed with his, held for two heartbeats, then she whipped around, giving him her back.

Buck watched the gown settle around her trim hips and the plump curves of her small behind.

Ignoring his comment on her stiffened nipples—which really had tantalized him—she stammered, "Y-you want to stay at my apartment for *two* hours?"

Distracted, he murmured, "Yeah, why?" And then, realizing how unenthusiastic she sounded, he added, "Is that a problem?"

She shrugged.

"Turn around, Sadie. I don't like talking to the back of your head." And he liked seeing her expressive eyes as she spoke, the way she watched him, how easily she blushed.

She turned, but kept the dog held high. "I don't think it's a good idea, that's all."

So, Buck thought, he was good enough to save her bald, bug-eating dog, but not good enough to feed? Did she find him so distasteful that she couldn't tolerate his company for two measly hours?

He shifted again, ready to grumble at her, then saw her eyes dip past his navel. She sighed softly before remembering herself and returned her gaze to his face. This time she didn't blush, but she did look defiant, as if daring him to mention her gaffe.

Given how she kept checking him out, maybe she didn't find him distasteful at all. Buck grinned. "You think I should just sit on my back porch twiddling my thumbs till Henry wakes up? In this wet underwear?" When she still looked undecided, he added, "With a Chihuahua on my lap?"

The mention of the dog did it.

"Oh." She frowned, shrugged her thin shoulders and tucked her silky hair behind her ear. "I, uh, I guess not." And she glanced at his lap again. "That wouldn't be fair to Butch."

If she didn't quit that, the monkeys on his shorts were gonna start dancing. Having a female, even a spinster-type female, stare at a guy's crotch usually got the action started. Seeing as he had no way of hiding it, he just knew her blush would brighten up a few notches.

With perfect timing to break the awkward moment, Butch barked, then stared at Tish while making that low humming sound again. Buck scratched the dog's ear, knowing just how he felt.

"There, you see? Butch isn't as…hardy as Tish. He's freezing and he wants to visit. I think he's even a little enamoured with Tish."

Sadie's chin went up. "Obviously *he* doesn't think she's ugly."

Oops. Had that remark he'd made about Tish insulted Sadie somehow? He hadn't lied. She was bald and fat. Anyone could see that. Still, given how Sadie doted on the dog, he should probably apologize if he ever hoped to make headway with her. "I didn't mean—"

Sadie gave him an evil look. "I think she's beautiful. She just needs some love and nourishment and then her fur will come back in and she'll be a beauty queen, you'll see."

Buck watched her loving the homely little critter, and knew that if anyone could make it happen, he'd put his money on Sadie. "You know what? I believe you."

He turned and started toward her door, but after a few steps, he realized Sadie wasn't following. He looked over his shoulder. She was staring at his butt. It was nice to be appreciated, but hey, the cold was starting to settle into his bones.

"Your fault," Buck accused, knowing his seat was wet, that the material was again clinging. "I've only had these on ten minutes, and now I'll have to change again."

Sadie stared at the boxers, an undisguised look of curiosity on her face.

"I sleep naked. I just put the boxers on to let Butch out."

"Oh." She blinked several times.

Knowing she didn't, but in the mood to tease, Buck asked in his most innocent tone, "Don't you?"

"What?"

She did have a problem concentrating. "Sleep in the nude."

She took a step back. "No!"

"Why not?" When she floundered for an explanation, Buck asked, "Get cold at night?"

She jumped on that. "Yes. I do."

He turned his back on her again, saying, "You need someone to sleep with. Sharing body heat is the best way to stay toasty." He heard her gasp, but luckily, she couldn't see his grin. Yep, things were progressing nicely this morning. "C'mon Sadie. Get a move on before I catch pneumonia."

"Right." Sounding breathless, Sadie scrambled to catch up. Her gown billowed out behind her, and at the last second, she passed him to reach the door first. With her bottom lip held in her teeth, she stood back so he could go in.

Ready and willing to take every advantage, Buck made a point of brushing against her as he entered.

He heard her indrawn breath, felt the stillness that settled over her, and then she moved away.

She flapped a hand toward the tiny kitchenette. "Make yourself comfortable. I'll go dress and be right back."

Buck hated for her to do that. She looked softer and more approachable in her nightgown. If she changed, he just knew she'd pile on the layers and do up all the buttons and start behaving like a spinster again.

But if he suggested she *not* change, then what? She'd probably throw him outside in his near-naked state.

Sadie was almost out of the room, Tish secure in her arms, when Buck said, "Grab me a big towel or something, too, will ya? I want to get out of these wet drawers."

She stumbled to a halt, her shoulders rigid, her spine straight. Without turning to face him, she put the little dog down, nodded and fled the room.

Buck stood there smiling, pleased and pondering Sadie's behavior. She was so easy to read, but also confusing in her different reactions.

Considering how many times he'd caught her at it, she liked looking at him, no two ways about that. But she blushed when she did it.

She hadn't hesitated to barge into his apartment and then order him out to get her dog. Yet, she'd been reluctant to let him into her place, and she seemed stunned silly whenever he got too close to her.

He'd never seen her date. And he'd be willing to bet she'd never seen a guy in his underwear.

Was she one of those women who only had sex in the dark? Not that he minded the dark on occasion, but generally, he liked to look at a woman as much as touch her. But if she preferred the dark, he'd make do.

There was only one problem. Dumb as it seemed, he kept wondering if she'd had sex at all. In so many ways, Sadie acted just like...a virgin.

But that didn't seem likely. Women these days were experimenting before they finished high school, and definitely by college. Sadie had to be—what?— midtwenties, probably twenty-four or twenty-five. The odds of her being *that* innocent were pretty damn slim.

But once Buck thought it, he couldn't get the idea out of his head. It teased him, sending a variety of possible scenarios flitting through his male brain, making him wonder about things he probably shouldn't wonder about.

Like just how much experience she might have. Kisses, surely. Everyone kissed. Even prim, spinsterish women.

But had she ever gotten a really *good* kiss, the killer kind that nearly pushed you over the edge and made common sense not too common?

Had a guy ever touched her breasts? Kissed her nipples? His jaw tightened just thinking about it.

Her breasts were modest, but then, she was a petite woman, so anything larger would have looked overblown on her frame. And seeing her nipples tight against that pale gown had really got to him. Before she'd hidden herself from him, he'd seen them clearly. They were small and tight…and he wanted to taste them.

Would he be the first?

That thought jolted him. Hell, she didn't even like him. He'd had to coerce her into letting him in her apartment.

And, of course, they had nothing in common. Buck wasn't even a dog person! But then, that hadn't stopped Riley from leaving Butch in his care, so did it really matter that Sadie had a lot of dogs coming and going?

He wasn't a spinster person, either, preferring women who were more like him, outgoing and full of laughter, willing to play. But from the day he'd met her, Sadie Harte had intrigued him. Because of her, there were some pretty vivid fantasies zinging around his brain. Watching her blush and listening to her stammer beat drinking coffee alone any day.

Tish trotted past him, drawing Buck's attention. He bent down to pet her, but she scampered away in obvious fear.

"It's okay, baby," he crooned, holding out his hand

for her to sniff. But she cowered in the corner, her ears down, her round eyes watchful. She was truly afraid of him, as if she expected the worst. That bothered Buck. A lot. It sort of reminded him of Sadie.

Unwilling to upset her, Buck slowly straightened and took a step away. It occurred to him that the little dog deserved special attention—just as Sadie did.

Butch struggled to be free, so Buck set him down near Tish. She probably outweighed him by two pounds, not that Butch minded. His eyes were huge, his ears raised on alert, and he definitely had courtship on his mind as he began sniffing Tish from one end to the other.

Truly, love was blind.

At least Tish liked and trusted Butch; her tail wagged in greeting. Like most guys, Butch wasted no time testing the water. Only Tish wasn't having it. She was anxious to play, but amorous attempts got shot down real quick.

"Typical," Buck grunted, thinking of how Sadie had ordered him out to get her dog, then tried to refuse him coffee.

Seeing that the dogs would get along fine, Buck decided to look around Sadie's apartment. It was nice, in a female-cluttered kind of way. Lots of silly knickknacks, lush plants, a few ruffles here and there, like on the white kitchen curtains and the tablecloth on her minuscule dinette table.

On her refrigerator were a variety of photos. No

men, no family, just cats and dogs of varying sizes and ages. It devastated him to think of what they had been through. It took a strong woman with a big heart to heal them. It took a special woman.

A woman without much of a social life.

Beside the refrigerator hung a calendar. Buck hesitated, he really did. But there was no sign of Sadie's return, and the temptation was too great. Because she was so standoffish, this was the best chance he'd likely ever get to know her better.

He walked over to the calendar and read the few notes she'd written in for September. Most of her days were empty, but there were four blocks with writing in them. She had marked an afternoon appointment with a vet, a trip to the dentist, a library book due back and carpet cleaners scheduled.

No dinner dates. No parties. Nothing exciting at all.

He flipped back to look at August and saw much of the same. Then back to July—and he froze.

July second, Sadie had met with a funeral director. Two days later, she'd met a lawyer. In her ladylike script were the words "Settle Mother's estate." And two days after that was "Secure death certificate."

Jesus. Buck swallowed, wondering if her mother's death had precipitated her moving into his apartment complex. The timing was right. He stared off at nothing in particular, trying to remember how she'd been three months ago, when he'd first met her. Quiet, alone. She'd spent nearly a week moving in, unloading her car each day all by herself. Back and forth she'd go, thin arms laden with cardboard boxes, lamps and small pieces of furniture.

What she couldn't carry she'd pushed or dragged in. She'd been relentless, tireless. Determined.

Buck had offered her a helping hand, but she'd refused, thanked him and gone back to work. That first day had seemed to set a precedent. No matter what he offered, she always refused.

The dogs came running past Buck's feet in a blur, ears flattened to their round heads, tiny bodies streamlined. They were a cute distraction. Tish enjoyed Butch's company, and Butch looked besotted.

Buck narrowed his eyes in thought. He had two weeks' vacation lined up, and no real plans because it'd all be spent with Butch. If being here made Butch happy, and being with Butch made Tish happy, then surely it'd make Sadie happy, too.

Maybe he could combine things to everyone's advantage.

He rubbed his hands together as the plan formed. Ms. Sadie Harte wouldn't be able to deny him any longer.

The best way to her heart was through her dog.

CHAPTER TWO

SADIE RAN THROUGH her morning routine in record-breaking time. She hated to admit it, even to herself, but she was half-afraid that if she took too long, Buck would leave. That he was in her apartment in the first place was nothing short of a miracle.

With ruthless determination, she brushed the tangles out of her hair and pulled it back into a quick twist. It wasn't the neatest job she'd ever done, but then she'd never done her hair with a big handsome man waiting for her in his underwear.

Oh, Lord.

Hands shaking, she cleaned her teeth, even gargled for safe measure—not that she expected to be too close to Buck, but… Several times, he'd invaded her personal space.

She stared at herself in the mirror, breathing hard, unseeing. Every single time Buck had gotten near, she'd enjoyed it. It likely meant nothing; he was a big guy and just naturally took up more room than most. But it still thrilled her, even when she knew she had no business being thrilled. Buck was not the kind of man she could start dreaming about.

But he smelled so good. Hot and musky-male. The freshness of the brisk morning air had competed with his scent, creating an intoxicating mix.

She closed her eyes, took a calming breath and quickly washed her face. She never bothered with jewelry or makeup, so less than ten minutes later she was dressed in a crisp pink blouse, a brown skirt with matching cardigan, and her comfortable weekend loafers. She had a bath towel—the largest she owned—draped over one arm.

Still she hesitated. Buck Boswell was just so… *much.* So much male, so much muscle, so much appeal.

And he was sitting in *her* kitchen. In his underwear. With his impressive, hairy chest, wide hard shoulders and flat abdomen all on display.

Sadie shivered in sensual delight. She felt terribly excited and anxious and apprehensive, all at the same time.

Never in her twenty-five years had a man sat mostly naked in her kitchen. Never. She'd had men over, of course. She wasn't a complete social misfit. But they were businessmen, guys from the shelter dropping off a pet for her to nurture, or the lawyer with papers for her to sign concerning her mother's affairs.

In some ways this was very, very different.

In others, it wasn't different at all.

Determined to face reality, Sadie reminded herself that Buck wasn't here for a date any more than the other men had been. Despite his frequent attempts to be friendly, he wasn't interested in her on a personal level; she'd seen the women Buck preferred, and they were nothing like her.

If she hadn't locked him out of his apartment, he wouldn't be here now. She'd ordered him outside to rescue her dog, then repaid him by locking him out in his underwear. She wanted to groan. He had reason to be furious with her.

She'd handled plenty of large male animals that'd been angry and fearful because of past treatment. She'd soothed them, petted them until they calmed down and eventually won them over. She only had a few scars to show for her efforts. Nothing dramatic. Nothing life-altering.

Besides, Buck didn't seem all that angry, and she doubted he went around biting women. And she definitely wouldn't be petting him.

Her heart gave a tiny little trip even as she formed the thought.

But no. He wasn't interested in intimacy, even if she felt that daring. And she didn't. Really. But the thought of stroking his powerful body made her flush, and then snicker at the absurdity of it.

Done being a coward, she forced herself to leave the room. When she rounded the corner of the hall, her eyes went immediately to the small kitchen table, and found it empty. Her heart sank before common sense took over. He wouldn't have left, not in his underwear. Not when he'd be insistent that she let him in.

Curious, she moved a little more quickly into the family room—and almost tripped over him.

Sprawled on his stomach on the carpet, taking up most of her minuscule floor space, Buck was trying to coerce Tish into coming closer. Butch sat beside him, impatiently watching, whining a little, and barking every now and then.

Her heart almost melted. From the day she'd met Buck, she'd been amazed at his size. He clowned around a lot, and he loved to tease and laugh, but there was no denying his strength. His biceps were so big, even using both hands she wouldn't be able to circle them. His shoulders looked like boulders and his thighs like tree trunks. He could intimidate most anyone just by standing there, and he'd certainly intimidated her.

Yet now he was trying his best to sweet-talk her little bald dog. Such an amazing contradiction.

In silence Sadie tracked the long line of his powerful body, from his rumpled brown hair, down the deep furrow of his spine framed by bulging back muscles, across his tight buttocks, along his thick thighs, his hairy calves and finally to his enormous feet.

He was the biggest man she knew. He was the only man she'd ever seen in his underwear. And he had the gentlest, sweetest voice—

"Want me to roll over so you can check out the other side?"

Sweetness changed to amusement when he addressed her, and Sadie's eyes nearly crossed. She glanced at his face, but he wasn't looking at her. He watched Tish, his lopsided smile giving him an endearing look.

She cleared her throat, summoned up a credible lie and said, "I was just trying to decide if this towel is big enough."

"Right."

Time to change the subject, and fast. Sadie coughed. "It's nice that you're trying, but Tish's really shy. She won't come to me willingly, either, and she's especially afraid of men."

"I'll win her over, eventually." He winked, then rolled to his feet and stood in front of her, towering, imposing.

Sexy.

When Sadie just stared up at him, he held out a hand. Reflexively, she jumped back, thinking he meant to touch her. One of his eyebrows lifted, and she saw his hand was held out, palm up.

Oh. She gave him the towel. "You can hang your shorts over the back of a chair to dry if you want."

He smiled, then started for the kitchen. "Sure. Give me one minute—and no peeking."

As if she would! Well…she might. If she knew she wouldn't be caught.

The dogs followed on his heels, and Sadie found herself alone in the tiny living room. She waited, peeked down the hall, and waited some more.

Incredible. A naked man was now in her kitchen. Her belly pulled tight as she pictured it all too clearly in her mind.

"Coast is clear," Buck called.

Being the cautious sort and already flushed from her vivid imaginings, Sadie crept in until she saw that he was indeed covered. Phew. What a relief.

Sort of.

Not that his wearing a towel was that much better than his wearing boxers, but it hid more of him, from beneath his navel to just below his knees. Still, he sat in the stiff kitchen chair, thighs open, one long leg stretched out.

She'd always heard that men had no modesty. This pretty much proved it. Right now, if she bent over just a little, she'd be able to see—

"The coffee smells good."

Sadie met his mocking gaze and had the horrible suspicion he'd read her thoughts. Mortified, she turned her back on him. "You could have helped yourself." As she said it, she got two mugs down from the cabinet.

"I wouldn't be so presumptuous."

That had her smiling. He was by far the most outrageous human being she knew, and she doubted he could spell *presumptuous*. She peeked at him. He'd hung the silly monkey-covered boxers over the back of a chair. The bright yellow in her white kitchen seemed as out of place as Buck himself.

"After saving Tish, I owe you. Especially since I locked you out."

He shrugged a massive shoulder as big and hard as a boulder. "I should have warned you that the door would lock. My fault."

Generous, too. And kind. Why had she never noticed these attributes before?

But she knew the answer. She'd been hurting from the loss of her mother and the upheaval of moving from the only home she'd ever known. She hadn't had the emotional strength to let anyone else into her life, especially not a man like Buck—so powerful and strong and…threatening.

At least to her peace of mind.

Besides, she'd known Buck wasn't the type of man to pay her much attention. He was big and sexy and he almost always had a smile on his face. He'd never been lacking female company, either. Sadie often saw him grilling steaks in his backyard with a woman draped around him.

She'd hear them laughing, and be drawn to look, regardless of her own sense of decorum. Buck liked to kiss and tease. He was a toucher, always stroking the women he had around. Not in a sexual way, though she was sure he indulged in plenty of that in private. But anytime he had a woman near, he was either holding her hand, casually caressing her arm, or running the backs of his fingers across her cheek.

He liked to tickle, too, she'd discovered. More often than not, that game would end up with Buck hoisting the woman into his arms and carrying her inside. Sadie would watch with a sick sense of yearning.

Not that it did her any good to pine after men. For the most part, they ignored her.

Only Buck wasn't ignoring her now.

"I really am grateful," Sadie told him. "I know we haven't always hit it off." To cover that halfhearted apology for past transgressions, she set a steaming mug of coffee in front of him and quickly inquired, "Cream or sugar?"

"Neither, thanks." He sipped, nodded. "Good. Maybe that'll help wake me up."

Tongue in cheek, Sadie asked, "Hard night?"

"Not in the way I would prefer." He tipped his head toward Butch, who trailed behind Tish like a caboose on a train. "I'm not used to having the little guy spend the night. My friend, Riley—you've probably seen him at my place before…?"

"With the red-haired woman, yes." She'd noticed Butch with him, too, of course. Not only was he smaller than most, but a red Chihuahua with black brindling stood out because of the unusual coloring.

"That'd be Regina. Or Red, as Riley calls her."

Riley was one of Buck's quieter, calmer friends. He oozed menace and confidence, but also gentle concern, especially with his wife. Still, even he took part in the boisterous laughing when three or more of the men got together.

"Riley's had Butch over plenty of times," Buck said, "but this is the first time I'm dog-sitting overnight. Butch keeps odd hours, which means I have to keep odd hours, too."

Sadie turned to the refrigerator to rummage for food. They had two hours together and feeding him would help pass the time.

"If he's the reason you were up so early this morning, I can only be grateful. Otherwise I'd have been dealing with that cicada on my own." She leaned around the door to see Buck. "And I hate to admit it, but I'm not sure I could have."

"Don't blame you. Cicadas have to be the nastiest bugs around."

That he'd agree with her made her feel less ridiculous. "Eggs and bacon okay?"

"Sounds great."

She heard her delicate little parlor chair creak as Buck settled back. "Now. About what you said…"

"Hmm?" Sadie dug out her frying pan. Cooking for a man would be a unique experience. Her father had walked out when she was young, leaving her mother to raise her alone. As an only child, Sadie had no brothers, and her mother had never remarried. Because her mother's health had always been frail, she'd never been a big eater. How many eggs would a man like Buck need?

She eyed his enormous form, decided on two, then changed her mind to three.

"About us not always hitting it off."

She nearly dropped an egg. She didn't want to discuss that, but apparently, she'd have to. She probably shouldn't have said anything, but after his heroic rescue this morning, she felt she owed him an apology.

To keep from looking at him, she began laying bacon in the hot skillet. "I'm sure that was more my fault than yours."

Buck leaned forward, bracing one elbow on the table. "Well, now, I don't want to rile you, but until today, you have always seemed kind of cold."

Sadie's back stiffened. "Cold?"

"Unfriendly," he said by way of explanation. "Standoffish. Maybe a little—"

"I get it." She glared at Buck.

He grinned. "Okay. Don't bite my face off."

Blast. She turned back to the stove. Her words had been sharper than she'd meant them to be. But just because she hadn't jumped all over him as most women did, he'd labeled her cold? She bit her lip, slapped two more slices of bacon into the pan, and said through her teeth, "Again, I apologize."

A loud, masculine sigh accompanied the creaking of the chair, and suddenly he was behind her. He didn't say a word, but the sensation of being cornered had her breath catching in her throat. Heat radiated off his big body, touching her all along her back. And she could smell him again, the delicious smell of warm male.

She couldn't turn to face him.

"I riled you."

"No." Sadie denied that with a quick shake of her head.

"I'd like to get to know you better, Sadie."

Oh, Lord. Her stomach dropped to her feet. She'd imagined this scenario many times, but the reality was a lot more nerve-racking.

His long hard fingers wrapped completely around her wrist, emphasizing the disparity in their sizes. He lifted her arm and his rough thumb coasted over a small scar, then another. "How'd you get these?"

With her heart ramming into her chest wall, speech was nearly impossible. "Dog." She cleared her throat. "Make that plural. Sometimes the dogs are…nervous with me."

"You let them bite you?"

"I don't exactly *invite* them to, no. But it happens." He was being so casual about touching her that she regained some—but not all—of her aplomb. "Most of the dogs I take in have been mistreated, abandoned, starved. Naturally, they don't trust humans, with good reason. Anything can startle them."

His thumb continued to caress her wrist, sending her senses rioting. "Hmm. Like what?"

He expected her to indulge in this conversation with him so close, his hands touching her, his expression intent? For most women, it'd be nothing out of the ordinary. For Sadie, it was unheard of.

She cleared her throat and tried to keep her voice steady. "Noise really bothers them. And when they're scared, they lash out. A dog might bite, a cat might scratch. They don't want to hurt me, but they're so afraid."

He frowned.

"It's not their fault. When I first bring them home, I try to give them security and quiet, lots of love and comfort. If they hear a loud noise while I'm trying to get them used to me—"

"A loud noise, like a laugh?"

He caught on all too quickly. She ducked her head. "Sometimes."

Carefully, Buck tugged on her wrist until she turned completely toward him. The top of her head reached his bristled chin. His mouth had gone flat and hard, his jaw tight.

She stared at his chest. He was just so…so *large*. And hard. And sexy.

What would it be like to run her fingers through

that dark, curling chest hair? She knew it was soft because she'd already touched him there, earlier when she'd demanded his help. At the time she'd been too worried about Tish to really appreciate the feel of him. If she nestled her cheek—

He lifted her other arm and examined it, too. "I'm a jerk."

She had to quit daydreaming. "No, you're not."

"That's why you don't like it when I have friends over and we make so much noise. That's why you won't ever join us."

After all his help that morning, she had to be entirely honest with him. It was horrible to admit, but she had to be fair. "The noise can upset the animals, yes. But I don't join in because I'm not very good in social settings."

He bent his knees, lowering himself to look her in the eyes. "Yeah? How come?"

He was so close that she breathed in the heat of his skin. She felt tight from her toes to her eyebrows, and everywhere in between was jumpy. But the big goof probably had no idea what he did to her, how his nearness turned her inside out. He wasn't flirting.

No man ever flirted with her.

Sadie stared at his right nipple and whispered, "Since moving here, I've been really busy."

Skeptical, he said, "Busy, huh?"

She nodded. "Between work and caring for animals, I don't have time to socialize."

"But I'm right next door."

He lifted her free hand and pressed it to his chest—right over the nipple she'd been ogling. Oh, Lord, oh, Lord. To not contract her fingers required all her concentration. She wanted to test his strength, knead him like a cat.

"You could bring your animals with you if you want."

For a moment, Sadie wondered if she was dreaming. Buck couldn't be serious. Not only was a man in her apartment, but now he was offering to let her visit, and with animals in tow?

Why would he make such a generous offer? "I'm…I'm usually not good company. Sometimes the dogs keep me up too late. They have nightmares just like anyone else and I get cranky without enough sleep."

She sneaked a glance at him and saw she'd amused him again. Forging on, she added, "When I don't make as much progress as I like, it gets to me. That makes me crabby, too."

With Buck holding one hand, and her other braced on his rock-hard chest, she had to blow away the lock of hair that had fallen in her eyes. She should have taken more time when pinning it up.

Buck was silent for a moment, watching her so intently, her knees felt ready to buckle.

In a voice that sounded remarkably seductive, he said, "You're a real sweetheart, you know that?"

Her gaze shot up to his face. "What?" Had he just complimented her?

He tucked her hair behind her ear for her, smiled and said, "I'll help cook while you tell me about Tish."

No! He couldn't say something like that and then act like nothing important had happened.

She wanted to know what he meant, but didn't have the nerve to push him. "You can cook?" She no sooner asked it than she felt like a dolt. He certainly didn't look malnourished.

"Yeah, I can cook." He lifted her hand from his chest, kissed her palm and then nudged her out of his way so he could reach the stove. "Nothing too complicated, but breakfast is a must." He turned the bacon with a fork before dropping butter in another skillet for the eggs. "You can make the toast. I'll take four slices."

Like a zombie, Sadie got out the loaf of bread and headed to the toaster.

"So why is Tish bald?"

That brought her around. Sadie glared at his broad back. At least he hadn't said "ugly" again. She glanced at the little dog, now curled in a ray of sunshine with Butch snuggled up to her back. If Tish moved, Butch jumped up in expectation, only to lie back down when Tish failed to do anything astounding. Too cute. Both of them.

"Her previous owner let her breed with a dog that

was too big. She had a really hard pregnancy and couldn't deliver the puppies on her own. The vet had to do a cesarean section."

"They do that to dogs?" He dropped eggs, two at a time, into the sizzling skillet. "Cesareans, I mean."

"When they need to. It wasn't just the size of the pups that gave her problems. She was undernourished, physically stressed in her labor, and someone had just left her on the shelter stoop."

Buck turned from the stove to stare at her with an unreadable expression. "The puppies?"

"Were fine. All five of them." Anger tightened her voice and left her stomach in knots. "Poor Tish didn't know what was going on. She was so afraid and in painful labor. The trauma of surgery, especially the anesthesia, can make the fur fall out. But it'll come back."

Buck paused, then he, too, looked at the dog. "Poor little baby."

At the sound of his voice, Tish lifted her head and stared at him.

Sadie's throat ached, and her heart hurt. "Whoever had her also hit her."

Without looking away from the dog, Buck stiffened. "How do you know?"

"The way she flinches if I lift a hand around her, as if she's expecting a blow. She's so afraid, she fights me every time I put her collar on her, and more often than not, she struggles until she can get out of it. I can't put it on her any tighter without hurting her, and that I won't do." She glanced at Buck. "That's how she got loose this morning."

Buck looked as disturbed by the truth as she felt. "So don't put a collar on her."

"If I don't, she might get away. I can't bear the thought of her getting lost and being alone again."

Buck turned away from the stove, a contemplative look on his face. Then he walked to her patio doors. Tish quickly darted out of his path, which meant Butch followed. Both dogs watched him from several feet away.

Sadie's apartment wasn't as upscale as Buck's. Where he had French doors, she had sliders. He looked out, rubbing his chin in thought. "I could build you a little fence for her. Nothing permanent, so it wouldn't get in the way when the maintenance guys cut the grass. But she's so small, it wouldn't take much to contain her. That way, you could wait to put the collar on her until she starts to like you."

Offended, Sadie said, "She already likes me. That's why she keeps bringing me gifts."

"Gifts?"

"The…bugs and stuff."

"She brings you a cicada because she likes you?" He grunted. "Good thing she doesn't hate you, then."

Ignoring that, Sadie explained, "We're getting along. Tish's just cautious."

"Like you?"

Sadie went still. She was cautious, but she had thought she hid it well. "What do you mean?"

Buck returned to the stove and expertly flipped the eggs. "Anytime I get too close to you, you poker up like you think I'm going to bludgeon you or something."

No, she pokered up like she thought she might jump his gorgeous bones. It didn't matter that she was plain and inexperienced. She was as curious as any woman, with all the same desires. But because of her natural shyness, the overwhelming responsibility she'd held for a sick parent, and her own high standards, she'd had very little chance to indulge those desires.

Sometimes she felt ready to explode with frustration. And putting her next to a guy like Buck, a guy who oozed confidence and sex appeal, was like waving a flame around a keg of gasoline. She didn't want to do anything to embarrass herself, so she tried very hard to contain her interest.

Naturally, she couldn't tell him any of that. "I, uh, that is…"

"You don't date much, do you?"

If by "not much" he meant never, then…

"Sorry," he said, not sounding the least bit sorry. "I don't mean to be nosy. Well, I guess I do. But I don't mean for it to embarrass you."

Sadie fell back against the counter. Her thoughts went this way and that, trying to figure him out.

What possible reason could he have for wanting to know about her lack of a social life?

The wall clock ticked loudly while she considered it. The dogs stared at her in expectation. Sadie straightened. She had a man in her kitchen. And not just any man, but Buck Boswell. He was showing interest. He was more naked than not. Shyness be damned, she had a right to ask.

She cleared her throat. "Why do you want to know?" Her voice emerged as a hesitant squeak.

He carried both plates to the table. "A guy needs to find out these things."

She looked at the dogs, and they looked back. No help there. They wore identical expressions of confusion. She turned back to Buck. "But...why?"

He moseyed over to the toaster and stared at it as if willing the bread to pop up. "We're neighbors. We're both single. Close to the same age." He looked up at her. "I'm thirty-one."

He seemed to expect some reply, so Sadie said, "I'm twenty-five," and he nodded.

"We both have Chihuahuas, too. That's a lot of stuff to have in common."

He had to be kidding. In truth, they had nothing in common.

"I was hoping to visit more," he said. "Hang out a little with you and Tish. But I don't want to intrude if you're going to be busy."

"Visit more? Hang out?" *Real intelligent, Sadie.*

Soon he'd consider her a blithering idiot, as well as a wallflower.

Buck shrugged away her stammers. "Yeah. Nothing formal." He looked down at her, his green eyes warm and speculative. "For now."

For now? Was he saying that, later, he'd want to get more formal?

"I mean, we have two dogs to deal with, right? Butch isn't nervous like Tish, but he doesn't much like to be left alone. No matter what I do, he's on my heels."

Sadie pointed out the obvious. "He's not on your heels now."

That made him grin. "No, he's busy trying to woo Tish, but I'm still in his sights. He might not like it if I left. So maybe we could hang out together at my place or yours. Maybe watch a few movies or something."

"Oh."

He smiled down at her. "You like movies?"

"Yes." She loved movies. They were a form of entertainment she could enjoy in her own home, with her pets nearby.

"Great. Seems like Tish would get used to you quicker if you were around more, right?"

Sadie bit her lip. "I didn't intend to leave her alone, except when I go to work."

"But see, that's the good part. I'm on vacation, so I don't have to go to work. I could be here while you're gone, and maybe she'd get used to me that much quicker, too."

His sincerity held her in place as surely as if her feet were nailed to the floor. "I suppose." She couldn't believe this. Buck Boswell, a hulking bachelor with a score of women at his beck and call, was trying to sell her on the idea of him spending more time with her.

Or was it that he wanted to spend time with Tish? Sadie frowned, more than a little confused.

"If I'm here enough," Buck continued, "she'll start to trust me. And if she trusts one human, she'll trust another, right?"

Sadie nodded. "That sounds, uh, reasonable."

"And then maybe…" He smoothed his big hand over her hair, once again tucking it into place. "You'll start to trust me a little, too."

No one, except her mother, had ever felt free to touch her so casually. To keep from falling over, Sadie took two deep breaths. She had no idea what was going on.

His voice dropped when he murmured, "Your hair is really soft." His thumb grazed her jawline. "Your skin, too."

Sadie's insides started a slow burn. She was about to melt when the toast popped up, making her jump a foot.

Buck reached for the toast before she could. "So

tell me, you seriously involved with anyone right now?"

She was seriously involved in a *fantasy.* "No."

He took a second to absorb her fast reply. "Casually dating anyone?"

Sadie shook her head.

He stared at her, brows slightly drawn, expression probing. "Dating at all?"

Why did she have to be so fair-skinned? Her blushes didn't make her look pretty. They just made her look scalded. "No."

"Why not?" Buck slathered an obscene amount of butter onto the toast while awaiting her answer.

What to tell him? The truth? She actually shuddered. No, some humiliations should be kept private forever. Like being stood up on prom night. Her blush intensified with the awful memory of standing there in her fancy dress with her fancy hairdo, feeling so giddy and anxious—and two hours later, finally accepting the reality that her date wouldn't show. Being the sophomore joke had been enough to last her through the rest of high school.

She locked her knees. "There hasn't been much time." Her eyes sank shut at that awful fabrication. She had all time in the world and he probably knew it.

"So you used to date, but don't much anymore?"

She refused to bare her soul, to totally expose herself and her lacks. She was a grown woman, not a wounded child. Her chin lifted. "Are we going to eat this morning, or keep talking?"

"Let's do both." He turned to carry the toast to the table, and almost tripped over the dogs. Butch knew better than to think he'd get table food, but Tish apparently had no manners. She jumped, barked, begged.

"So now you like me?" Buck inquired of the little dog with a smile.

"Sorry." Sadie hurried to the cabinet and got out the box of doggie treats. "When we first got her, she was so thin that everyone hand-fed her, just to make sure she'd eat. Now she thinks any food near a hand is hers for the taking."

"It fattened her up, so I'd say it worked."

Sadie couldn't take offense at that comment; Tish was as plump as a little penguin. She dug out a small bone-shaped treat, then thought to ask, "Is it okay if I give Butch one, too?"

"Sure." Buck set the food on the table and again crouched down to pet Tish. She lurched away with a yelp, making him sigh. "That's okay, baby. I understand."

The way he knelt left his towel wide open over his spread knees. Sadie leaned forward to peek, but could only see his upper thighs. Nice, muscular thighs.

Buck turned to smile up at her. Either he didn't notice what she was doing, or he chose to ignore it.

"I *really* want to hold that little dog."

"I know. Me, too. Eventually she'll let us."

He turned back to the dog. "I'm always patient when I want something."

His tone of voice was sweet and gentle. Tish watched him, creeping closer, inching toward the table.

"Good girl," Buck crooned softly.

Slowly, he reached out to her. He was almost touching her when Tish snatched his colorful boxers off the back of the chair and ran off.

Startled, Buck shot back to his feet. "Hey!"

Sadie watched her run around the corner and into the living room. "Uh…"

Butch ran after Tish, and Buck was next in line. Sadie followed. The dogs had gone under her couch. When Buck knelt down to look underneath, both dogs barked at him, trying to warn him off.

"What the hell is she doing with my underwear?"

Sadie stared at the picture he made, on his knees peering under her furniture. "I don't know." And as Buck stood to face her, she said, "I can get them for you later, when she comes back out."

Buck hesitated, then, amazingly enough, stood, slung his thick arm around her shoulders and led her back to the kitchen.

"I suppose that'll be okay."

Awareness made Sadie so stiff she could barely walk. Buck's arm was heavy and warm, his embrace casual. He kept her tucked in close to his side. When they reached the kitchen, he pulled her chair out for her, waited until she got seated, then joined her at the table.

"So tell me what you do. I know you work at the shelter, but what's your job there?"

He began eating, not paying her much mind, and that made it easier to converse with him. "I work as a vet's assistant."

He nodded. "I sort of figured it'd be something like that."

"I've always loved animals."

"It shows."

He was so open and friendly, he made it easy to talk. "I'd always wanted to be a vet, but I never got my schooling finished for it."

"How far did you get?" In two large bites, he finished off a piece of toast.

Watching him eat amazed Sadie. Without looking like a glutton, he polished off the food in short order. She pulled her gaze away from him to taste her own eggs. Delicious.

"I got accepted to a veterinary college," she admitted, and hoped she didn't sound boastful.

"Yeah? You have to have a really high GPA for that, right?"

She remembered how thrilled and proud her mother had been. Buck sounded almost as admiring. "Yes. Admission was selective, but I'd already completed a pre-veterinary curriculum with a strong focus on the sciences. Anatomy, physiology, chemistry, microbiology and some clinical sciences."

"Wow. Heavy subjects. So what happened?"

Sadie toyed with her fork. "My mother needed me at home." So that he wouldn't misunderstand and think her mother selfish, she rushed through the rest of the explanation. "She'd raised me on her own. For as long as I can remember, it was just the two of us. She did a great job, but she was sick for years."

"Sick how?"

"Cancer." Just saying the word made Sadie relive the hurt. "She'd go into remission, feel a little better, then go downhill again. Each time it got worse and worse, and her recovery from treatment took longer. The cancer began to spread." Her voice started to shake. It hadn't been that long since she lost her mother, and talking about it still hurt. "I didn't want her to be alone."

Buck pushed his empty plate away. His brows were drawn with concern and sympathy. "You took care of her?"

"Me and a nurse who visited three times a week."

"How old were you when she first got diagnosed with cancer?"

Looking back, it seemed her mother had always been ill, but Sadie knew that wasn't true. It was just that when most young women were breaking away from home, striving for independence, she'd had to stay close to her mom. "We first found out she had breast cancer when I was almost fifteen. She had surgery, and things seemed okay for a year or so. Then they found more cancer. Lung. Bone." She swallowed and pushed her plate away. She couldn't eat another bite. "Eventually brain cancer."

Buck reached across the table and took her hand. "Must've been really rough."

Watching her mother weaken over time had been a living hell. But she'd borne it all alone. There'd been no one, other than peripheral strangers—doctors, nurses and a variety of legal people—to offer her any support or assistance.

For years, she'd been hungry for human contact, and to compensate for that lack, she'd turned to the animals she'd understood best. But now Buck held her hand as if he really cared. Sadie was amazed, and very grateful.

"Toward the end, she had very few good days."

Buck turned her hand over and rubbed her palm with his thumb while looking into her eyes. Sadie felt touched everywhere. Not just on her skin, but in her heart, too. For once, the icy memories didn't linger. They got soothed away by the intrusion of other, warmer emotions.

It was the oddest feeling, like falling into a deep, heated pool. Silence stretched out between them. She saw Buck's eyes narrow marginally, saw his shoulders tense.

He said, "Finish your breakfast, okay?"

"I am finished." Her upset was over, but now she was too excited and anxious to eat.

The dogs came back into the kitchen, distracting them both. Tish crept, keeping her eyes on the humans. Butch just pranced beside her, waiting as Tish dragged the colorful cotton boxers to a sunny spot in front of the sliding doors. She laid them down, used her nose to push them this way and that, digging, tugging with her teeth, before circling three times and dropping into the middle of the material with a grunt.

Butch, openly confused but unwilling to be left out, glanced at Sadie and Buck, back at Tish, then curled into her side.

A slow grin came over Buck's face. "I think she likes me."

Sadie actually giggled. "If she's willing to sleep in your underwear, then she must."

He turned to face her, still holding her hand captive. "And what about you?"

"I don't want to sleep in your underwear."

Buck accepted the joke with a laugh. He tugged her closer, leaning toward her at the same time. "But do you like me, Sadie? Because I like you. A lot."

And to Sadie's utter shock and excitement, he kissed her.

CHAPTER THREE

Buck felt as though someone had just knocked him onto his terry-cloth-covered ass. It was a simple kiss, a featherlight brush of his mouth on hers. No tongues. No real heat.

And his whole body was buzzing.

He pulled back just a little to take in Sadie's expression. Her eyes were closed, her feathery lashes leaving shadows on the smooth texture of her flushed cheeks. She swayed a little toward him.

Damn.

When he'd started all this, he'd meant to go slow, to get to know her better, figure out why she didn't seem to like him.

Given her expression now, she liked him all right. But Sadie had more burdens than any single woman should have to bear. She was shy and sweet and so damn generous.

He leaned in again, but this time he let his nose graze her throat, inhaling the sweet female scent of her. You'd think a woman who played with animals from sunup to sundown wouldn't smell so nice. But she did. He felt…intoxicated.

And if his friends knew his thoughts, they'd laugh themselves silly.

Ethan and Riley and Harris, his best buddies for some time now, all considered him too goofy to ever settle down. Their wives probably agreed. He'd once heard Rosie call him a "goober." And then Clair, Harris's wife, had qualified that he was a "big lovable goober." Whatever the hell that meant. It didn't sound very complimentary, but the women had said it with affection, not insult, so Buck hadn't taken offense.

He knew he wasn't intense like Riley, and he sure as hell wasn't heroic like Ethan and Harris, who were both firefighters. He was just himself, easygoing, ready to laugh. He loved his lumberyard, his family and his friends. He loved women, and he especially loved sex. He was fortunate in that he'd inherited some good genes, resulting in a body that was tall and strong and well-muscled. All the men in his family were big—and plenty of women appreciated that.

He enjoyed good health and business success, so he'd never needed to take life too seriously. But bless her heart, Sadie hadn't been given that choice.

As he'd told her, she was a sweetheart. Petite and shy and loving. Determined and smart, but so withdrawn. He wanted to bring her out of her shell. He wanted to watch her laugh.

He wanted to get her naked and feel her softness

everywhere, and he wanted to hear her scream with a mind-blowing orgasm.

Yeah, he wanted that most of all.

"Buck?" Her voice was tentative, confused.

He sniffed his way up to her ear, brushed his nose across the downy hair at her temple. "Yeah?" he whispered, feeling more aroused by the second.

She cleared her throat, very stiff and still. "What are you doing?"

"Smelling you." He leaned back to see her face. "You smell good enough to eat."

A rush of scarlet filled her cheeks. "I, uh…"

"I don't mean right this second. We'll save that for later."

She looked ready to faint, prompting him to chuckle. He fingered the high neckline of her cardigan. "Aren't you too warm in this?"

"No." She clutched the neck together in a protective gesture.

"You sure?" Slowly, using the same care he'd shown with Tish, Buck pried her fingers loose. "It's comfortable in here, Sadie." Her top two buttons were undone, so he let his fingers drop to the third button, right above her breasts. It slid free. "I'm only wearing a towel and I'm not cold." Just the opposite, in fact.

Her eyes were wide and slightly dazed, her breath low and uneven.

When he finished undoing all the buttons, he

urged her to her feet and carefully pried the sweater off her shoulders. She was so fine-boned and fragile, he took extra care with her. Standing by her made him feel like a great ox.

She stared at him with wary apprehension and what he could have sworn was hopefulness.

He dropped her sweater over the back of her chair. "Okay?"

Practically panting, she licked her lips, blinked twice and nodded. Her breasts rose and fell beneath the pink blouse.

So damn sweet. He cupped her face. "Can I ask you something really personal?"

She stared at his mouth. "What?"

"When was the last time someone kissed you silly?" He waited, wondering if it'd been a week, a month, or longer. She seemed very unsure of herself and what he had planned.

On stiff legs, Sadie took a tiny step closer to him, then another. With incredible caution, she lifted her hands and let them touch his chest. Her fingers spread out, tangling in his chest hair, while her thumbs rubbed small inquisitive circles on his skin.

It drove him wild.

With her attention on her hands, all he could see was the top of her head. "Look at me, Sadie."

She did, tipping her head way back. Her lips parted.

"Answer my question."

Her expression was shy, embarrassed, resigned. She lifted one delicate shoulder and sighed out her reply, "Never."

"Never?" Disbelief made his voice sharper than he'd intended.

She shook her head and admitted with a grimace, "I've never dated. Never had a boyfriend. Never... done any of that stuff."

Conflicting emotions raged through Buck. Tenderness was at the forefront, so strong it nearly choked him. Damn, but he wanted to pull her onto his lap and cherish her.

Lust ran a close second. He was only a man, and knowing that no one had done *anything* with her before him turned him on. He'd be her first in every way, and there were so many things he could show her, teach her, let her experience.

Pity was there, too, because no woman should have been so ignored. He wished like hell that he'd forced his way over sooner, instead of letting her remain alone for so long. He'd stupidly wasted three months.

Behind everything else he felt was the need to stake a claim. Not just a friendly, neighborly-type thing, either. He wanted to somehow bind Sadie to him, and the easiest way presenting itself was through sex. Because of her inexperience, intimacy would mean more to her than it did to the women he usually spent time with.

"I'm going to kiss you, silly, okay?" It felt strange to announce his intent, but he needed to know that she understood, that he wasn't taking advantage of her naiveté.

"If…if you really want to."

Oh, yeah, he wanted to. He cupped her face, tipped her chin up and tried to quiet the wild drumming of his heart so he could do this right. "I want to."

It'd been a hell of a long time since he'd had to concentrate on a kiss. Usually it was the way he touched a woman, with the purpose of bringing her to orgasm, that made him concentrate. Not the foreplay, and for sure not the preliminary kissing.

The urge to devour her mouth was strong, but Buck managed to go slow, moving his mouth over hers until she softened and sighed. He licked her bottom lip, liked it enough to do it again, then gently nibbled. Her breath caught.

"Open up for me, Sadie."

With an excited little moan, she did, and Buck again cautioned himself to go slowly. He held her still and tentatively explored the moist heat of her mouth, letting her get used to his tongue, to the added excitement of a French kiss.

Damn, he'd forgotten how much fun kissing could be. He'd forgotten the sexiness of it. He opened one big hand over the back of Sadie's head to keep her close, and slanted his mouth over hers, deepening the kiss, feeling the heat rise between them. He realized he could kiss her all day and not get enough.

Shyly, her tongue came out to touch his. He felt a sexual jolt so powerful he couldn't hold back his groan.

He lifted his head and looked at her, amazed by his own reaction. He'd had plenty of hot, wet-tongue duels in his day, most that he knew would lead to hotter, wetter sex. But none had affected him quite like this.

Sadie's eyes were only partially open, her cheeks warm, and as he watched, she slowly licked her lips, as if savoring the flavor of their kiss.

Another groan tried to crawl up his throat. He wanted to lower her to the kitchen floor and show her just how clever his tongue could be.

Instead, he pulled her into his chest to hold her close. It took him a full minute to find his voice. In the meantime, he stroked her back and rubbed his chin against the crown of her head.

Finally, wondering at her thoughts, he asked, "Well?"

"Wow."

She sounded as breathless as he felt, which made him smile. "You liked it?"

She snuggled closer before asking, "Could we do it again?"

She'd be the death of him. "Oh, yeah. But I gotta take a break first."

Sadie reared back, blinking fast. "I'm sorry. I didn't mean to be—"

Buck put a finger to her mouth to hush her. Her lips were full and soft, slightly swollen. "If I kiss you again right now, I'm going to lose it. I don't want to rush you."

With no hesitation at all, she said, "You're not."

Her fast reply was so endearing, his grin went crooked. "I will be if we don't slow it down a little."

"But I don't mind."

Damn, she obliterated his control. "Sadie—"

"You don't understand, Buck. I didn't think anything like this would ever happen to me."

She looked so vulnerable, it bothered him. "That's just crazy." He knew damn good and well that other men had wanted her. But her eyes were now wide and sincere.

"No, it's not. Men like you don't look at me twice."

"Men like me?"

"Nice men. Attractive men." She again ducked her face, leaving him to look at the top of her head. "I've been asked out a few times, but it was by men I wasn't interested in. Maybe my standards are too high. Maybe I expect too much. But I just couldn't encourage a man I wasn't attracted to."

"Who asked you out?"

Her little nose wrinkled. "There's this one guy who cleans at the shelter. He…smells funny. And his hair always looks dirty."

In a dry tone, Buck said, "Cleanliness doesn't qualify as part of a high standard."

"There's also this man who won't get his cat spayed. Three times now he's dropped off litters at the clinic." Her brows puckered. "I don't like him."

"Anyone who doesn't take proper care of their pet is a jerk, and of course you wouldn't date a jerk." He tipped his head to see her face. "What about in high school or college? Surely—"

She shook her head, cutting him off before he could finish the question.

"Well, why not?" *Everyone* dated as teenagers. Even if she'd just gone to a few school dances, they counted.

Her bottom lip was caught in her teeth. Sadie touched his chest, absently toying with his chest hair. Buck didn't think she even realized what she was doing.

"Sadie?"

"I didn't date then, either."

Buck could tell the topic was difficult for her. He had a feeling it was important, though, so he pushed her. "You said you trust me."

Her sigh was long and exaggerated. "Back in high school, a few guys asked me out. But I had to turn them down."

"Because?"

"They just asked me as part of a dare. Like a…a joke."

Suspicions rose. "What makes you say that?"

"Because once, only once, I said yes." She lifted her chin, catching him in her dark gaze. "It was prom night, and I got stood up. That next week in school, everyone was laughing about it."

Aw, hell. His gut cramped. Stupidly enough, he wanted to find the punk who'd bruised her feelings and pound on him. "It was his loss."

Sadie smiled, then laughed. "I doubt he saw it that way."

"So you're attracted to me?" Buck deliberately took her off guard with that question, changing the subject at the same time.

"What?"

"You said you couldn't get involved with a guy you weren't attracted to. And since we'll be getting involved…" He waited, but she didn't deny it. "I figured you must be attracted. Right?"

She stared at him in disbelief. "Of course I am. What woman wouldn't be?"

He had to laugh. The confusion on her face was priceless. "Honey, plenty of women turn me down."

"But…why would they?"

Buck tucked her face into his shoulder so she wouldn't think he was laughing at her. "You're going to make me conceited."

He felt her lips touch his skin. "No. But you are sexy and strong and handsome and funny."

"Sadie, stop."

"It's true."

Her compliments should have pleased him, except that he knew she drew unfavorable comparisons between them. "You're not too strong from what I can tell, but you're definitely sexy."

She snorted, and coming from Sadie it seemed a very odd sound.

Buck caught her face and turned it up toward his. "It's true. You're about the softest thing I've ever touched." He kissed each of her eyelids and felt the flutter of her long lashes. "Your eyes could eat a man alive."

She looked away in embarrassment.

"And your big heart just turns me to mush."

Her gaze swung back to his. "My big heart?"

"The way you love the animals." She'd shared so much, he figured he should share a little, too. "Do you know, I've stood at my window and watched you with them? A few times, I even hung out in the yard, wanting to join in." He flicked the end of her nose. "But you never asked me to."

Her brows shot up. "I didn't think you'd want to."

"So now we're both learning something."

Tish let out a squeaky bark, drawing their attention.

Sadie groaned. "Oh, no. She wants out again."

The dog stood on Buck's underwear, her ears back, waiting.

"I can help you get the leash on her."

"Easier said than done. She runs from me, and as you've already seen, she's hard to catch."

Buck decided to try his luck. But sure enough, as soon as he got close to Tish, she grabbed up his underwear and ran off with Butch in hot pursuit. They shot under the couch and out of reach before Buck could stop them.

Sadie stepped up behind him. "See? This is why I had to buy a carpet shampooer."

"Why?"

"Because she wants out, but she's afraid of me, so she sneaks off and ends up...piddling on the floor."

Buck grinned. Piddling, indeed. "Let's put our collective minds to this one. We're bigger, definitely smarter and human. I might not be the swiftest guy going, but no way am I going to be outwitted by a Chihuahua."

Sadie sat on the chair opposite him. "Any ideas?"

Buck bent and looked beneath the couch. Butch, normally so nice to him, had turned into Demon Dog. He snarled and growled, placing himself in front of Tish.

"You'd think I was a marauder of Chihuahuas the way he's carrying on," Buck complained.

"He thinks he's guarding her."

"Easy boy. She's all yours." Butch was not reassured, given the way he continued to bristle. Then, a thought coming to mind, Buck said, "Wanna go out? C'mon, Butch. Wanna go out?"

Butch's ears perked up and he barked in excitement. He started to crawl out from under the couch, but when Tish didn't follow, he whined.

Buck moved to stand behind Sadie's chair. "Let's be really quiet. Don't move, okay?"

She shrugged.

"C'mon, Butch old buddy. Let's go outside."

Again, Butch came out, then grumbled and whined until Tish poked her little bald head out. She had Buck's underwear clamped in her teeth. She eyed the humans, then crept toward the patio doors.

"Where's the leash?" Buck asked.

"On the wall by the door. But don't pounce on her. If you do, she'll never learn to trust me."

"I haven't pounced on you, have I?"

"Uh…no."

"Remember—trust." He slipped out from behind the chair. Butch saw him and started yapping in happiness. Slowly, Buck knelt down about five feet from the dogs. "Come on over here, Butch. If you do, she might."

Butch never turned down a nice pet session, so he did as instructed. Buck spent a long time just stroking the dog, playing a little, lavishing attention on him. Tish watched from a safe distance in fascination and obvious yearning.

She reminded Buck of Sadie.

He turned to her. "Sit with us. Slowly. Tish knows you better than she does me."

Sadie sidled over to them, took the leash off the peg on the wall, then knelt down beside Buck. She scratched Butch behind his big ears. Finally, after a long, long time that strained Buck's patience but didn't seem to bother Sadie at all, Tish took a few steps toward them.

She halted, eyeing them warily.

They deliberately ignored her, hoping that without their attention on her, she'd feel safe and join in. Eventually she got close enough to lean on Sadie's foot. The yellow underwear hung from the side of her mouth, looking like a flag.

Sadie cautiously reached out and scratched the dog's chin. As long as she didn't raise her hand or move too fast, Tish was tolerant. But the second Sadie went to pet the top of her head, Tish flinched away.

Buck's voice was soft, hiding his frustration. "It's okay, baby girl. No one's going to hurt you." He held out his hand, palm up. Tish sniffed, but wouldn't rejoin them.

Butch didn't like being ignored and again insisted on going outside as promised.

Very, very slowly, Buck caught Tish. She went spastic, howling and moaning and kicking.

He held on to her, and she held on to his underwear.

If it hadn't been for the dog's fear, Buck would

have been amused. "You can keep my drawers, baby girl. Whatever you want."

Sadie, fretting like a worried mama, hurried to get the leash on her and open the door. Buck scanned the yard, thankful it was empty, and set Tish outside. To their surprise, she didn't fight the leash as long as Butch stayed beside her.

And Butch, bless his savage little animal instincts, didn't move more than an inch away from Tish. It was almost comical watching them. They kept bumping into each other, tripping over Buck's colorful boxers.

Sadie sat in her one and only lawn chair, and Buck stood beside her, holding the reins on the dog. "Tish makes a better leash for Butch than the one Red usually uses for him."

Sadie grinned. "He's protective."

Buck bent and kissed her temple. "Most of the male species suffers the same affliction."

Because the dogs were happy, they spent a long time outside. The sun shone directly on them, warming their skin and burning the chill out of the morning air until the day felt pleasant. The dogs were sometimes playing, sometimes just lying in the sun-warmed grass. Tish forgot all about her leash.

Sadie watched the dogs with a pleased smile, and Buck watched Sadie.

The sunlight did amazing things to her hair, and showed the perfection of her skin. In the bright light,

Buck could see that her lashes were tipped with gold, and there were a few faint freckles over the bridge of her nose. He thought she looked beautiful, especially when she smiled so sweetly.

After a while, he lifted her from the seat, sat down, then situated her on his lap.

"Want to make out?"

"Here?" Her scandalized gaze darted around the empty yard. "Someone might see us."

"Who? Most everyone is still in bed, and even if they're not, they still couldn't see us. My apartment is empty, and your apartment is on the corner."

He enjoyed seeing her face heat with guilt.

"Come on, Sadie," he teased. "You know you want to."

She hesitated only a moment. "I do."

The dogs were currently dozing, so Buck was able to engage all her attention.

It was wonderful.

True, he wore no more than a towel. But it was his vacation and doing nothing more important than smooching with Sadie just felt right. It was frustrating, to be sure. He hadn't indulged in this much innocent kissing since junior high school. Sadie's enthusiastic involvement made it even harder. She followed wherever he led. If he kissed her throat, she murmured in delight, then reciprocated, putting her soft lips against his heated skin. If he stroked her narrow waist, she followed suit by smoothing her hands over his chest to his abdomen.

Her innocent exploration was more exciting to him than the lovemaking of other women.

When enough time had passed, Buck reluctantly went inside to call Henry. The manager grumbled and groused, but finally agreed to meet Buck at the back of his apartment when Buck explained he was damn near naked.

Sadie giggled at his predicament. But she quickly sobered when Buck picked up a disgruntled Butch and started to leave. She walked him to the door, her feet lagging, her eyes downcast.

They stopped at the door. "Have lunch with me?" Buck asked.

Immediately her expression brightened. "Yes."

He shook his head. She wore her heart on her sleeve, leaving herself so open to hurt. It worried him. "I have a few errands to take care of, but I can be done by noon. You like pizza?"

"Yes."

"I'll pick it up. Wanna come to my place?"

She shook her head. "I can't leave Tish…"

"So bring her with you." He leaned forward and took her mouth in a warm kiss, already anxious to see her again. "You're a package deal, right? No problem. Butch would chew my ankle if I didn't invite her along."

Laughing, Sadie said, "All right, then. We'd be happy to accept."

CHAPTER FOUR

Buck had just returned from buying groceries when a knock sounded on his front door. Thinking it might be Sadie, he opened the door with a fat smile—which twisted to a scowl when he saw the faces of his friends Ethan and Harris.

"What are you two doing here?"

Harris shoved his way in. "What kind of welcome is that?"

Butch rounded the corner in a near-hysterical tangent, slid to a halt when he saw it was only Harris and Ethan, and immediately quieted. His tail stopped wagging, and his little face showed his disappointment.

Buck decided that he and Butch were in a bad way. They were two bachelors who'd accepted their fates, but hadn't yet informed the ladies of the new plans.

Ethan stepped past Buck. "Hey, Butch." Then to Buck, he said, "You been torturing the little guy? He doesn't look too happy."

"He probably thought you were Tish."

"Tish?" Harris straightened in interest. "What the hell kind of name is that for a woman?"

"I think it's cute," Ethan argued. "She sounds like a woman with big boobs."

Harris laughed. "And an IQ of two."

"Look who's talking," Buck accused. "Has anyone accused you of being bright lately?"

Smug, Harris said, "Yeah. Clair."

"She doesn't count," Ethan argued. "She married you, so she has to keep your ego healthy."

"Actually," Buck interjected, before they could start a debate on Harris's intelligence or lack thereof, "Tish is fat and bald and this morning, she stole my underwear."

Both men wore comical faces of horror, until Buck began to chuckle. "She's my neighbor's dog. A Chihuahua. Butch took one look at her and fell madly in love."

"Poor guy," Ethan said sympathetically. "I know just how rotten that feels."

"Right," Harris sneered. "You knew Rosie *forever* before you realized you loved her."

"Wrong. I always knew I loved her. I just didn't realize I was in love with her. Besides, you're no better. It wasn't until you saw naked photos of Clair that you got the love bug."

Harris, ever sensitive about the photos Clair's past boyfriend had taken without her knowledge, grew taut with anger.

"No fighting. It'll upset Butch." Buck turned his back on them and headed for the kitchen. "So do either of you yahoos believe in love at first sight?"

"No," Harris said.

"No way," Ethan agreed, then he added, "But Riley must."

Buck paused in the middle of putting cans of cola into the fridge. "That's right. He took one look at Red and was a goner, wasn't he?"

"In a big way," Ethan agreed. He snagged a cola before Buck could put it away. "It was almost embarrassing, the way he branded her right off."

"I wish he was here."

Harris and Ethan looked at each other. Slowly they grinned with conspiratorial humor. Harris, being the bigger goof of the two, said, "Tell Uncle Harris what ails you."

"Go to hell."

"A woman ails him," Ethan said. "I know the signs."

"It was only a matter of time, you know." Harris grabbed a can of cola, and together, he and Ethan made a toast. "Here's to happily married men."

Buck said, "Marriage hasn't matured either of you at all."

Ignoring that gibe, Ethan said, "So tell us who the lucky lady is." His brows pulled together in consideration. "Is it Beth? I remember you were partial to her, but I gotta tell you, Rosie doesn't like her much."

"Rosie doesn't like any woman who smiles at you, Ethan, but no, it's not Beth."

"Then it must be Rachel." Harris held his hands out in front of his chest as if juggling melons. "There's a lot of her to love."

Buck narrowed his eyes. "Clair's gonna kill you when she hears what you said."

"Well, for God's sake, I was just kidding around. Don't tell her!"

Just then, a knock sounded on Buck's French doors—and there stood Sadie with a squirming Tish in her arms. Buck's underwear was half wrapped around the dog. Belatedly, Sadie noticed Ethan and Harris and appeared ready to bolt.

Buck wondered if he could somehow magically make the guys disappear. He ran through his options—but one look at them told Buck a team of wild horses couldn't drag them away. He gave up and opened the door.

Taking her by surprise he whispered, "Hey," and bent to press his mouth to hers in a warm kiss.

When he lifted his head, she looked speechless, breathless and too warm. She glanced at Harris and Ethan, who smiled at her in turn, and her blush intensified.

"I can come back later," she blurted. "I didn't mean to interrupt—"

Harris literally leaped forward. "You're not. Come on in."

Ethan pulled a chair out for her. "Have a seat. Can I get you a cola?"

She looked overwhelmed by her welcome. "Well…"

Buck had to grin. Damn, but he had great friends. They were total idiots at times, which was part of their charm, but he could never doubt their loyalty.

Butch came barreling around the corner, saw Sadie and Tish, and there was no curbing his exhilaration. He turned circles, barked maniacally, and all but demanded that Sadie put Tish down.

"Young love," Harris crooned with a hand over his heart.

He tried to pet Tish, but she almost threw herself out of Sadie's arms trying to get away. Sadie juggled her to the ground, Tish snatched the underwear away from her, and together with Butch, she made her hasty escape.

Harris stared. "My God, she hates me."

"Probably heard about your reputation." Ethan grinned.

"Ha, ha." But Harris was both appalled and wounded by the dog's rejection. Buck knew just how he felt.

Sadie tried to reassure Harris. "She's very shy. She hasn't even gotten used to me yet. It wasn't personal."

"She was mistreated," Buck explained.

"Mistreated?" Ethan demanded. "Who would

mistreat that little thing?" Buck told them all about what Tish had been through, then he went on to describe Sadie's role in caring for the animals. He left nothing out, extolling her dedication and caring.

She blushed as Harris and Ethan heaped praise on her for her generosity. Within minutes, the two men were settled at the table, drinking his cola and eating his pizza and hanging on Sadie's every word. Whenever she paused, they asked another question. Their interest was genuine, but Buck also knew they were deliberately welcoming her, trying to make her feel at ease.

There was something about Sadie that brought out a man's protective instincts. Her big heart, yes, but also her naked vulnerability, the way she left herself so emotionally exposed.

Buck thought about throwing them out, then decided it'd be nice for Sadie to get to know them better. He'd have her alone soon enough.

Or so he thought.

Two hours later, Harris and Ethan were still going strong. The dogs had reappeared for a drink and a doggie treat, then gone off again for the alone-time Buck craved.

He'd done little more than think about making love to Sadie. At first, he'd resisted the idea, thinking it might be better to ease her into it. Maybe spend a week just necking, then a week petting…but he knew his control wasn't strong enough for that. Not with Sadie.

And there was the very real concern that if he waited, she'd misconstrue his impatience for lack of interest. He couldn't have that.

He brought his attention back to his guests in time to hear Sadie say, "Yes, it's incredibly hard to give the dogs up, but I always make sure they go to a wonderful and appropriate home."

"So," Harris asked with visible hesitation, "would I be eligible to take one? Clair's been talking about getting a pet since we'll be moving into our own house soon." Then to explain, he added, "Ethan's wife, Rosie, is a realtor and she's always finding great deals on houses. The one we offered for is a handyman special, and since Buck is a real handyman, I couldn't pass it up."

Ethan nodded. "Rosie made kids and a dog and a damn picket fence all a stipulation before saying yes to my proposal." He winked. "I've been working most diligently on the kid part. Since that's not happening real fast, maybe I could surprise her with a dog. What about us? Do we qualify as suitable?"

Because Sadie barely knew Harris and Ethan, she glanced at Buck.

He nodded. "You're visiting with bona fide heroes, honey. Firefighters. Ethan's even been written up for daring deeds, and Harris once went back into a fire to save a kid's guinea pig. Neither one of them would ever neglect or abuse an animal. And their wives are terrific, too. You couldn't find a better home for a dog."

Harris pretended to sniff. "Damn, Buck, now you've made me all weepy."

Ethan laughed. "True friends always make each other sound good."

"Thank you," Sadie said with a smile. "I'll definitely keep you in mind."

Buck took Ethan's elbow. "Speaking of friends and what they do for each other—it's time for you two to hit the road."

Ethan allowed himself to be hauled out of his seat. Harris rose on his own steam with a lot of feigned offense. "What? No dessert? No coffee? See, this is why you need to get hitched. You're a lousy host."

Buck surprised them both by saying, "I'll see what I can do." He didn't turn to see Sadie's reaction. He'd find out how she felt about a real relationship soon enough.

As he practically dragged Harris and Ethan to the front door, they yelled back their farewells to Sadie, then started sniggering and elbowing Buck as he tried to shove them out onto the stoop.

Buck gave up. "So what do you think?"

Bobbing his eyebrows, Harris whispered, "Still waters run deep."

"Very sweet," Ethan added. "And gentle."

Buck was so relieved, he grinned. He'd been half

afraid his buds wouldn't recognize Sadie's appeal. It wasn't in your face, like a lush figure or a stop-traffic face. She didn't have a load of sexual confidence or snappy charisma. She wasn't a fashion plate.

Sadie was subtly attractive.

So much so, he'd been afraid they might not see her appeal at all. God knew he'd missed it at first. But through Sadie, he was learning the truth about cats, dogs…and women. He was learning the truth about himself, and what he really wanted out of life.

He wanted Sadie.

Anyone so quietly kind and caring deserved a lot of love.

Buck had a hell of a lot of love to give.

"Thanks," he told his friends. "And goodbye."

Harris had his mouth open to say more when Buck shut the door. For good measure, he locked it. He could hear the male laughter of his friends as they strode away.

Bending down, he peered under his couch. Butch and Tish were curled tightly together in the yellow underwear. He could hardly tell where one Chihuahua started and the other ended. Cute.

Tish opened one eye, saw him and inched farther back.

"It's all right, baby girl. I won't bother you. Go back to sleep now." She kept watching him as if waiting to be pounced on.

Sighing, Buck decided that sooner or later, he'd win her over. He really, really wanted to hold her.

Sadie stood in the kitchen doorway. "The dogs are hiding?" she asked.

Buck straightened; their gazes met. Sadie's lips were parted to accommodate her fast breathing. His muscles tensed, his abdomen clenched.

It was time—and they both knew it.

"Yeah." He walked to her and held out a hand. "How long will they nap, do you think?"

Sadie put her hand in his. Her attention was on his mouth. "Long enough. At least, I hope so."

His smile felt silly and right and full of anticipation. His heart turned over. Damn, but she was perfect.

And starting now, she was his.

SADIE WENT DOWN THE HALL to Buck's bedroom with her heart tripping, her stomach fluttering and her thighs shaking. Anticipation stole her breath.

Her hand felt tiny in his. She watched the play of muscles in his broad back beneath the soft cotton shirt. He was so sinfully, deliciously, unbelievably gorgeous.

And he wanted her.

Sadie didn't care if it would be for an hour, a day, a week. It didn't matter; she wasn't about to turn him down. Whenever she fantasized, it was of a man like

Buck, a man who was physically big and strong, but emotionally gentle and loving, who filled her dreams.

No other man she knew had ever been so concerned for an animal. When he spoke to Tish, it was as if he related to her. That took confidence, in himself and in his masculinity. Though she'd deliberately kept her distance, she'd always admired him. And after seeing him with her dog, her heart was lost.

He tugged her into his bedroom and shut the door. Facing her, his gaze molten and very direct, he murmured, "I don't want the dogs to wander in."

"No?"

"I'm not into exhibitionism."

He liked to joke. "I doubt they'd understand."

She didn't understand. Not yet anyway. But soon.

He leaned against the door. "You put your cardigan back on."

Excuses tripped on her tongue, but nothing coherent came out.

Lazily, Buck reached out with his long arms and began undoing the buttons for the second time that day. "It's okay. I like undressing you." His eyes lifted briefly to her face, then returned to her sweater. "Do you mind?"

Did she mind what? Nervousness took hold, making it hard for her to think beyond the obvious desire to know him physically.

"Would you be more comfortable in the dark? I

can shut the blinds, but the truth is…I'm dying to see every soft, pink inch of you."

Oh, God. If he said things like that, she'd never get through this. Sadie licked her lips. "No one's ever looked at me before."

His expression heated even more. "I know."

He pushed away from the door, and with his fingers busy on the last button of her sweater, took her mouth. The kiss was unlike the ones earlier in the day. He ate at her mouth, consumed her, made her burn.

"Damn." His laugh was shaky as he stripped off her sweater. "I should be honest and tell you that your virginity is an enormous turn-on. I can't wait to take you, to see your face when I push inside you, when you come…"

Sadie sucked in a startled breath. She couldn't wait, either. "You first."

Buck paused. "Me first what?" He half laughed. "If I come first, I'm afraid the gig is up. I'd need at least an hour to—"

"No." Her face burned. "I meant…would you undress first? Then I won't feel so…naked."

He shrugged one hard shoulder. "Sure. Modesty isn't one of my virtues." Reaching back, he grabbed a fistful of his shirt and yanked it off. He dropped it onto the floor beside them. Smiling at her, he lifted one foot and tugged off his shoe and sock, then removed the other.

Sadie's heartbeat accelerated. Buck wasn't an overly hairy man, but there was a nice patch of brown curls between his well-developed pecs, and farther down, trailing from his navel into his jeans. She already knew that hair was silky soft and that his skin was warm and taut.

He opened the snap of his jeans.

"Okay?" he asked, watching her closely.

"Yes." More than okay. She'd already seen him in his underwear and a towel. Now she wanted to see everything.

He shoved the jeans down, taking his underwear off at the same time. He kicked them aside, straightened—and let her look her fill.

Holy moly. Everything in her felt tight and liquid and hot. Embarrassment ebbed, replaced with fascination. Sadie had never seen a naked man up close. It was so nice that her first was the epitome of masculine perfection.

Raising her gaze to his face, she said, "You're amazing."

A startled laugh escaped him. "Look all you want, honey, but you know, you can touch, too."

That was all the encouragement she needed. "Thank you." She leaned up against him. "Kiss me again, okay?" It'd be easier for her to explore his body if he wasn't looking at her with such probing expectation.

His tone was more serious than she had expected when he said, "Anything you want, Sadie."

And then his mouth was over hers, treating her to a long, slow, tongue-teasing kiss that made her toes curl in her shoes.

Sadie started with her hands on his shoulders. His skin was hot and sleek, but she preferred the feel of his hairy chest. When her palms grazed his nipples, he gave a small growl of pleasure, and then his hands were on her breasts, too.

Even through her blouse, she could feel the heat of his palms, the strength. He cuddled her breasts, shaped them, and finally his thumbs moved over her nipples, circling, barely stroking, but eliciting a gasp of surprise at the sharp intensity of the sensation.

"Nice, huh?" he murmured against her mouth.

"Yes." She knew her reply sounded a lot like a moan.

"You'll like it even more once we get your clothes out of the way."

As far as hints went, that was pretty clear. "All right."

He showed his appreciation of her reply with another voracious kiss, while his hands left her breasts to tackle the buttons on her blouse. These were smaller than the ones on her sweater, and not as easy to undo. But Sadie had little thought for her own clothes with Buck's powerful body bared for her pleasure.

She let her fingers trace the tense muscles of his abdomen, tease the silkier hair beneath his navel, then she dipped lower. His penis jutted out, hard and warm. Fascinated, she cupped him in both hands.

With a low growl, Buck seemed to forget about undressing her. He dropped his forehead to hers. In a rasping whisper, he said, "I love having you hold me, Sadie."

A little awed, she spoke without measuring her words. "You're so hot and so soft."

"Not soft at all."

"No, I didn't mean that. Your skin is velvety. I didn't expect that." She continued to explore him while Buck made sounds of mingled pain and pleasure. "And you feel alive. You're even throbbing."

His hand curled over hers, forcing her to squeeze him a little tighter, then stroke. Once. Twice. "Okay. That's enough of that." With a raw, broken laugh, he pulled her hands away, kissed each palm, then put them on his shoulders. "Safer ground, at least for now, okay?"

Confused, Sadie asked, "I did it wrong?"

"You did it too *right*. And no way in hell do I want to come early on your first time."

"Oh." He was so frank in his speech, she should have been embarrassed again, but somehow, his lack of embarrassment reassured her.

She'd forgotten about him unbuttoning her blouse

until he dragged it off her shoulders. Her bra was plain white cotton with no decoration at all.

But Buck didn't even seem to notice. Once the blouse was gone, he reached around her and un-hooked her bra with practised ease. He stepped back, leaving the bra to hang loosely on her slender frame. His gaze burning, he used just his fingertips trailing over her shoulders to drag the straps down her arms. The bra slipped, then fell free past her elbows. Sadie let it drop to the floor.

Refusing to be too timid, she put her shoulders back and kept her spine straight.

Buck's gaze was so hot, so admiring as he stared at her breasts, that she didn't feel too small despite her modest bust. Throwing his own words back at him, she whispered, "I don't mind you looking, but you're welcome to touch, too."

"Yeah?" he asked with a slow grin. "Thank God. I'm not sure I could mind my manners right now."

But he didn't just touch her. No, he shocked her senseless by catching her waist, lifting her to her tiptoes while he bent down, and then his mouth was over her left nipple, his rough tongue licking, curling around her, and then he sucked.

"Buck." Sadie tunneled her fingers through his hair, holding on for dear life.

He gave a rough groan and moved to her other breast.

She felt the draw of his mouth everywhere, in

each of her breasts, in her trembling thighs, and most especially low in her stomach, where a tingling ache expanded on waves.

"We gotta lose the skirt now, too, baby." He set her back on her feet and hurriedly opened the zipper down her side. "I'm sorry, I know I'm not being very patient." He went down on one knee and pulled her skirt to her ankles. "But it's crazy how bad I want you."

Sadie stared down at him, touched, flattered, turned on. "Whatever you want, Buck."

He helped her step out of her shoes and skirt. "I want this. Don't faint on me, okay?"

That was all the warning Sadie got before he cupped her fanny in his hands, pulled her forward and kissed her through her white cotton panties.

"Ohmigod."

"Yeah," he murmured, and even his breath felt erotic and tantalizing. "You smell delicious."

Never in her life had Sadie imagined a man saying such a thing while doing such a thing.

His tongue pressed against her, seeking, and her knees wanted to buckle. "I…I need to sit down."

"Not yet," he growled. "Once you're on the bed, things are going to get out of control pretty quick." He squeezed her bottom, kneading her, then hooked his thumbs into her waistband and eased her panties down. "Step out, Sadie."

She had to brace herself on his shoulders to do

that. When she stood before him naked, she expected him to stand. He didn't. He put his thick arms around her and hugged her close, with his cheek on her belly, his hands opened wide on her back.

"You're beautiful."

Sex talk, Sadie thought, and smiled. While her muscles turned to mush, she stroked his hair and wondered how long this euphoria could last.

It wouldn't be long enough for her.

Buck leaned back and looked up at her. "You don't believe me?"

Her smile twitched. "It doesn't matter." She cupped his jaw in her hands. "You can't know how happy I am to be here with you. Not just with any man, but with you, Buck."

His gaze holding hers, he dragged his palms down her back to her bottom, then the back of her thighs. "Why?"

"Besides the obvious?"

His fingers rose higher again, this time between her thighs. His gaze never wavered. "What's the obvious?"

"That you're sexy and handsome and have an incredible body."

That gave him pause, but only for a moment. Sadie felt his fingertips touching her intimately from behind. Another thing she'd never imagined!

"What's not so obvious?"

"I…I can't talk while you do that."

"Yeah, you can."

One finger teased at her tender lips, gently probing without quite entering her. Sadie felt her own wetness and had to close her eyes to think.

"Tell me," he insisted. "Why me and not some other guy?"

"You're good to Tish. You're gentle with Butch." She opened her eyes so she could make sure he understood. "And you make me laugh."

He pushed his finger deeper, his expression strained, his breathing harsh. "You're so damn tight."

Sadie tipped her head back and moaned, as much from what he said as what he did.

"Am I hurting you?"

She shook her head. "No." She knew in her heart that Buck would never hurt her. Not physically. But he was bound to break her heart when their time together ended.

He kissed her belly. His tongue dipped into her navel, trailed a damp path down to her pubic curls, then he used his thumbs to open her. "You're wet, Sadie, but I want you wetter. I want to know for sure that I won't hurt you. You're just so damn small, and I'm not—"

"No," she agreed with a smile. "You're not." That she could smile at the moment, that even now Buck amused her and made her feel lighthearted, was nothing short of a miracle. He was a miracle. And for now, he was all hers.

She felt his tongue searching, and had to lock her knees. "Buck, I really need to lie down."

"In a minute." He worked a second finger into her, pressed deep, slowly withdrew, and pushed in again.

"Oh, God." Giving up, Sadie automatically widened her stance and let him do as he pleased, because what he did pleased her, too.

He nuzzled closer, his breath burning, his tongue damp and soft, seeking until he curled it around her clitoris. Her heart and lungs threatened to explode. Her body shivered all over.

And then he was suckling again, this time with such devastating effect that she almost couldn't bear it. Sensations grew, twisting inside her, shaking her, all the while expanding, receding, then coming back stronger—and she knew what was about to happen.

She clenched her fingers in his hair to stay upright and let the awesome shock waves roll over her.

Somehow she ended up on her back on Buck's bed. His mouth was now at her breast, sucking strongly, while his fingers remained inside her, keeping her orgasm alive. Sadie twisted and groaned. She couldn't silence her cries or hold herself still.

Finally, after long agonizingly amazing moments, Buck kissed his way gently up to her temple. He pulled her close and just held her.

Sadie stared at the ceiling in blank surprise. She'd never dreamed...never quite imagined... "Buck?"

"Hmm?" He kissed her ear and hugged her.

"That was *wonderful.*"

He shoved up on one elbow and, though he wasn't smiling, she saw the glint of humor in his green eyes. "You're something else, you know that?"

She shook her head. She'd always thought she was pretty darn ordinary, in a plain, easy-to-ignore way.

Buck looked down at her breasts and began tracing one nipple with a fingertip. "I expected you to be really shy."

"I am."

"I expected you to be uptight. I thought I'd have to work at getting you to relax." He bent and gave her a quick kiss, which made her blush considering where his mouth had just been. He grinned. "But you're a hedonist at heart, aren't you?"

Sadie considered that. "I enjoyed what you did." She turned a little toward him so she could stroke his chest and abdomen. "And you make me feel comfortable. You're so matter-of-fact about everything. I didn't quite know how this would work, but it just seemed natural with you."

He nodded, looking far too grave. "Right. With *me.*" He sat up and opened the bedside drawer. "Remember that, okay?"

Sadie watched as he located a condom and rolled it on.

"You're going to finish making love to me now?"

"No. I won't finish now. I'll take my time. But I am dying to get inside you. And after we both come, maybe we'll nap or get a snack or watch a movie." He stretched out over her, held her face and kissed the bridge of her nose. And in a voice husky with arousal he said, "Then we can start all over again."

"Really?" Sounded like a great plan to Sadie.

"Oh, yeah. You're spending the night, okay?"

Before she could answer, he kissed her deeply. He went on kissing her until she punched his shoulder and demanded he get a move on.

Laughing, Buck said, "Yes, ma'am." He reached down between their bodies, opened her and slowly pressed in.

Her breath caught.

His jaw clenched.

He was big, and she felt incredible pressure.

"Stay with me, Sadie." He braced himself on stiffened arms, which increased the pressure between her legs. He squeezed his eyes shut, clenched his jaw, then had the nerve to say, "Relax."

"I don't think I can."

He groaned. "Bend your knees, honey. Lift into me." To help her, he lowered himself onto one elbow and wedged a hand under her hips. "That's it."

His fingers clenched on her bottom, he let out a long, exaggerated groan, and then he sank deep.

Sadie cried out, not in pain but with mind-numbing pleasure. Buck didn't slow or give her time to get acclimated to his size. He pulled out and drove in again. Both hands went to her bottom, tilting her up to take more of him. His body was warm and heavy. The friction was incredible.

She wrapped her arms around his neck, her legs around his waist, and tried to follow his rhythm.

But far too soon, he stiffened. Sadie knew he was about to climax and curiosity distracted her. Until he opened his mouth on her throat and gave her a love bite. It was so wicked, such a sexual act of possession, she felt her own orgasm swelling again and she embraced it. It was different this time, with Buck a part of her. It was more powerful, and more satisfying, to be able to squeeze him tight inside her body.

Her limbs trembled and throbbed. Vaguely she was aware of Buck trembling, too, his muscles all straining, his growls raw and broken. Moments later he lowered himself onto her, but immediately rolled onto his back so that she was on top.

For several minutes they lay there like that. Then Sadie felt him pull out of her, and even that was an enjoyable experience.

"My backside is cold."

He grunted and blindly reached for a sheet, dragging it up and over her. "Sleep woman. I need to recoup my strength."

His heartbeat was a steady thumping beneath her cheek. His arms were around her, his hands now cuddling her bottom, presumably to warm it. And she felt so lax, so utterly replete, that she dozed off without a single care on her mind.

CHAPTER FIVE

TWO NIGHTS LATER, Buck accidentally woke Sadie in the middle of the night when he climbed back into bed. They'd spent the entire weekend together, alternately playing with the dogs, eating, watching movies, and making love.

Just that evening, after she'd gone limp in his arms from a long, screaming climax, Sadie had told him that she hadn't realized life could be so relaxed and enjoyable. She broke his heart when she said things like that, and made him more determined than ever to make up for her selfless and lonely childhood.

On the outside, Sadie continued to look shy and timid. But deep inside, she was wild and without reserve. She made no bones about loving sex. She wanted to try everything, claiming she had a lot of catching up to do.

Buck was more than happy to oblige her.

He wanted to cherish her, and toward that aim, he kissed her all the time, for no reason and for every reason. If she fixed coffee, it deserved a kiss. If she yawned, he thought it was cute and had to nibble on her lips.

When she struggled with Tish or had to clean up a mess from the dog, he offered to help. And when Tish dragged a hideous half-dead bug into the house, Buck got rid of it for her, then hugged her and kissed her again and again until she stopped making awful faces.

He'd even tackled another cicada for her. He hoped she realized that, with his aversion to the red-eyed monsters, he wouldn't have done that for just anyone.

Sadie obviously hadn't heard him leave the bed earlier, given her suspicious look now. "Where've you been?"

For a woman who'd spent her life sleeping alone, she'd quickly accustomed herself to having him take more than half the bed. She compensated by sprawling over him. Buck liked that.

He deliberately snuggled close, making sure his cold feet brushed hers. She yelped and pulled her feet up to his calves.

"I was outside."

"Doing what?"

"Herding Chihuahuas." He smiled and kissed her shoulder. She had the silkiest, most baby-fine skin he'd ever felt. She was soft everywhere, and it made him nuts. "Butch wanted out, and of course, Tish had to follow. But she got past me without her leash, and then Butch shot out, too. I chased Tish, and Butch chased me."

Sadie snickered at the picture he painted.

In mock annoyance, he said, "Hey, catching her again wasn't easy. But at least I had enough sense to pull my jeans on this time."

Still grinning, looking tousled and sexy and sweet, she sat up. "You should have woken me up."

Buck pulled her back down into his arms. "You were dead out, so I didn't want to bother you." He cupped her naked breast, loving the feel of her.

Loving her. *Damn.*

"Buck?"

"But you're awake now," he drawled.

Sadie's voice went deep and she sank down against him. "I am. Very awake."

Buck pulled her beneath him. Words of love tried to break free, but he knew it was too soon. Sadie needed a little time to get used to the physical side of having a man in her bed before he dumped the emotional stuff on her, too. Even while kissing her shoulder, he murmured, "It's four-thirty in the morning. I should let you sleep."

"I have to be up for work in an hour anyway."

He trailed kisses along her throat. "That's an extra hour you could sleep." He'd already learned Sadie's secrets and knew that she was especially sensitive on her throat, behind her ear, and beneath her breasts.

Of course, she went wild when he licked at the inside of her thighs, too, and higher—

Her hand closed over his cock and Buck stilled.

"Know what I'd rather do in that hour?"

Oh, he could just imagine. She was a generous lover, but also wicked enough to enjoy tormenting him. "I don't know if I can bear for you to tell me."

With her free hand, she pushed against him until he obligingly went onto his back—giving her free rein over his body.

"I want to kiss you all over."

Excitement trembled along his nerve endings. He'd never live through this. "Okay."

Smiling with newfound female power, Sadie climbed atop him. She did seem to enjoy his body; she made plenty of comments on his strength and size.

"You relax, okay?"

He laughed. "Not a chance, honey."

Her lips grazed his. "Then at least hold still."

Lord help him. He locked his hands behind his head and promised to try his best. It sure as hell wasn't easy. Twenty minutes later, Sadie was on her knees between his thighs. She'd been slowly—and he did mean slowly—working her soft mouth down his body.

Now she held his cock in one hand, his balls in the other, and it was heavenly torture. "Hussy," he teased with a low groan. "Put me out of my misery before I break."

Laughing, she whispered, "All right." And then she bent, kissed the head of his erection, opened her mouth and swallowed him.

Buck stiffened with a wrenching growl.

Her tongue swirled, gave one final lick and she lifted her head. "Hold still."

"Can't."

Her small fist stroked. "Keep trying." And she took him in her mouth again, all the while cuddling his balls, working him. She was a fast learner, and teaching her was its own form of pleasurable agony.

To make matters worse, the moonlight shone through the window, putting her small round breasts on display. It was enough. Too much. He caught her shoulders and pulled her up onto his chest.

"Buck," she complained.

"Sorry, babe." He groped on the bedside table for a condom, while holding Sadie still with his other hand. He ripped it open with his teeth, then handed it to her. "Here, put this on me."

"Oh." She straightened, eyed the protection and smiled. "Okay." She wore that concentrated, fascinated expression that made him hot as a chili pepper. "Like this?"

With awful precision, she rolled the condom halfway down his length.

His teeth clenched. "You little tease." He hurriedly finished the job while Sadie chuckled, but she stopped laughing when he lifted her, positioned himself and drove up into her.

Her fingers curled against his chest, stinging in force while proving her own measure of excitement.

"Do whatever you want, Sadie," he managed to say. "Fast, slow, I don't care, as long as you keep moving."

Luckily for his peace of mind, she was in a fast mood. Buck held her breasts, lightly tugging at her nipples while she labored over him, rising and falling, again and again. He was so deep this way, and he loved being able to watch her face as her climax overtook her. She didn't hide from him, but at the crucial moment, she did fall onto his chest and let him take charge.

All she could do was moan.

Buck loved it. He loved her. He even loved her difficult little dog.

Soon she'd fall in love with him, too. He was counting on it.

SADIE ENJOYED HER JOB at the shelter, but because she always had a pet waiting, she never lingered after work. The need to rush home was even more urgent with Tish, because she knew that, more than most, the little dog needed reassurance and human contact.

That hadn't changed. But now she also had Buck to come home to. So she smiled as she drove, think-

ing of how he'd hug her when she walked in, how
the dogs would run to greet her. Everything was so
perfect, it scared her.

If she told Buck she loved him, would he misunderstand? Would he assume her feelings were no
more than an infatuation, because she'd never been
intimate with another man? Or would he realize just
how special he was to her?

She didn't know, and for that reason, she hesitated
to put her feelings into words.

Until Buck, she hadn't known how much was
missing in her life. But knowing was a two-edged
sword, because now she knew what she could lose,
too, and that was one reality she didn't want to face.
She'd faced enough already.

Sadie was so lost in thought as she turned
down her street she almost missed Buck on the
sidewalk in front of the complex's parking lot. She
slowed the car to take the turn, and stared in awe.

He wore a big smile filled with pride. And no
wonder. He had both dogs on a leash—and Tish
wasn't fighting him.

Exhilaration exploded within Sadie. She pulled
into her parking space and turned off the ignition.
Buck was striding toward her, both dogs politely
trotting along, to greet her.

Sadie got out of the car and stared. "She doesn't
look afraid."

"Nope." Buck couldn't stop grinning. "It was a

chore getting her to try the walk, but having Butch next to her helped. At first she kept watching me, but soon she was too busy trying to keep up with Butch."

Sadie laughed. "She has your sock in her mouth."

"I know." He shrugged. "She stole it out of my laundry, which is gross. I tried to give her a clean one, but you know how she is. I figured as long as her mouth was full, she couldn't chomp on any bugs. It's a fair trade-off."

The sight of Buck, all six-feet-plus inches of him, bulging muscles and obvious strength, walking two very tiny dogs, made her throat tight with emotion. He was so secure in his masculinity that he could love two Chihuahuas without hesitation.

How could she not love *him?*

Sounding a little hoarse, she said, "You're a miracle worker."

"Nah." He tipped his head and his eyes were warm with affection. "I learned patience from you."

He said that with so much sincerity and affection, she felt tears sting her eyes. "Thank you."

"No big deal." He grinned down at the dogs. "These two are like chick magnets. Women of all ages were beeping their horns, stopping to chat, oohing and aahing at me. One older woman called me 'sweetie' and patted my cheek. Another, um, younger woman slipped me her phone number." Buck retrieved the crumpled piece of paper from his pocket.

Before Sadie could get too worked up about that,

his grin widened. "'Course, some guys passing by laughed their asses off at me, too."

Sadie watched him toss the phone number into a nearby trash can. Relief washed over her. "That wasn't nice of them."

"They're just jealous." He knelt down and held out his hand. Butch came right to him. Tish lowered herself until her belly touched the ground, flattened her ears and wiggled nearer until Buck could tickle her chin. In a voice as soft as butter, Buck said, "They wish they had dogs as fine as these two."

Well, Sadie thought. If she hadn't been in love before, that would have done it.

Buck pushed back onto his feet. "Come on, gang. Let's get inside and see about dinner."

He strode to Sadie, put his arm around her, kissed her warmly, and together they went into his apartment.

BUCK SPENT EVERY FREE MOMENT of his two weeks' vacation with Sadie. While she worked, he kept the dogs. When she got home, he greeted her at the door. She'd see him, smile and throw herself into his arms.

Tish continued to steal Buck's things. Whenever she could manage it, she'd grab something and pull it under the couch to make a bed. Good thing Buck had a big couch to accommodate the yellow underwear, the sock, a T-shirt, dishtowel, ragged work glove and leather shoelaces from his favorite boots.

The last hurt, and he half blamed Butch for that, because both he and Tish liked to chew the laces. Buck learned real quick to put his boots in the closet, well out of reach of small jaws.

They fell into a routine of sorts that seemed to work for everyone. Buck made sure the dogs had been out before Sadie got home so they could fix dinner together without doggie interruptions.

She was a good cook, but then so was he, so they took turns, and every so often they had dinner delivered.

After dinner, they took the time to play in the yard with the dogs. Before bed, they'd sit on the floor. Buck would hold Butch while doing his best to entice Tish into his lap. So far, it hadn't worked. She'd stopped being so jumpy, but she remained a long way from trusting.

Still, to Buck, they felt like a family—and he wanted to protect that. He wanted Sadie and Tish to be happy. But tomorrow, Riley and Regina would return home. They'd take Butch, and that would be one more thing for Tish to adjust to.

The September nights were unseasonably cool, making it necessary to wear a jacket or flannel when sitting outside. But neither Buck nor Sadie wanted to give up the time outdoors with the dogs. Buck had created a removable, adjustable fence that covered about ten square feet. Each day they set it up differently so the dogs could explore new areas.

The fence worked out great, except that with more freedom, Tish found more bugs. At least half the time she went outside, she caught a spider or a grasshopper or a night crawler, which she always presented to Sadie.

Thankfully, she hadn't located any more cicadas. Butch was a more discriminating Chihuahua and didn't care for bugs. He even seemed a little creeped out when Tish caught them, but he always ended up helping her, as if it were a game.

The little dogs had become inseparable friends, and Tish seemed happiest when she was with Butch.

Now Sadie sat curled next to Buck on her small back porch. Without looking at him, she wondered aloud, "Maybe I should bring in another dog, just so Tish won't be lonely when Butch has to leave tomorrow."

Buck swallowed. He hated that idea. "Oh sure, that's fine for Tish. Maybe she'll even forget about him. But what about Butch? Think how lonely he'll be." He glanced at the dogs, and had the perfect opportunity to prove his point. "Look at the little guy. He's snuggled up against Tish as if she's his better half."

Sadie sighed. "I know. Maybe…that is, if you wanted to…"

Buck waited, almost holding his breath. "What?"

"You could bring him over every so often to visit."

He scowled at her. Her suggestion was far from

what he'd hoped to hear. "I could do that." He stared at her, trying to read her thoughts. "Or I could take Tish to see him. The wives have everyone over at least once a week."

"The wives? That's what you call them?"

"That's what they are." Sadie had already been to one of those gatherings last weekend to meet Clair and Rosie. The dogs had played while the people had conversed. Sadie had seemed to like them, and Buck knew they liked her. Things were moving along in that regard. "We, meaning the guys, had kinda figured the wives would put an end to us hanging out together. But we were wrong. We still hang out, we just usually do it with the wives there. Not that they mind if we take off to fish or play cards late one night or something."

Sadie stared at him, arrested by this outpouring of confidences. "I'm sure they're very understanding. Why wouldn't they be?"

Buck felt like an idiot. "All I'm saying is that Regina wouldn't mind if we brought Tish with us, and even when Rosie's the one doing the cooking, or Clair, they like Butch, so I know they'd love Tish, too."

They'd better, because Tish was going to damn well be part of his family. As he'd told Sadie early on, he understood they were a package deal. The little dog had been through enough without being left behind.

Buck was waiting for Sadie's reaction when Harris and Clair rounded the corner of the building. "There you are," Harris said, as if he hadn't just interrupted Buck's attempts to settle the future.

"We knocked at Buck's," Clair explained, "but when we didn't get an answer, we decided to check out here."

Butch raced to greet them, and Harris knelt down close to the low fence. Tish cowered back into the farthest corner of her contained play area.

"She's still so shy," Harris said with a worried frown. "It just breaks my heart. I swear, Sadie, I don't know how you do this."

Butch allowed Harris to pat him a few times, then he ran back to Tish.

Sadie sent a fond smile to Tish. "Some cases are harder than others." She stood. "Can I get you something to drink?"

Harris shook his head. "No, that's okay. We just stopped by because I have a suggestion." He gave Buck a surreptitious glance and then cleared his throat. "There's a house for sale next door to Riley's."

Buck stilled. His brain went blank. "There is?"

"It's small," Harris hurried to explain, "and like the one we picked, it needs some work. But if you bought it, the dogs would be close together." He winked—and Buck caught on.

Bless Harris, even he had a good idea every now and then.

Clair knelt down and offered her hand for the dogs to sniff. "Assuming you'd want to keep Tish," she told Sadie. "I mean, I know you're supposed to be getting her ready for a family, but she's...special." She glanced at Sadie. "Isn't she?"

With her bottom lip caught in her teeth, a sure sign she felt unsure of the situation, Sadie nodded. Her voice was faint, and touched with emotion.

"Very special. I'd already thought of keeping her." She glanced at Buck, then away. "She's going to need a lot more care before she's comfortable with being held. She's shy by nature, I think, and whatever she went through set her back more than I'd realized."

Harris cleared his throat. "If she was able to see Butch every day, that'd help, don't you think?"

"Yes, being with Butch comforts her."

Buck watched Sadie, foolishly wondering if she loved Tish enough to marry him, buy a house and make a home.

"How much is the house?" Sadie asked. Then she added, "I'm not sure I could afford it."

Harris again glanced at Buck. "With your combined incomes..."

Buck stood, cutting off Harris's suggestion. He wanted Sadie, more than he'd ever wanted anything else in his life, but damn it, he didn't need his friend to propose for him, and he didn't want a house to be the reason she married him.

She had to love him.

"You said you were just stopping by. You on your way somewhere?"

Taking the hint, Clair said, "We're having dinner with my boss and his wife. We just wanted to tell you about the house." And because Sadie had asked, Clair turned to her. "It's cheap enough that Rosie doesn't think it'll stay on the market long."

"Thanks. We'll check into it." Buck stepped past Sadie. "Come on, I'll walk you to your car."

Sadie also stood. "Thank you," she called to them before Buck could haul them away.

After they'd rounded the corner and were out of earshot, he thumped Harris on the back. "Thanks."

Clair smiled. "We figured it couldn't hurt to put the thought in your heads."

"The thought's been in mine almost from the first. Sadie's the one who needs to be convinced. And I'm working on that."

"Work fast," Harris suggested. "Riley and Red will be back tomorrow, and the house won't last."

"Gotcha." But Sadie didn't deserve to be rushed. She deserved a slow, romantic courtship. Still, when he thought of Tish alone, without Butch as a companion...

When he returned, Sadie was sitting in a sunny spot inside the fence, stroking Butch and crooning to Tish. With his arms crossed over his chest, Buck stopped to stare down at her. "So, what do you think?"

She continued to pet the dog. "About what?"

His temper edged up a notch. He pointed a finger at her. "You know damn good and well about what. The house."

She ducked her head and shrugged. "I don't know. What do you think?"

Frustrated, Buck stepped over the fence and sat beside her. "You are planning to keep Tish, aren't you? Because I gotta tell you, if you don't, I will."

Sadie's head jerked up. "Really?"

"Damn right. She needs someone to love her a lot. Forever. She needs calm and quiet. In just the two weeks I've known her, she's gotten back more fur."

Sadie looked caught between laughing and crying. "She looks like a sleek little seal now, doesn't she?"

"She's beautiful." Buck touched Sadie's cheek, and he was appalled to see his hand shake. "Just as you said she'd be."

Sadie's eyes were sad, and her smile wobbled. "She's fatter, too."

"She reminds me of a little sumo wrestler, especially when she's sneaking up to steal something from me." He peered down at her. "She's not exactly graceful."

Sadie leaned against Buck and laughed.

Buck melted.

And suddenly, Tish crept over.

They both froze. The little dog had her ears flat on her head, her big brown eyes watchful—and hope-

ful. She slowly, so very slowly, did an army crawl…
right into Sadie's lap.

"Ohmigod," Sadie whispered.

Butch blinked his big eyes in stunned surprise at
this change. Since he'd been in Sadie's lap first, Tish
was now half sitting on him. She outweighed Butch
by at least a pound, and for four-pound Butch, that
pound was a lot.

But he didn't complain.

"Slow," Buck whispered. "Go real slow." He
reached out with one finger and tickled the dog's
chin. Her worried gaze transferred to him, and her
tail lifted in a one-wag thump. She looked very undecided about things, but she didn't run off.

Holding his breath, Buck carefully tickled his way
over her muzzle, to her ear, and then to the top of her
little round head, which was no longer bald, but soft
with chocolate-brown fur.

Tish let out a long, doggie sigh, dropped her head
onto Sadie's thigh and closed her eyes.

"You did it, Sadie." Buck's heart swelled so big,
it felt ready to pop out of his chest.

Enormous tears swam in Sadie's eyes. "This is
stupid," she whispered on a shaky laugh, "but I feel
like bawling."

"Yeah," Buck admitted, "me, too."

Sadie leaned on his shoulder. "Butch has to have
most of the credit."

Reminded of his goal, Buck was quick to agree.

"It'd be a damn shame to separate them now, don't you think? I bet Regina would love the idea of letting them play together. She's taken only freelance jobs lately so she could be home more with Butch. And when she has to be away for regular business hours, she or Riley come home at lunchtime. If we were right next door—"

With her head still on his shoulder, Sadie squeaked, *"We?"* She twisted to see him. "You think we should buy the house—"

"Together." He smoothed his hand over the dogs, taking turns petting them. "It's a good plan."

She stared at him in mute surprise.

That irritated Buck. "You know the dogs would like it."

Sadie nodded. "Yes. But…would you like it?"

He touched her cheek. "I'd love it."

She bit her bottom lip, drew a deep breath, then nodded. "I'd love it, too."

The tension left Buck in a rush. Then Sadie said, "Because I love you."

His back snapped straight. "What did you say?"

His strangled voice startled the dogs, and he rushed to calm them with soft pats.

Sadie held his gaze. "I love you, Buck Boswell. You're the most wonderful, loving, giving man. Even in my imagination, I didn't think anyone like you could exist. But here you are, sitting in the yard, petting little dogs and offering to buy houses and being so wonderful…how could I not love you?"

He almost hyperventilated. "I love you, too." He wanted to grab her up and swing her around and laugh out loud. But he didn't want to upset Tish. "I've loved you since the day you ran into my place in your nightie, demanding I go head to head with a killer cicada."

She blushed. "I am sorry about that."

"I'm not. If Tish hadn't caught the nasty bug, we might not have gotten together. And I never would have realized that you and one tiny bald dog were the very things missing in my life."

She didn't laugh the way he expected. Instead, she bit her lip.

Buck kissed her, licked her bottom lip to soothe it, then asked, "What is it?"

"Will you marry me?"

He stared at her, then burst out laughing. The dogs barely paid him any mind, but Sadie blushed hotly. "I would have been on one knee within the next five minutes. Thank you for saving me the trouble."

Her cheeks turned pink. "I'm sorry. I didn't mean to…"

"I love you. Everything about you," he reminded her. "Thank you for proposing to me, and yes, I accept."

"There'll probably be more dogs. I can't give up what I do."

The cautious warning only made him grin again. "Okay by me. After all, the dogs are nothing compared to my loony friends."

Her smile warmed his heart. "Your friends are wonderful."

"Yeah, they are."

"Do you think we should get ahold of Rosie and make an offer on the house right away?" She bubbled with new enthusiasm.

"Yeah." He stood, pulled Sadie to her feet, and then his voice lowered to a husky rumble. "We'll get right to that."

"After?" Sadie asked, and her voice, too, grew rough.

"After," he agreed.

A FEW MONTHS LATER, they closed on the house. Once they moved in, Sadie did indeed bring in more dogs. But with the means to keep them, she couldn't bear to give them away.

They ended up with three—which Buck claimed was fair, since he had the same number of buddies.

Ethan ended up with two dogs, and Harris had a dog and a cat. Every get-together did resemble a zoo—not that anyone minded.

In fact, the men began speculating that the dogs needed kids to play with. And judging by the love and attention they gave their pets, the women had no doubts that they'd make doting fathers.

Butch and Tish remained the best of friends. Whenever there was a crowd, they crawled under a couch together—curled up in Buck's yellow boxers.

Sadie claimed that Tish saw the boxers as a security blanket.

Buck saw Sadie the same way. His life had always been good.

Now, with Sadie as his wife, it was perfect.

* * * * *

AN HONORABLE MAN

CHAPTER ONE

CHAOS REIGNED IN the classroom as the kids returned from their second recess. Liv Amery listened to the comforting sounds of their bustling activity, the scraping of chairs, the continued childish chatter. The cold mid-May weather had made their small faces ruddy, and had resulted in several runny noses. Wind-ruffled and still wound up from the recent play, they were utterly adorable.

Only an hour remained in the school day, and then the kids would head home. She had just enough time to finish going over the math lessons. Giving them time to remove their jackets and settle in their seats, Liv retrieved several papers from her desk. When everyone had quieted, she stood and went to the chalkboard, ready to start the afternoon lessons.

That's when she heard it—the even, very precise cadence of military footfalls echoing down the tiled hallway. She'd grown up hearing that sound, the memory of it buried deep in her heart. But hearing it now, here in an elementary school, nearly stopped her heart.

With one hand raised, a piece of chalk still in her now limp fingers, she faced the blackboard, listening as those steps came closer and closer and finally stopped at the door of her third-grade room.

Heart pounding, throat tight, she began silent prayers. A visit from the military now could only mean one thing, and the idea that her most dreaded nightmare could have happened, that she might have lost him before she'd ever really had him.... No. She couldn't accept that.

Then her senses picked up more subtle nuances. Not just any military walk, but one so familiar that, almost on cue, her stomach did a small flip and her lungs expanded with relief. They were telling reactions, an inbred response to one particular man.

Hamilton was okay. *Thank you, God.*

But because he'd come unannounced, not to her home, but to her school, her uneasiness remained. *He* was fine, but his visit here today could only mean one thing.

Wanting to shut out the moment, Liv started to close her eyes, and the door opened. With a mix of dread and awful yearning, she turned.

There he stood: Lieutenant Colonel Hamilton Wulf. Tall, strong, commanding. Exactly as she remembered him.

His brown eyes zeroed in on her face and stayed there, as probing and intimidating as ever. He wore no smile of welcome because this wasn't a social call.

Shaken, Liv pulled her gaze from his and looked him over, making note of the hat tucked under his arm, his polished shoes and the razor-sharp crease in his dress blues.

Hamilton was fine—but her father wasn't.

Knees going weak, Liv felt herself swaying, and suddenly Hamilton was there, his big hands warm and steady on her shoulders, keeping her upright. Close to her ear, he murmured, "Come with me, Liv."

He didn't wait for her agreement before finding her purse under her desk, pulling her sweater off the back of her chair, and leading her quietly, efficiently from her classroom. Her fractured senses scrambled to understand the situation, to absorb the enormity of what she knew to be true.

"Easy," Hamilton said, redirecting her thoughts with his presence. "Just keep walking."

Liv became aware of Betty Nobel, a teacher's aide, taking charge of her students; aware of the children staring in wide-eyed wonder at the awe-inspiring figure Hamilton made, and aware of the strained hush in the air.

When they reached the front lobby of the school, the fog lifted and she pulled up. From as far back as Liv could remember, the military had ruled her life. But she'd finally broken free, and no one, not even Hamilton, could come back and start directing her again. She'd known this day would come. It had only been a matter of time. She'd prepared herself, living in dread day in and day out.

She could handle this. What choice did she have?

Hamilton waited while she dragged in two deep breaths. His hand remained on her elbow, his gaze steady and unblinking, the force of his will settling around her like a warm, heavy blanket.

Liv tipped up her chin to see his face. Although she already knew, she wanted it confirmed. "It's Daddy, isn't it?"

The second her gaze met his, Liv felt the old familiar connection. She felt his sympathy and his understanding and his need to comfort. It had always been that way with Hamilton, regardless of how she fought it.

His expression remained stern, but his voice sounded oddly gentle. "Outside, baby. Then we'll talk."

Liv looked beyond him to where another uniformed man and a uniformed woman stood on the front steps. They both appeared to be younger than Hamilton, probably in their early thirties, while Hamilton now edged close to forty.

Being a military brat, Liv automatically sought out the truth. She noted the young man had a religious symbol where Hamilton had wings, and the woman carried a small medical bag.

A chaplain and a military doctor. Did she need any more confirmation than that?

"Come on." Hamilton's arm went around her, pulling her protectively into his side and before Liv knew it, he had her outside in the brisk wind with the blinding sunshine in her face. Slipping on aviator sunglasses, Hamilton hustled her to the car.

Indicating the doctor, he said, "Liv, these are friends of mine, Major Cheryl Tyne and Captain Gary Nolan."

They both nodded, their gazes respectful and sympathetic.

"Father, Doc, meet Weston's daughter, Liv Amery."

Liv tried for a smile, but had no idea if she'd succeeded. Major Tyne settled behind the wheel while the chaplain opened the rear door. Hamilton urged Liv into the back seat. Before she'd completely seated herself, his body crowded in next to hers, giving her no room to retreat, no room to react. He was so close, Liv breathed in his familiar scent, felt the touch of his body heat everywhere.

With a strange tenderness, especially considering his size and capability, Ham put his arms around her, gathering her to his chest.

She waited, breath held.

"I'm sorry, Liv."

Odd, how she'd held out the faintest, most ridiculous hope. Now her hopes sank and around her distress, she felt burning anger. *"No."* She tried to push away from Ham, but his thick, strong arms kept her close. "No, no, no—"

"Shh." His hand cradled her face. "He had a heart attack, Liv. There was nothing anyone could do."

A heart attack? Surprise silenced her. The military hadn't taken him as she'd always feared? But how could his health have failed him when he'd always prided himself on being in prime physical condition?

It seemed…ironic. And so damn unfair.

Sick to her soul, Liv slumped against Hamilton, felt his hand stroking through her hair, his breath on her cheek.

Visions of her father—strong, proud, coldly distant in his discipline—warred with the image of him struggling for breath, a hand to his chest. "Did he…?"

"It was quick, baby, too damn quick." To Major Tyne, he said, "Doc, take us to my motel room."

"Sure, Howler."

Howler? She hadn't heard Ham referred to by his call name in a very long time. Some day, she'd find out why they called him that.

But for now, while her thoughts might be muddled, she still knew she didn't want to go anywhere with Hamilton. She needed solace, to cry in private, to deal with her grief where no one could see or judge her.

She needed to find her backbone, to dredge up her independence. "My class…"

"I took care of it."

She stared up at him, and even though he still wore the aviator glasses, she felt snared by his gaze.

Hamilton lifted a hand as if to remove them, and Liv caught his wrist. Sunshine flooded the car windows, making her squint. But Hamilton's eyes were especially sensitive after so much time flying high above the pollution, being overexposed to the sun. He needed the glasses, and she knew it.

Diverted, his hand again settled against her cheek, his thumb stroking over her jaw. "You're not alone, Liv."

A near hysterical sob threatened to break free. Of course she was alone, just as she'd always been.

Shamefully, she felt mired in self-pity—and she hated that Hamilton always knew her most private thoughts. Her mother had died when she was young, and the military had owned her father. His death was a crushing weight on her heart, but she doubted she could miss him any more in death than she had in day-to-day life.

Looking out the window in an effort to compose herself, Liv whispered, "You're wrong, Ham. I've always been alone."

Her statement bothered him, and he tightened his hold. "Don't do that, damn it. Don't buck up like a good little soldier. You don't have to, not with me."

Liv didn't reply. If she spoke, the tears would come and she'd be even more humiliated.

But her lack of reply didn't deter Ham. "Listen to me, Liv. I'm here and I'm staying." Before her hopes could fully surface, he burst her bubble. "I have two weeks' leave."

As if two weeks could matter in the scheme of things. Deep inside herself, pain twisted and prodded. Memories raced through her mind, memories of past years, of lost opportunities.

When he pulled her toward him, Liv rested her forehead against his chest. Typical for a man to think he could handle anything in two weeks. In so many ways, Hamilton was like her father—confident, capable, a man other men looked up to.

A man forever lost to her because the air force was his life.

Hamilton tipped up her chin. "I know that look, Liv. I know what you're thinking." His hand opened, his fingers curling around her nape. "I'll be here with you, to help with the arrangements, to talk to, to… be with. If you need or want anything, if there's anything I can do, you only have to tell me."

Liv closed her eyes, unable to bear Hamilton's close scrutiny. Want anything? She'd wanted *him,* but she couldn't bear the constant moving or the constant worry she associated with the air force. She'd seen so many military marriages break up. Good people on both sides, just unable to handle the pressures of separation. Often the wives had no family close by for support. And she knew firsthand what a tough way it was to bring up kids.

She wanted constancy and close friends and a husband who came home every day. She wanted kids who felt secure, who wouldn't have to go through what she had.

So she'd resigned herself to life without him.

Just as she'd resigned herself to life without a father. As a colonel with the Office of Special Investigation, Air Force Intelligence had taken Weston to some pretty spooky places over the years, and kept him away from her for long periods of time. Too long, and too many times. Liv couldn't go through that again.

Already Hamilton had been in Kosovo, Afghanistan and Iraq. He'd even flown in Desert Storm as a newly trained pilot in a B-52. Sometimes, ignorance was bliss, and where Lieutenant Colonel Hamilton Wulf was concerned, the less she knew about his duties, the dangers he faced and the volatile situations he willingly put himself in, the better.

Once long ago, she'd been wildly in love with him, hopeful of a future, her dreams filled with the possibility of a tidy house in the suburbs and all the trimmings—kids, pets, rosebushes and a picket fence. They'd both been military brats, and even though Hamilton was nine years older, she'd been closer to him than to anyone else in her life.

After her mother's death, Hamilton was the one she'd turned to. When her father had missed her birthday, a gift had always arrived from Hamilton. And when a boy had broken her heart, Hamilton had been there, convincing her that she was better off without him.

When she'd turned twenty-one, he'd kissed her for the first time…and kept on kissing her. She'd had boyfriends and a few serious flirtations, but kissing Hamilton had proven a revelation. For the first time in her life, she'd felt like a woman.

Liv had asked him to make love to her then, but he wouldn't. Instead, he'd just driven her crazy with desire, showing her how it could be between them without ever fulfilling the promise. For years, they'd played that ridiculous game, until at twenty-seven, Liv had made it clear what she wanted—and what she didn't.

A military life fell in the "didn't want" category, and that had effectively ruled out a relationship with Hamilton. Not that he'd given up on her. Stubborn to the core, he insisted on thinking he could have it all without consideration of her wishes. He made no bones about his feelings—he still kissed her on the rare occasions when Liv softened enough to let him, and whenever duty kept him from her, he stayed in touch with correspondence, cards and phone calls.

It might have been enough, except that year after year had passed, promotion after promotion—and still he'd stayed in the air force. Her heart broke each and every time.

Now at thirty-seven, as a lieutenant colonel, a B-2 stealth-bomber pilot, and second in command of a B-2 bomb squadron, Hamilton was career air force through and through, and Liv couldn't seduce him away from his first love: flying.

The reality crushed her and made her more determined to live her life without him.

With a sigh, Liv pushed herself upright, away from Hamilton's warmth and the lure of his comfort. She *was* alone, and she had to deal with her father's death without allowing Hamilton to get too close.

Hamilton sighed, too, the sound ragged with exasperation, but he said nothing. He was the most contained, enigmatic person she knew—which made him perfect for the military, but difficult to understand in a relationship.

Liv's father had admired Hamilton's cool regard, while forever accusing her of being too emotional. And she couldn't deny it. She *was* passionate about her work, determined with her students, and despite everything, she'd loved her father so much that now she felt physically wounded.

She wanted to be alone, but at the same time, she wanted Hamilton to stay close and keep on holding her. *Forever.*

The drive to his motel took them within minutes of her home, which was a ten-minute drive from Denton Elementary. She could travel the entire length of the town in less than a half hour. But right outside of town, better hotels existed.

She should have guessed that Hamilton would be staying close by in the shabby lodging rather than putting any distance between them. His organizational skills had served him well in the military. But they would not color her life.

"I want to go home, Ham."

He looked at her, his eyes shielded by the reflective sunglasses, his expression impossible to read. "Not yet. We have some talking to do first."

Shaking from the inside out, Liv whispered, "I don't want—"

But he'd already opened his door and stepped out. Seconds later, he strode to her side of the car and with both Major Tyne and Captain Nolan in attendance, Liv refused to make a scene.

Hamilton opened her door and helped her out. He didn't move away from her or give her any space. With his arm around her waist keeping her pressed to his side, Liv felt his strength and his determination.

Major Tyne glanced at her, then asked, "Should we accompany you?"

Why? Liv wondered. Did they expect hysterics from her? Should she fall apart over a father who hadn't cared, a father who'd willingly walked away from her time and time again? A father who... who...

Damn it, the tears fell, taking her by surprise, closing her throat and making her chin tremble. She sniffled, struggling to stifle the emotional display, knowing it would have disgusted her father.

But she couldn't. And even while it humiliated her, she felt helpless to pull herself together.

Quietly, Hamilton said, "That's not necessary," while gathering Liv close. Warmth and security surrounded her, and pushed her over the edge. Her shoulders shook with her sobs. Damn him, why did her father have to die before they could reconcile? Why hadn't he come to see her just once?

Why hadn't she gone to see him?

With her face tucked against Ham's chest, she heard his quiet conversation with the others. He told them to go ahead and get settled in their rooms.

Captain Nolan put a hand to Ham's shoulder. "If you need me, Howler, give a yell."

"I'll be in touch," he replied. Once the two officers had gone inside, Ham's mouth touched her ear, and he whispered, "I am so sorry, Liv."

She shook her head. He had nothing to be sorry about. Ham, like her father, had gone with his heart. They were both warriors through and through, dedicated to their country, ready, willing and able to defend and protect.

Ham tipped her back and mopped at her face with a snowy-white hanky. "Look at you. You've ruined your makeup," he said with a small sad smile. Then his forehead touched hers. "God, Liv, please don't. Seeing you cry just about kills me."

He wasn't judging her? Her father would have lectured, would have told her to be strong and dignified. To be brave and suck it up.

Ham just cuddled her.

Feeling like a fool, Liv half laughed while taking the hanky and blowing her nose. "So I'm capable of doing what weapons can't, huh? Wow, I feel powerful."

He tugged off his sunglasses, his expression far too serious. "You have no idea how powerful you are when it comes to me."

While she reeled from that cryptic comment, he started them on their way again, across the blacktop lot and toward the brick building.

Tears continued to track down her cheeks. Liv mopped them away and considered what Hamilton might have meant. Surely if she had any real power over him, he'd have been happy to settle with her.

With his long stride shortened to accommodate her, Hamilton glanced at her and frowned. "I'm sorry about the motel. Denton doesn't have much in the way of luxury."

Taking that as an insult to her home, Liv lifted her chin. "It has everything I need and everything I want. It's small and quiet and everyone knows everyone." And then, to ease up on him a little, she said, "It's a place to put down roots. A place to raise a family."

Hamilton paused in the process of opening the glass lobby doors, but only for a moment. His arm went around her waist again and he ushered her down the worn carpeted hallway to the door of his room. The motel was old enough that they still used keys instead of key cards. Hamilton jiggled the lock until the key clicked into place, then held the door open for her to enter.

He must have come straight to the school, Liv thought, noting his unpacked bags and the stuffiness of the air. Automatically she walked to the window to open it, letting in the fresh spring breezes.

Hamilton tossed his hat and sunglasses onto the bureau, leaned back against it and watched her with an intensity that should have been reserved for enemy captives.

Feeling conspicuous, Liv seated herself on the edge of the full-size bed. "Now what?"

Seconds ticked by before he answered, as if he had to give his response serious thought. "Have you eaten?"

"I'm not hungry." Using the hanky, she tried to remove what she could of her ruined mascara. Crying had always been useless, a lesson she'd learned long ago.

Ham's gaze moved over her, from her wind-tossed hair to her sensible teacher-type pumps. Disregarding her words, he asked, "You haven't changed that much, Liv. I know getting upset makes you hungry."

"Everything makes me hungry." Luckily, she had a fast metabolism that kept her from being more than pleasingly plump. "But I can eat at home. Alone."

"You need to talk."

Pushing both hands through her hair, Liv decided to face his arrogance head-on. "No. I need time to think, and I suppose I have to figure out funeral arrangements—"

"The military will take care of it."

She knew that. A military funeral would be what her father had wanted, certainly what he deserved. Nodding, Liv said, "I still have to make plans. I can't do that sitting here and chatting about food and sniveling like a child."

"Showing that you care isn't childish."

She half laughed. "My father would have disagreed with that. I can't tell you how many times I got compared to soldiers. How many times Dad pointed out the differences between my soft bed and a battlefield, my security and the danger in every war."

Hamilton stared at her hard. "He was wrong, Liv. You're one of the strongest women I know."

The compliment warmed something cold deep inside her, but still she said, "Not strong enough to play second fiddle to the air force."

The silence swelled, tinged with anger and frustration. Hamilton pushed away from the bureau to stand directly in front of her, every muscle tensed, his eyes blazing. "I've missed you, Liv."

Oh, God, don't do this, don't do this....

Catching her arms, he pulled her upright and against his chest. "I'm sorry that I'm here under such awful circumstances. God knows I wish you didn't have to go through this. But it happened and we can't change that."

She started to turn her face away, and he whispered, almost warned, "Don't shut me out, baby. Not now. I *need* to help."

Something in his tone penetrated her sorrow. In so many ways, Hamilton had been closer to her father than she had. They'd had so much more in common, he had to be grief-stricken, too. How could she selfishly add to his hurt?

Fingers splayed against his shoulders, she conceded. "All right."

His hands loosened on her arms, became caressing. He shook off the vulnerability as if it had never been there, adopting instead the confidence and arrogance that better suited him. "I'll take care of the funeral arrangements. All you need to do is tell me where you want him buried, and what you want posted in the local paper."

Her lips began to tremble again. From hurt. From long-buried hope. "I'd like him buried here with my mother." The sad truths of her life intruded. "I know it's not officially my home." How could it be, when her entire life had been spent moving from place to place?

Rather than question her decision, Ham said only, "I think that'd be best."

"Thank you." Again, she felt the emptiness, the loneliness compounded by her most recent loss. Her words sounded sad and shaken to her own ears. "All my mother's relatives are now gone, but I still remember the stories she told of walking to the bakery, riding her bike to the same school where I now teach. I know the playground and the movie theater and…" A deep breath helped to steady her voice. "It's the closest thing I have to roots. Mother is buried here, and so I want Daddy here, too."

Hamilton pressed a kiss to her forehead. "That's what I figured." His gaze searching, concerned, he said, "The body will be here tomorrow. I think it might be possible to have the funeral on Friday. Is that okay with you?"

So soon. Again, her heart clenched, the pain close to crippling. Her daddy was really gone. Between his lack of interest and her own stubbornness, so much time had been wasted. She could have gone to see him, whether he wanted her there or not. She could have insisted he come to her college graduation, or…

This time Hamilton's kiss landed on her lips. A light, barely there kiss, but it obliterated her distressing thoughts, overcoming them with pure sensation.

"Don't do that, Liv," he murmured, his mouth still

touching hers. His hands tangled in her hair, angling her face up to his. "Don't beat yourself up with regrets. Nothing was ever your fault."

She'd believed that—until now. "I haven't seen him in so long. I should have—"

"No, baby. *He* should have." Hamilton kissed her again, harder this time, a kiss of resolve and heartache, a kiss that nudged at the grief and curled her toes. "Weston made a damn fine colonel, one of the best. He was brilliant and strong, a natural-born leader." Hamilton swallowed and his jaw worked. "He was an asset to our country, but we both know he could have been a more attentive father."

"He gave everything he had to the military."

Trying to force her to his will, Hamilton held her gaze. "But plenty of guys balance it, their careers, their families. It doesn't have to be one or the other, all or nothing."

"For me it does."

Her statement fell like a sledgehammer, and suddenly new emotion darkened Hamilton's eyes. "This is hard for you. That's why I want to help get you through it. I don't want you worrying about it. It hurts me to see you hurt."

Liv caught her breath—and then his mouth was on hers, devouring, seducing, coaxing. No simple kiss, this. He consumed her, devastating her emotionally and physically. His taste stirred her, his dark, distinctive scent filled her head.

He teased with his tongue, then sank in to make love to her mouth. Before Liv even realized it, she had her hands on his neck, feeling the muscles there, his short-cropped hair, his heat. Time apart, hurt feelings and resentment all melted away. This was familiar. Necessary. Sadness morphed into desperate aching need.

With a groan, Hamilton slipped one arm around her waist, angling her in close to the hardness of his body. There'd only been a handful of times that he'd ever held her like this, and not at all since she'd become determined to get by without him. Not once, not ever, had she forgotten how wonderful it felt to be in Hamilton's arms.

His strong steady heartbeat reverberated against her breast. His heat wrapped around her, making her light-headed and too warm. Overwhelmed by her own powerful response, she tried to retreat, but he tangled his fingers in her hair with his free hand and held her head still while his mouth ate at hers with voracious hunger.

Too many sensations rioted inside Liv. She couldn't fight them, not now. His tongue stroked, his teeth nibbled, and she wanted him, had always wanted him.

Rising on tiptoes, she aligned her belly with his groin, pressed in against his throbbing erection—

And suddenly Hamilton stepped away from her.

Without his support, Liv would have stumbled

back onto the bed if he hadn't quickly caught her shoulders. Just as quickly, he released her again. He breathed deeply. His nostrils flared, his cheekbones burned. She stood, shaky, devastated.

One look at her face and he swore softly, running a hand over his short dark hair, his other hand curled into a fist. Sexual tension rippled in the air, and heat poured off him.

Giving her his back, he growled, "I'm sorry. I didn't mean to do that."

It sure felt like he'd meant it.

Licking her swollen lips, Liv tried to come up with a coherent response. Her body throbbed and her heart raced, and a sweet ache had invaded her limbs. Given the circumstances, lust should have seemed a disgraceful thing, but she'd never felt shame with Hamilton. He was the only man who could make her forget herself, her surroundings and any sense of propriety.

The fact that he'd lost control, too—a rare event indeed—made her own loss easier to take.

When she said nothing, he glanced over his shoulder at her. Assessing her with a probing look that scanned from her tear-reddened face, her laboring chest, to her unsteady legs, he cursed again. "Stay put. Give me one minute to change and we'll get out of here."

Her chin lifted. "Away from temptation?"

Narrowing his eyes, Ham said, "Don't fool yourself, Liv. You always tempt me, no matter where we are."

Stomach doing a free fall, Liv sucked in needed oxygen. Because leaving on her own seemed unlikely, given she didn't have a car and she looked like hell, she dropped to the edge of the bed. She didn't have to reply to Hamilton one way or the other. He'd already grabbed up his bag and gone into the bathroom. The door closed with a quiet click.

With a feeling of helplessness, Liv covered her face. The next two weeks would try her resolve, but she'd get through it. She'd made a life for herself in Denton, Ohio, and no one, definitely not Lieutenant Colonel Hamilton Wulf, would rob her of the peace she'd found.

CHAPTER TWO

LOVE, TENDERNESS AND carnal need still gripped Hamilton as he drove to Liv's house. Calling himself three times a fool, he looked over at her. Eyes swollen from tears and dark from smudged mascara, she kept quiet, her thoughts contained. She held her shoulders stiff and her back straight in true military fashion—thanks to the teaching of her father, *a father she'd just lost.*

And he'd come on to her. One minute more, and he'd have had her stretched out on the bed, his hand in her panties, his mouth on her breast....

His timing couldn't have been worse, but God, it infuriated him whenever she ranked him in the same category as Weston. Hamilton had a load of respect for Weston Amery as a military officer, but very little for him as a father.

How in hell could a man ignore his own daughter as thoroughly as Weston had?

She'd never been a priority in his life, and once Liv's mother had passed away, she'd lost her father, too. Weston had quit any pretense of paternal regard beyond the occasional criticism, and had thrown himself into his field operations. Career military—yeah, that described Weston all the way. Only he'd made career military seem like a nasty thing to Liv, an excuse to disregard family obligations when nothing could be further from the truth.

The military husbands and wives that Hamilton knew were *more* dedicated, *more* caring, because experience had taught them the value of family. They knew exactly what they missed while on assignment. They knew the hardship their partners endured, the number of responsibilities that they carried alone. It was all tough, but for them, separation was by far the greatest trial in serving their country.

Because of what they saw and did during wartime, they lived with a reality that few civilians ever had to face. They understood how easily a loved one could be lost, and they compensated by pouring more attention and affection on their wives, husbands and children. They didn't take their lifestyles for granted, and they couldn't be complacent about the gifts in their lives.

But thanks to Weston and his callous attitude toward his own daughter, Hamilton was stuck trying to work his way past her understandable prejudices against the air force.

He had two weeks. Fourteen lousy days to make her understand that they belonged together.

Hell, they were both of an age that they should

have settled down. Hamilton knew why he hadn't. Other women could relieve a temporary ache. He could lose the sexual edginess, but the awful loneliness remained because Liv Amery was the love of his life, a woman who'd taken up residence in his heart.

She was stronger than she realized, too. She had the balance of backbone and empathy necessary to be a lieutenant colonel's wife, to pick up the familial slack when duty took him away from home. She had enough guts to weather the storms of war, and the loyalty to wait, to pray and worry, and accept him when he returned.

But he loved her enough to want to spare her that.

Yet, given that, at twenty-seven, she'd never had a serious relationship, Hamilton had to believe she loved him, too.

His Liv was stubborn; she had that in common with her dad. She was also beautiful, inside and out, another fact to which she seemed oblivious. Again and again, his gaze was drawn to her. Seeing her seated rigidly as far from him as she could get in his rented car put an ache in his heart, and expanded his determination.

Pale brown hair hung to her rounded shoulders, tangled by the wind and her own frustrated hands. Red highlights glinted beneath the sunshine, though Liv always denied any red in her hair. Her eyes looked bluer than ever after the rush of tears. Her lips were puffy, her cheeks blotchy…and he wanted her so much, restraining himself took Herculean effort. He'd given his body to other women, but never his heart. And until he could give Liv both, he wouldn't feel complete.

Thank God for the aviator sunglasses that hid his innermost thoughts. Liv had always been able to see through him. One look and she'd know what he wanted and how he intended to get it. Ruthless— that could describe his current frame of mind. But damn it, he'd waited long enough. He couldn't wait anymore.

All he needed was some reassurance. Before he spilled his guts and made melodramatic vows of lifetime love and commitment, he wanted her to admit to her own feelings.

He needed that much in exchange for what he intended to give up.

Luckily, she'd paid no attention when he'd dropped his key at the front desk, or when he'd put his bag in the back of the car. He knew she'd assumed he'd stay at the motel, but no way would he keep that much distance between them. He'd missed her so much that he wanted to take advantage of every second of his two weeks' leave.

But he didn't want to take her completely by surprise with his plans. Tightening his hands on the steering wheel, he said, "Liv?"

"Hmm?"

Her disinterest and distraction cut him, and made

his words harsher than he'd intended. "When we get to your house, I'm coming in."

Her head turned and she stared at him with a mixture of incredulity, annoyance and…need. "Whether I invite you in or not?"

"That's about it." Needing to touch her, he reached out his hand and left his palm open, waiting, and finally her small hand slipped into his. The sign of acceptance gave him hope and turned his voice gruff. "You shouldn't be alone right now. I want you to eat. Rest." He squeezed her fingers. "I want to be with you."

She hesitated. "I'm surprised an important man like yourself could get two weeks off."

Was that sarcasm in her tone, or did she maybe understand just how much red tape he'd gone through to be with her? As second in command of a squadron, he had plenty of responsibilities on his plate. But Liv always came first in his heart.

Whenever possible, he wanted to be with her. "You know the routine. It's typical to send a commander, a doc and a chaplain. I filled in as commander."

Her gaze still on him, she said, "The doctor and chaplain aren't needed."

"You never know."

She ignored that to say, "But you were closer to Dad than I was, so it makes sense for you to want the duty."

Anger surfaced, and Hamilton corrected her with a growl. "I came for *you,* Liv, not Weston." When she remained quiet, he took his eyes off the road to glare at her. "Damn it, do you honestly think I'd let anyone else tell you? Do you think I'd do that to you?"

Her bottom lip trembled, making him regret his temper. Then she shook her head. "No." Her eyes were huge, accepting but sad, her voice no more than a whisper. "You wouldn't do that."

His damn heart constricted. "Liv, baby, I'd stay longer if I could, but you know that's not possible."

He waited for her to ask him about his duties, about the current assignments that would keep him away. She didn't. He knew she resisted asking because she didn't want to worry.

And she didn't want to further their involvement into intimacy.

"Liv..." Her name emerged as a word of warning, a signal of his frustration.

"I understand, Colonel."

"You don't." He squeezed her fingers again before releasing her. "But before I leave here, you will."

"Is that reassurance, or a threat?"

"Just plain fact."

They made the rest of the short, silent drive along narrow, tree-lined country roads, over a two-lane bridge that spanned a swollen creek, past a family-owned grocery store and a textile plant, until finally Liv directed him down the road to her home.

The houses were small, most of them well-kept but older and situated near to the street. Enormous elms and maples spread leafy branches to form a canopy from sidewalk to sidewalk. Birds darted around and squirrels scurried across phone wires. Ham noticed at least three antique shops, and the post office flew a flag from a towering pole. Farms butted up alongside businesses.

Life, laughter and enthusiasm burst from the area.

And Hamilton felt regret, because this was what Liv had always wanted, and he intended to take her away from it.

"That's my house right there."

Hamilton slowed the car to turn into the narrow gravel driveway as she indicated. The drive wrapped around to the left of the home, leading to an aged one-car detached garage, but Hamilton stopped, still facing the front porch.

Damn.

Surprise left him all but speechless.

"It's…" *Exactly the type of home he would have chosen for them to live in.*

The small, two-story structure could use a little work, but otherwise it looked well loved. Homey, like Liv.

A knot of uncertainty settled in Hamilton's gut.

Knowing all of Liv's hopes and dreams, he'd counted on the lure of a house to help sway her to his plans. But even an idiot could see that Liv had set down roots, and knowing how important that was to her, getting her to move wouldn't be easy. He turned off the car and sat there, staring at the steep roof and its display of loose, damaged shingles, the wraparound porch in need of fresh paint and the tall trees begging for a good trimming.

As a full-time teacher, there were things Liv didn't have time for, things she couldn't afford and things she couldn't do on her own. He'd help her during his visit, and enjoy doing so.

But there were other things, like the sparkling clean multipaned windows. And wind chimes hanging from the porch. And a fat, floral wreath on the door. He hadn't expected…what? That she could truly be content without him?

He'd come here with the staunch belief that he'd finally have her for his own. When he set his mind to something, he never failed.

Now, failure loomed, and damn it, he didn't like failing.

Liv turned toward him. "Daddy never saw it. I sent him a letter, telling him I'd moved. But I never heard back. I think he was on assignment somewhere." Her shoulders lifted and fell, and she took a deep breath. "Now he'll never get to see it—and I'm not even sure he would have wanted to."

Swallowing damn near hurt because it felt like he had to swallow some of his own arrogance, his own confidence. "It's nice, Liv. Real nice."

"Then what's the problem? You look annoyed."

Hamilton shook his head. "You'd accuse me of being an ass if I told you."

Her smile quirked on one side. It was a smile he recognized, and one he'd missed. "Odds are I'll accuse you of that even if you don't fess up."

"True." He smiled, too, but when he touched the side of her face, feeling her warmth, her vitality, his smile faded away. "I've looked at a few houses lately, too. It's uncanny how much your home resembles the ones I liked best."

Her beautiful blue eyes widened. "You...you looked at houses?"

"Yeah." He curled his hand around her neck, under the silky fall of her hair. "God knows I want you happy, Liv, but I guess I just hadn't expected to see you so settled in."

Her breath shivered, her eyes closed. And abruptly she turned away, jerking the door open and lurching out of the car. Emotional to the core, she slammed her door and hurried up the walkway to her front door.

Hamilton dropped his head back against the seat with a groan. But he didn't linger in disappointment long. If he did, she might lock him out. He caught her on the first step of her porch. Restraining her with a gentle hold on her arm, he chided, "Stop running from me, Liv."

She whipped around to face him, her eyes no longer sad but filled with fury. "Then stop making me sorry. Stop making me want things I can't have."

His heart skipped a beat. Anticipation tightened his muscles. Holding her gaze with his, he ordered, "Tell me what you want."

She punched him in the shoulder—the equivalent of a fly landing. But what she lacked in physical force she made up for with antagonism. "You know damn good and well what I'm talking about."

He caught her upper arms, overcome with a turbulent combination of fury, hope...desperate need. *"Tell me anyway."*

Going on tiptoe, she said, "Yes, sir, Colonel Wulf."

Her sarcasm pricked his frayed mood and his spine stiffened. "Liv..."

"First and foremost, I want a life free from worry."

Leave it to Liv to want the impossible.

Shaking his head, Hamilton said, "Ain't gonna happen, Liv, no matter how you dodge me. Everyone has worries, about money, about family, about job security. It comes with being alive, with being cognizant of our surroundings and our own mortality." Ham caressed her shoulder. "I know how hard it is. Wives worry about their husbands—and husbands worry about their wives. But the military does the best it can to ensure everyone can at least feel safe from the violence that plagues a lot of other countries."

He didn't mean to preach, but for as long as he

could remember, he felt unwavering pride in his country and the armed forces that kept it strong and kept it free. In his younger days, he'd thought about joining the army or the marines. Then, when he was fourteen, he joined the Civil Air Patrol and got his first chance to fly an airplane.

Instantly hooked, he changed his focus to the air force.

When he met Weston, he also met Liv. In time, his love of the air force grew, as did his love for Liv. Now at thirty-seven, nothing had changed. He still wanted them both. He'd never stop wanting them.

With bitterness reeking in her tone, Liv said, "I know all about the military, but my perspective is just a little different from yours. I know about wishing my dad could be home on my birthday, or when I was sick, or when I just missed him and didn't want to be alone."

"He should have been there." But a variety of missions had kept Weston away. Since he often couldn't be there in person, he should have at least been there in spirit. A card, a gift...

He'd never made Liv a priority. He'd never attempted to make his time away easier on her. He'd never let his daughter know that he cared, that he thought of her and worried and wanted what was best for her.

Liv made a rude sound of disagreement. "Air Force Intelligence had more important duties for Dad than placating a whiny little girl." Duties that put him at an awful risk. "Some of the places he went to were terrifying, and he stayed there for so long that there were times when I went to bed at night that I wouldn't know if he was dead or alive."

"That was Weston's choice, honey, not a code of military conduct."

An angry laugh preceded angrier words. "When I asked him about it, when I told him I missed him, he accused me of being selfish." Big tears swam in her eyes and she furiously blinked them away. "He made me feel so…so…" When her voice broke, so did Ham's heart. "I felt guilty for wanting him to spend time with me."

"Shh." Ham desperately wanted to ease her pain. But all he could do was reassure her, as many times as it took. "I'm not him, Liv. I'm not Weston, not OSI, and I would never let you worry if I could help it."

Incredulous, her mouth fell open, then snapped shut. "You wouldn't let me worry? That's rich." She swiped at her cheeks, dashing away the tears. "Do you have any idea what it did to me when you went into Kosovo? Or what about Afghanistan? And oh, God, I can't even think about Iraq without shaking and feeling ill and…" Her loss of control only added to her fury. Hamilton knew how much she hated to be seen crying.

"Liv." He tried to tug her into his arms.

She shoved away. Giving him her back, she spoke

quieter, softer. "I can't keep going through that, Ham." And with iron resolve, she added, "I *won't* keep going through that."

Hamilton struggled with himself, but he wouldn't give everything away, not yet. Timing was everything. "Regardless of how we're involved, it sounds to me like you go through it anyway." He settled his hands on her shoulders and pulled her resisting body back into his chest. "We have a lot of talking to do, Liv."

"Right. Talking about what I want?"

"Yes." They could be together, not here, not where she most wanted to be. But if she truly loved him—

When she pulled away, he let her go, but went with her up the porch steps.

"Here it is in a nutshell, Colonel. I want a home and stability, friends I can keep forever and a community that knows me."

Ham started to describe the possibilities, but she held up a hand. "I have that now, right here. And I'm not about to give it up."

Did she even care about what he wanted? Hamilton stood right behind her, crowding close while she unlocked the front door and stepped into the small foyer. Did she realize that the air force was in his blood?

He felt challenged enough to point out the obvious. "What about a husband and kids, Liv? I remember you used to want them, too."

"I still do," she remarked, giving him a quick glance over her shoulder, "and eventually I'll have both."

Jealousy raged through him, setting his blood on fire. *Only if you marry me,* he silently vowed.

Before he returned to base, Liv Amery would accept that he'd always put her first. She'd admit to her feelings, she'd trust him, and then they'd find a happy compromise in the military—one that would leave them both content, with exactly what each of them wanted. On this mission, he wouldn't fail.

But for now, it'd do him well to back off a little, to show her, rather than tell her, how much she could enjoy life with him.

His plan to give her some space lasted about three seconds, right up until Liv said, "Jack must be sleeping. But you'll get to meet him in just a second."

LIV BECAME AWARE of Hamilton standing frozen behind her, and she turned to face him. Having him in her home left her filled with unmeasured emotions. *He liked her house. He'd looked at some just like it.*

She couldn't, wouldn't, buy into that. What did a lieutenant colonel care about setting down roots? Her father had never cut grass, never voted on school levies or concerned himself with holiday decorations. And Hamilton, for all his assurance otherwise, was as military-minded as her father. "What's wrong, Ham?"

Stony-faced, his brown eyes fierce and hot, he stared at her. In a low, harsh whisper, he demanded, "Who the hell is Jack?"

The question reeked of possessiveness, and Liv couldn't help feeling just a touch of satisfaction. At least she knew she wasn't the only one uncomfortable with their current nonrelationship. "Jack is the new love of my life. But he must be sleeping. I swear, he sleeps like the dead." Smiling, she called out, "Jack?"

Two seconds later the rush of nails on hardwood floors thundered through the hallway. Jack, her nine-month-old shepherd-rottweiler mix, bounded around the corner in unrestrained joy. He jumped up and his sixty-pound body landed against hers with enough force to take her to the ground, except that she'd learned to prepare for Jack's welcomes, and always braced herself.

More than ever before, she appreciated the unrestrained welcome. Liv put her arms around him, buried her face in his scruff and just held on. She felt emotionally ravaged and vulnerable when accepting comfort from Ham, but Jack loved her unconditionally. And she loved him the same.

After accepting a few licks of greeting, Liv eased the dog down. He ran in circles, howling, barking, his tail swatting hard. Touched and oddly proud— just as a parent might be—Liv turned to Hamilton to make the introductions. "Ham, meet Jack. Jack, this is Lieutenant Colonel Hamilton Wulf."

With a priceless look on his face, Hamilton knelt down and held out his hand. "Glad to meet you, Jack."

Jack, not in the least discriminating, ignored the extended hand and jumped up against Hamilton's shoulders, almost unseating him. To Liv's surprise, Hamilton laughed and rubbed the dog, patting his sides, stroking his back and just plain enjoying himself.

"Good boy." Then he asked Liv, "How long have you had him?"

Bemused, Liv cleared her throat. "I got him the day I moved in."

"Yeah?" Hamilton looked up at her, handsome, happy, the epitome of a strong man with a big heart. "I remember you always wanted a dog."

True. And her dad had always refused.

Ham gave in to Jack's enthusiasm and sat cross-legged on the floor. The dog crawled right into his lap, still wiggling and turning and exuding elation with every pant and bark.

"You're just a big baby, aren't you?" Hamilton smiled at Liv while rubbing the dog's fur. "You've had the house—what? About six months now? I know you didn't have it when I visited last time."

"That was eight months ago." A short lifetime filled with many sleepless, lonely nights. He'd sent letters since then, and photos and cards. But correspondence wasn't the same as a warm body to hold, and never would be. "I've been moved in for six months now."

"And Jack is still this excited to see you whenever you get home?"

For some reason, that made her heart ache, probably because for as long as she could remember, Jack was the only one to give her such a welcome. "He loves me. I love him. Of course he's happy to see me." Then reality kicked in and she added, "Oops. He always has to go out right away, so I wouldn't keep encouraging his enthusiasm."

At a less distressful time, Ham's expression of alarm would have made her laugh. He quickly stood, distancing himself from the dog and any possible accidents.

Liv went into her living room, crossed through the dining room, and opened the sliding door to the backyard. She was a tidy housekeeper, thank goodness, so her home was in order, presentable to guests. Not that Ham could be considered a mere guest.... "Come, Jack. Let's go out."

The dog raced—which seemed to be the only speed he knew—through the rooms and out the door into the small fenced yard. As usual, he took his time sniffing every bush and several patches of grass before finding a spot that suited him.

Amused by the familiar routine, Liv settled

against the doorframe and gazed outside. A brisk spring wind buffeted her face, and she noticed that the sun had slipped behind dark clouds, and a distinct chill now filled the air. A storm was creeping in, and that meant her roof would leak. She hated for Hamilton to see the flaws in her house, but there'd be no avoiding it if he stayed with her—and he did seem intent on staying.

Besides, if she busied herself with preparations for the rain, she wouldn't be able to linger on regrets, and she wouldn't find time to indulge foolish hopes.

Hamilton stepped up behind her, too close for comfort, but then, being around him was never comfortable. Exciting, yes. Turbulent and heated and ex-hila-rating, but far from easy. He drew too many strong emotions from her, most of all love.

"He's a beautiful dog, Liv." While speaking, he took her sweater from her, then stripped off his leather aviator jacket. He laid both over a kitchen chair.

"Thank you." Liv glanced back at him. Before they'd left the hotel, he'd changed into jeans and a white T-shirt that hugged his muscular frame. The cotton shirt appeared soft, urging her to rest her cheek against his chest, to wrap her arms around his waist. He looked almost too good to resist. His biceps bulged and his forearms were twice as thick as hers.

And his hands...

Liv remembered those hands touching her in so many different ways, holding her, hugging her, smoothing her hair and on occasion, exciting her. Hamilton had strong but gentle hands that could guide a B-2 stealth bomber with precision, or make a woman hot with pleasure.

If she ever made love with him, she knew it would be incredible. And unforgettable. Already, her convictions wavered whenever he got too close. Sharing that much intimacy would rip away her last shred of resistance, and she'd find herself in the same position she'd resented most: alone and lonely, worried, and when the country needed Hamilton, forgotten.

Thinking about the future, about the life she'd always dreamed of, left her empty deep inside, especially when what she'd always wanted most was him.

"Liv?" With the edge of a fist, he tipped up her chin so that she had to look at him. A breeze heavy with humidity washed in through the open door, moving over her skin and sending her hair across her face. With a gentleness that felt decidedly intimate, Hamilton tucked the loose curls behind her ear.

She thought he might kiss her again, and she both wanted him to and feared the possibility.

Instead, his big thumb drifted high on her cheekbone. "Why don't you take a quick shower before the storm hits? I'll get something together for dinner and then we can relax and talk."

She'd missed lunch and hunger made her jittery.

Or maybe it was Hamilton's nearness, his touch, the very warm look in his eyes that kept her on edge.

A hot shower would be heaven, and it'd give her an opportunity to collect herself. "Thank you."

Jack ran in past her legs, still excited, but moderately so. He plopped down beside her and stared up with doggie adoration.

Liv rubbed his ears. "Let me feed him first, and then I'll…"

What? The pain surfaced again. Following her mundane routine seemed somehow disrespectful. She'd just lost her father, and the man she'd loved forever loomed in her kitchen, storming her already lacerated defenses. She didn't quite know *what* to do, or think or feel.

"Go on," Hamilton said. "I'll take care of Jack. It'll give us a chance to get better acquainted."

Crossing her arms under her breasts, Liv said, "Do you think that's a good idea?"

He matched her stance, until they had the appearance of two combatants squaring off. "Why wouldn't it be?"

"When you leave again, like you always do, he might…miss you." *Just as I always miss you.*

Hamilton worked his jaw, his annoyance obvious. "I'll be here two weeks, honey. We're bound to become friends." He held out his hand to Jack and the dog immediately abandoned Liv to go to Ham's side. In a tone that should have warned Liv, Hamilton added, "I told you I'd been thinking about a house recently. Well, I've thought about getting a dog, too."

Animosity rose in Liv, to the point that she trembled. Did he think her a fool? What did he hope to accomplish by mocking the things that gave her satisfaction? "A dog in the air force? I doubt that."

Hamilton didn't look at her, choosing instead to peer around her kitchen. He made note of the colorful drawings held on her refrigerator by magnets. Gifts from her students, signs of affection that she cherished.

His eyes narrowed in speculation. "A lot of people living in base housing have pets, Liv. It's not a problem."

Disbelief rose up. She knew pets were allowed; many of her neighbors in housing had dogs and cats. But her father had discouraged any additional commitments, claiming it wasn't fair to the animal when they never stayed in one place for long. "My dad said—"

Hamilton's gaze locked on hers. "Forget whatever Weston said, okay?" Slowly, he straightened to his full height until he towered over her. Oozing machismo, he stepped so close she inhaled his hot male scent with each deep breath. "Entire families live on and off base and yeah, they have pets and the kids ride bicycles and the men love their wives—" He drew a steadying breath. His voice dropped. "And the wives love their husbands."

Defensively, Liv pointed out, "It's difficult to move with an animal."

"So if you had to move—"

"I won't."

"But if you *did,* you wouldn't take Jack with you?"

"He's mine," she snapped. "Of course I'd take him."

Satisfaction gleamed in Ham's eyes. "Of course."

Feeling cornered, she started to turn away, but Hamilton moved with her, crowding closer still, backing her into a corner of the kitchen. "You're meant to be a mother, Liv. Kids love you, and you love them."

She clasped her hands together to keep them from shaking. "I have an entire classroom of kids. I don't need to birth them to—"

"It's not the same thing and you know it." His nose brushed the delicate hair at her temple. "Why won't you admit it? Why hold on to your old fears?"

"Because I know them to be true."

"No." His lips brushed her ear, sending a shiver down her spine. "You have a unique perspective, but it's not the norm. Marrying into the military isn't a heinous thing, no matter what you want to believe."

Her heart heavy, Liv whispered, "For me, it would be."

His breath came out in a sigh. "Liv, honey, there's always room for compromise."

"Dad said—" Liv caught herself. She winced,

then cleared her throat. "There are no compromises in the military. There are rules and regulations, a code of ethics. But no compromise."

For several heartbeats, Hamilton just looked at her, but Liv could feel the force of his frustration and her convictions wavered.

Jack whined, breaking the spell.

Drawing a deep breath, Hamilton stepped back. "To show you how good I am at compromising, I'm going to let that topic go—for now. At the moment, you've got enough to think about without me debating the pros and cons of married life in the air force." He tried a smile that lacked sincerity. "Go take your shower. Jack and I'll be fine."

Taking the opportunity to escape, Liv agreed. "His food is in the pantry. Two cups full. And give him fresh water."

Utilizing a touch of irony, Hamilton saluted her.

If only she could have him forever, her life would be perfect. But perfection aside, she had a job she loved, a house that suited her, a dog for companionship and friends galore. No husband and no children of her own, but she had a classroom full of kids that she truly cared about.

Not the same, but close.

It was a good life, full of consistency and security. She was content.

At least she had been before Lieutenant Colonel Hamilton Wulf had once again invaded her life.

CHAPTER THREE

LIV TOOK ONE look in the mirror and cringed. Tears stained her cheeks, her makeup either gone or where it didn't belong. She could only imagine her father's reaction if he saw her like this.

But Hamilton hadn't seemed to mind. No, he'd kissed her silly. Held her. Supported her.

Why did he have to be so wonderful?

And why did she have to love him so much? Through the years, other men had wanted her attention, but nothing had ever come of it. Liv tried, she really did. She gave each man a chance to wiggle into her heart. But no one compared to Ham. There were times when she doubted any man ever would.

If she could do things over... No, she wouldn't remove Ham from her memories. Without him, her childhood after her mother's death would have been unbearable. Her moments with Ham made up some of the best of her life. Whether he ever became part of her future, he'd left an indelible mark on her past.

Her most immediate future involved the preparation for her father's burial. She should probably call the funeral home today. Liv rubbed her forehead, knowing that once again, Ham deserved her gratitude. He'd come to help, when this couldn't be easy for him, either.

Taking her time in the shower, Liv let the hot water ease her tension and wash away the remnants of her tears. When she heard the loud rumble of thunder, she turned off the shower and climbed out. In addition to funeral arrangements to make, she also needed to leak-proof her house.

Trouble was, her bones felt useless and her head ached and she had a great, crushing void inside her. She and her father might have been estranged, and true, she'd often been lonely for a caring father. But in her heart, she'd always known he was still there, just a distance away. Now he was gone forever, along with the opportunity to reconcile. She should have gone to her father, she could have *made* him care.

Squeezing her eyes shut and holding her breath, she waited for the wrenching pain to subside. It didn't, but at that moment, Ham tapped on the door.

His deep baritone vibrated through the door. "You okay, honey?"

She had to clear her throat before she could answer. "I'm fine."

He paused before murmuring low, "You don't sound fine."

No, she didn't. She shook her head, swallowed

hard and lightened her tone. "I'll be right out. How's Jack holding up? Storms scare him."

"He's right beside me, but he's not fretting about *himself,* so don't insult him that way. He's worrying about *you.*"

That made her smile. Yes, Jack would worry. Whenever she got sad, he crowded close and whined and looked as miserable as she felt.

And talking about sad… Her appearance in the mirror left a lot to be desired. With a red nose, puffy eyes, and still damp hair, poor Jack might disown her. No telling what Hamilton might do….

"Liv?"

Resigned, she pulled on a hooded sweatshirt and flannel pants and opened the door.

Hamilton leaned in the doorframe, staring down at her, solemn and observant. His gaze moved over her before settling on her face. "I ordered some food. It should be here soon."

She was grateful because she had way too much on her mind to ponder what to cook. "I have to—"

"Eat." His hand glided over her hair to her shoulder, then fell away. "You know you get shaky when you go without food."

"True. But I don't have time to worry about it."

Satisfaction brought a small smile to his face. "I know. That's why I took it on myself to order some *Kartoffelsuppe* from *Hofbräuhaus.*"

At her wide-eyed surprise, he laughed and tugged

on a lock of her hair. "I thought that'd get your attention."

Kartoffelsuppe was a delicious potato soup topped with sour cream and cheese. She'd fallen in love with it the first time Hamilton had taken her to eat at Hofbräuhaus. But the closest restaurant was more than an hour away. "How...?"

"I have a buddy who lives down that way. We were in college together at the Citadel and completed the ROTC program the same year."

Which no doubt made them lifelong brothers. "So you just called him up...?"

"That's one of the calls I made while you were showering. He agreed to send the food here in a taxi." And with deeper meaning, Ham added, "The military is one big family, Liv, always willing to help out when they can."

Unwilling to acknowledge the truth of that, Liv studiously ignored his statement. "It's so much trouble for soup."

"Not just soup. We'll be sharing a *Schmankerlplatte,* too."

The mention of smoked pork chops, roasted chicken and fried cabbage had her mouth watering. "Okay, so maybe I can take time to eat after all."

His smile settled into a frown. "It won't be too much for your stomach, will it? Maybe I should have considered something lighter and blander."

"It's perfect." And so thoughtful—so typical of Ham. "Thank you."

Again, he touched her hair, tunneling his fingers in toward her scalp. For the longest time he said nothing, then with a sigh, he whispered, "Liv," while bending down to take her mouth.

She prepared herself for another explosive kiss, but instead, he kept the touch of his mouth sweet and gentle, exploring, comforting. Before she knew it, he had her cuddled up against his chest, his strong arms around her, and Liv wanted to stay there forever.

Keeping her close, he said, "I made another call, too."

His tone alarmed her. She tried to press back, but he wouldn't let her. "What did you do?"

"I contacted the funeral home. I found there's a real advantage to being in a small town. Everyone can make the time, and make things work, when they know you and care about you. And everyone here cares about you very much."

A little stunned, Liv said only, "You contacted Martin…."

"He sends his condolences, and gave us an appointment for tomorrow morning. He confirmed that Weston can be buried Friday afternoon. If we call within the next hour, they can still get the announcement in the obituaries. I'd have done that, too, but I thought you might have something particular you wanted to say."

For some reason, his autocratic behavior struck Liv as humorous. He'd be here two weeks, so that didn't factor into his rush.

"With the funeral behind you," Ham said, as if he'd read her thoughts, "you can put the grief behind you, too. Then you can start planning for the future."

A future that included him? Is that what he wanted?

Is that what she wanted? She just didn't know, but she did know that Hamilton held himself tense, awaiting her reaction. "You expect me to be angry."

"Well…yeah. I know it was presumptuous of me to sort of take over. But I'm only trying to make things easier on you."

She gave him a fierce hug. "And I appreciate it. We can decide on the announcement together, if that's okay with you."

Ham drew back, his surprise evident, and then he kissed her hard. "We'll get through this, Liv." His mouth still touched hers, his breath warm and fast. *"Together."*

That sounded nice. If only it could always be that way. But the very nature of military service guaranteed that Ham wouldn't always be there—no matter what he promised.

Did she dare to settle for less, to compromise her own convictions…?

More thunder rumbled, closer this time, prompting Liv to hurry. After girding herself, she confessed, "Could we work on the announcement now?"

"If that's what you want."

"It's not that I mean to rush, but…my roof needs work."

He shrugged, confused as to what one had to do with the other. "I noticed."

"You did?" He'd been so openly admiring, she hadn't realized. "The roof's not that old, but it did get hit with some storm damage. A few of the shingles are loose or missing. There are replacement shingles in the garage, but I haven't had time to get to it yet."

"I told you I'd been looking at houses lately, remember? I've seen more than a few that needed some repairs. As long as it's nothing structural, who cares?"

Liv wanted to ask him *why* he'd been looking at houses if he had no intention of leaving the military. An officer's mobile lifestyle made putting down roots impossible. But before she could find the right words, he added, "That storm is coming in fast. I gather the roof leaks?"

Back in the moment, Liv nodded. "In more than a few places. Luckily, there's no furniture upstairs, and not much in the way of carpet. But I don't want to see the hardwood floors get drenched either, so I need to put some buckets down to catch the worst of it."

Ham pressed another kiss to her mouth, then one to her forehead. His casual touches kept her off balance while at the same time providing the human touch she needed in the face of her loss.

"I'll help." He drew her toward the kitchen. "But first…do you have a pen and paper anywhere?"

It took them over twenty minutes to get together the facts that summed up her father's life. Hamilton called the funeral home to give the information, and Martin assured him he'd be able to get it to the paper on time.

Ham made everything so much easier. With him by her side, she couldn't imagine dealing with her father's death alone.

After he hung up the phone, Hamilton asked, "Are the buckets in the garage?"

"Yes. I'll show you." Everywhere they went, Jack followed. The second they stepped outside to the narrow path connecting her house to her detached garage, the dark sky closed in around them, thick with moisture and static with electricity.

Ham lifted the heavy, warped wooden door with an ease that brought home the contrasts in their physiques. Liv had a replacement garage door on her list of things needed for the house, but like the missing shingles, she hadn't gotten around to it yet.

The dark, dank interior of the concrete-block building smelled musty and Jack, the big baby, pressed into her side. "On the shelf over the lawn mower."

Ham grabbed up three buckets. "Are these enough?"

Half-embarrassed, Liv reached past him and took up two more. "Unfortunately, no."

Ham frowned a little in thought, then urged her back out of the garage. The wind caught his words, rushing them past her as he brought the door back down to close it securely. "If the rain holds off, I'll check out the roof. Maybe I can patch it so the leaks don't damage your ceilings too much."

Unlike her father, who had hated repair work, Ham offered with no hesitation. Such a simple thing; shoot, most men were happiest with a tool in hand. But it was more than that now. She couldn't analyze Ham or the way he made her feel, not now with her emotions so close to the surface. Her independent nature rebelled, but more than anything, she wanted to turn herself over to Lieutenant Colonel Hamilton Wulf's tender care.

Dangerous. Very, very dangerous—most especially to her heart.

They reentered the kitchen just as the rain came in a deluge, washing over the windows and filling the house with noise. Jack whined and tucked himself closer to her legs, nearly causing her to stumble.

"I guess I won't be patching the roof today."

Liv wanted to comfort Jack, but leaks were a major priority. She put a hand to the dog's neck and started for the hallway. "Don't worry about it. I was going to hire someone next week, anyway."

"Fibber."

Affronted, Liv jerked around at the base of the stairs—and saw the gleam in Ham's eyes. He always saw right through her.

She scowled at him.

He smiled crookedly and shook his head. "You can't lie to me, Liv."

"All right," she grouched, stomping up the steps to avoid his astute gaze. "It's a fib. Big deal."

"Why tell it in the first place?"

"Because I don't want to be indebted to you." The second the words left her mouth, she felt the change in the air.

"Don't push it, Liv." At the top of the stairs, he caught her elbow and drew her around to face him. Jack looked between the two of them, alert to the new tension in the air, wary. "There's something between us. It's been there for years." His voice lowered, his expression hard. "It will always be there."

"No."

"Yes." To make his point, he backed her up to the wall, looming, imposing. He still held the buckets in his hands, so he used his chest, pressing in on her, keeping her immobile. His mouth grazed her throat, up the side of her neck to her ear, where his tongue gently explored.

"Ham…" Her protest came out a breathless plea.

"Anything you need, Liv," he whispered, "anything you want, you can always get from me."

Her heartbeat drummed and her mouth went dry. Against the hard muscled wall of his broad chest, her nipples drew tight. Her stomach bottomed out when his thigh pressed against her belly....

And he stepped away, not far, but enough that their bodies no longer touched. "This is a tough time, honey, I know that. Your world has just been turned upside down. And for that reason, as much as any other, I won't let you keep your distance."

Speechless, Liv stared up at him. With every fiber of her being, she wanted him. It didn't matter that she knew firsthand how much heartache resulted from loving an officer. She well remembered her mother's tears and prayers when her father was away. It had been awful then. It'd be ten times more so with Ham.

On the ridiculous hope that by not seeing him, she could distance herself a little from his emotional pull, her eyes sank closed. She sucked in several deep breaths to steady herself, to shore up her wavering resolve.

When she opened her eyes again, Hamilton was halfway down the hallway. As he sauntered away, apparently unaware of her inner turmoil, she stared at the long line of his back, the muscled length of his thighs. His too-tight tush.

Emotionally she wanted him.

Physically she craved him.

Mentally, she knew he could break her heart for good. But the yearning swelled inside her, almost unbearable.

Maybe, just maybe if she indulged her needs— *all her needs*—when he left again, it wouldn't be so bad. She'd have memories to comfort her through the lonely years, memories to cling to if, God forbid, he never returned.

And maybe, if the worst happened, it'd also be a balm to Hamilton in his last moments. He'd always been there for her. He was here for her now. He'd always given to her, and now, she had the opportunity to give back.

The excuses sounded lame even to her, but deep down, she'd known what would eventually happen. And right now, she was just plain too weak to fight his appeal.

HAMILTON FELT HER STARE, her interest. Little by little, he was wearing her down. Soon, with any luck and continued patience, she'd admit to her true feelings. She'd tell him she loved him—and then he could tell her about their future, a future of compromise. A future he'd designed just for her.

A future that he felt sure would keep her content.

He glanced into the first small room, devoid of furniture but with a growing stain on the ceiling and a puddle forming on the floor. "I've got this one," he called back to her, aware of her standing immobile right where he'd left her.

Shaken.

Aroused.

When he spoke, his voice was even, his tone level, but his calm was deceptive. The feel of her warmed skin, her stiffened nipples and fast breath had fired him in return. He had an erection that almost hurt, from months of celibacy and years of wanting. His muscles were stiff, his abdomen rigid with restraint.

Walking away hadn't been easy, but damn it, he had his pride, too, along with his own share of fears.

Even as a child, Liv had been bright and observant, so she knew Weston was the closest thing to a father he'd ever had. His own parents hadn't factored heavily into his life, more prone to ignoring him than caring for him. If it hadn't been for Weston and the air force, Hamilton knew he would have been alone in the world, and probably more in trouble than out of it.

He loved Liv, more than anything life could offer, but the air force had become a vital part of him, harnessing the wildness and refining his leadership instincts. It gave him a purpose that meshed with the most intrinsic part of his personality. And flying fed his soul. It was as simple as that.

If Liv refused to see it… He shook his head, unable to abide the idea of leaving himself open to cold rejection. He knew, deep down inside, that she cared for him, too. But with her refusal to admit it, how could he possibly throw his heart at her feet? How did he know if she loved him enough?

He needed her to confide in him. He needed her trust. And then he could trust her in return.

After placing three buckets beneath drips that left large, dark wet spots on her ceiling, he reentered the hall. Liv was in the room across from him, another small bedroom with no furnishings.

Seeing her on her knees, mopping up a spill before placing the bucket beneath it, brought out all his protective instincts. Ham rubbed the back of his neck, trying to relieve his tension. "Liv?"

She went still, then glanced up. Eyes wide and watchful, and full of some indefinable emotion, she waited.

"It occurs to me," Ham said, "that you only have one bedroom."

Slowly she came to her feet. A look of expectancy replaced the wariness in her expression. "Yes."

Not yet, Ham cautioned himself. If she wanted him physically, it'd help to ease her into an emotional commitment. "I can camp out on the couch."

She said nothing to that.

"But is it all right if I store my stuff in this room? I don't want to leave it cluttering your foyer."

"All right."

So enigmatic. Ham crossed his arms over his chest. "You sleep downstairs?"

"In the only furnished bedroom, yes."

Close to the couch. But close enough?

She said abruptly, "Jack is spooked." Moving past Ham, she led the dog back toward the stairs. "When I sit with him, he feels better."

But rather than follow her, Jack paused at Ham's side and whined.

"Come on, Jack," Liv said, but still the dog hesitated. Ears back, head low, he whined again.

At least the dog was on his side, Ham decided. "I guess he wants us all together."

Liv opened her mouth, but nothing came out.

Hiding his smile, Ham patted the dog. "Let's go, boy. The lady is waiting."

Jack followed Ham downstairs, then back upstairs again as he stored his things in the spare room. "I should change your name to Shadow," Ham teased the dog. But when he saw Liv standing at the window, watching the pouring rain, his heart went out to her. She appeared so dejected, so…alone, that he felt guilty having her dog's attention.

A loud boom of thunder shook the house, and in a flash, Jack was at her side. Liv's nurturing nature took over and she spent several minutes calming the dog. Ham absorbed the picture she made, gentle and sweet and patient. He could easily see her with a classroom full of kids, relating, guiding, teaching.

He could also see her with a baby in her arms— *his* baby. She would be a phenomenal mother. He imagined the four of them, himself and Liv, Jack and a toddler, settled into the cozy little house in Colorado Springs. She'd be happy there, because he'd make it so.

He'd only seen the house in Internet ads, but as soon as he'd been approached with the offer to be a permanent professor at the academy, he started weighing the pros and cons.

God knew he'd miss being squadron commander, but he'd be promoted to colonel. He'd stay on active duty longer, but they'd never have to move away from the Air Force Academy. The two years it'd take for him to get his Ph.D. would be trying, but he'd stay on full pay during that time, and if Liv knew the end result, that they could be the kind of family she wanted...

Once he convinced Liv, they could check out the house together. She'd enjoy buying new furniture, or planting flowers.

The doorbell rang, announcing the arrival of their food and releasing Ham from visions of a perfect future. He answered the door while Liv got out dishes and drinks. She knew him well enough that she automatically poured him milk with his dinner.

Jack curled up beneath the table, determined to stay close but mannered enough not to beg or make a nuisance of himself. The entire setting felt cozy, especially when the lights flickered and then went out. At the dinner hour, it normally wouldn't have been so dark. But the storm-filled sky, thick with black clouds, lent the sense of midnight.

Liv stilled with her glass of iced tea near her mouth.

"Do you have any candles?"

She swallowed her bite of fried cabbage and nodded. "In the drawer by the sink. Matches are there, too."

Ham located a fat scented candle and set it in the middle of the table. Liv watched him as he lit it. Soft illumination danced across her features, and he felt prompted to say, "Does this remind you of that time in California, when an earthquake took out the electricity?"

Memories surfaced, and she gave a small smile. "Daddy was off somewhere, but you came over to stay with me until the worst of it was over."

Ham remembered that he hadn't wanted to leave at all, even hours later when things were again calm. But she was young then, and he'd had too much respect for her and her father to ever overstep himself.

"You denied being scared." He grinned. "You were what? All of eighteen then—a woman, but still so young. Cute as hell. And so damned independent I thought you were going to throw me out in the middle of the quake just to prove you didn't need me there."

Chagrined, she rubbed away her smile. "I didn't

want you to know how nervous I was. Daddy didn't like it when I gave in to fears."

Reaching across the table, Ham took her hand. "Everyone gets afraid sometimes."

"Not you."

He half laughed until he realized she was serious. Then he shook his head. "Hell, honey, I live with fear."

Her somber eyes filled with sympathy. "Because of the danger in what you do?"

"No." Being totally honest, he said, "When I'm in a plane, instincts kick in. There isn't time for fear, because I'm too busy reacting. I'm well trained, the air force has seen to that, and there's a level of arrogance in knowing how qualified I am, sort of a feeling of invulnerability."

She watched his face and her fingers tightened on his. "You love it, don't you?"

Not like he loved her. "It's hard to explain, Liv. What I do… It's a calling to protect and serve my country, a calling I've felt compelled to follow since I was a kid. Just as you feel the need to teach. The air force is me, and I'm the air force."

He felt her need to understand. It was there in her gaze, in the way she clutched at his hand, the sadness in her eyes. "I guess I have enough fear for both of us."

Ham wanted her love and loyalty. Perhaps he

should start by giving to her first. "So you want to know what does scare me?"

"What?"

He leaned closer. "You."

"Me?" Her laugh was nervous and self-conscious.

"Yeah, you. You're the most important person in the world to me, Liv, don't you know that? You're my family, and my friend. You're the woman I think about when missiles and antiaircraft fire are thick. I fear leaving you alone. I fear never seeing you again."

Her bottom lip began to quiver, and tears again threatened, breaking his heart. She was so precious to him, and she didn't even realize it.

Damned emotion clogged his throat and he paused to swallow. Deliberately lightening the mood to spare her, he said, "Look at all this good food going to waste. Let's finish up because I have something I want to show you."

She accepted the change in topic gratefully. Pulling her hand away, she bit her lip and nodded. But then she paused, raising her face to his. "Ham?"

His heart pounded. "Yeah, baby?"

The seconds ticked by, and the tension grew.

"Thank you," she whispered, "for being here with me."

"Always." He touched her chin, smoothed her jaw.

Her smile wavered, softened. With reluctance, she gave her attention back to her food.

When their plates were almost empty, she asked, "So. What are you going to show me?"

Another touchy subject, but one that couldn't be avoided. "Before we see the funeral director tomorrow, I wanted to go over your dad's belongings with you. I took some photos off his desk that might be nice to have at the ceremony, some commendations, too. The photos might be nice to display."

"Daddy would like it to be a big event."

Ham nodded. "Regular military funeral. Bugler, twenty-one gun salute…"

"The works."

"Yeah." He watched her face, and felt her pain. "You've been to military funerals before."

"Too many." She gripped her hands together. Knowing that many military members would attend the service, she said, "Whiteman is an eight-hour trip, at least. Will that cause a problem with the funeral set so soon?"

"A tanker will bring the wing commander and most of the men from your father's office. The word will get around, so there'll be others, too. Those he's served with who are at other bases, and local retired military and their families—they'll all want to pay their respects. Military folks are tight, you know that."

"Yes." She drew a breath. "I've never handled a funeral before."

Hating to see her tension, Ham reached for her

hands, drew her up from her seat. "Weston died on active duty, Liv, so the air force will provide funeral benefits and arrange the burial ceremony."

She turned her face up to his, brave and beautiful and his—if only she'd realize it.

"Even now, the air force plays such a big role in his life. But this time, I have to admit that I'm grateful."

More thunder rumbled. Rain lashed the windows and lightning flickered. He cupped her cheek. "I told you, we're one big family." And then he kissed her—and he didn't want to stop.

CHAPTER FOUR

LIV KNEW SHE DIDN'T want to sleep alone that night. Ham was right—it didn't matter if she admitted how she felt or not because no one would ever replace him in her heart.

She made up her mind as Ham struggled to rein in his hunger. Not once in the many years she'd known him had he ever shirked what he considered his duty. He was honorable to the core, dedicated to caring for others, driven by a deep and patriotic love of his country.

How could she not love him?

His forehead touching hers, he whispered, "I shouldn't keep doing this."

"This?" Liv stroked her hands over the soft cotton T-shirt he wore, across his chest, up and over his shoulders.

"You aren't thinking straight."

She laughed, feeling lighthearted for the first time since he'd arrived at her classroom. "Does that mean my thinking is bent?"

He squeezed her. "It means I picked a bad time to keep coming on to you."

"I think it's the perfect time." And she went on tiptoes to kiss him again.

Ham groaned, taking control of the kiss, pulling her into the hard lines of his body. Their breathing soughed in the quiet night, vying with the violent storm.

He wrenched away. "Liv, wait...."

"Why?"

He caught her face and held her still. Eyes smoldering with heat, he asked, "Do you love me?"

Liv recoiled from the idea of giving away so much. If she told him her deepest feelings, that she'd loved him forever and probably always would, there'd be no going back. She knew Ham, knew how he thought and how determined he could be.

She licked dry lips. "I want to make love with you."

Something in his expression chilled and became distant. He stepped back. Every bit the officer, he held himself straight and proud—yet somehow wounded. "Let's sit down and I'll sort your dad's things with you."

"Hamilton..."

"You need time," he insisted. "Time to deal with your loss and to come to grips with your feelings. You need sleep. You need..." Unblinking, he stared at her, then shook his head. "You need me to stop pressing you. Come on." He picked up the candle with one hand and reached out for her with the other.

Given that she had electric heat, the house had quickly begun to cool during the power outage. The spring storm had brought with it chilly temperatures and window-rattling wind. She wore a sweatshirt, but Ham wore only a T-shirt. He didn't look the least bit uncomfortable though.

The moment they left the table, Jack scooted out from underneath and chased after them. Candlelight danced and spread out, leaving dark shadows in her small family room. Once Liv sat on the couch, Jack dropped across her feet with a lusty doggy sigh. It wasn't the most comfortable position, but she enjoyed his nearness as much as he enjoyed being near.

Ham fetched a box that he'd left on the table in the foyer. Sitting beside her, he opened it and pulled out the framed photograph on top.

"This stayed on your dad's desk, in the lefthand corner. It was as much a part of his office as his chair and bookshelf."

Liv recognized the five-by-seven photo as one Ham had taken of her years ago. It was only months after her mother had passed away. She'd been baking, determined to make her father a "welcome home" meal that he'd never forget. Long curls, damp with sweat, hung in her face, and her clothes were limp and disheveled.

"That night, Daddy told me I was as good a cook

as my mother." She smiled, remembering one of the good times. "He didn't even complain that the meatloaf was dry or the rolls a little burned."

"He bragged to me that you were one hell of a fine cook."

Laughing, Liv said, "I bet that's exactly how he put it, too."

Ham's arm slid around her shoulders, comfortable and familiar. "Word for word."

Liv challenged him with a teasing look. "Is that why you had it framed for him?"

Caught off guard, Ham stalled, and finally rolled one shoulder with a guilty grin. "He liked the photo. Whenever anyone came to his office, they'd look at that picture and ask about it. Weston would hold it with pride and tell everyone that you were his daughter."

Desperately, Liv clutched at this small proof of affection. "Did he talk about me much?"

"Truthfully? He wanted me to court you."

A surprised laugh bubbled out. "*Court* me?"

"He considered me worthy of his one and only daughter." Ham pulled out another photo. "This one sat on his bookshelf. He'd always point out what a handsome couple we made, and believe me, your dad didn't have an ounce of subtlety."

Skeptical, Liv accepted the smaller, three-by-five shot of her with Hamilton at a military function. She smiled at the camera, but Hamilton stood in profile, his absorbed gaze on Liv's face. Seeing the picture, and his expression, actually made her blush. "I don't recognize this one."

"I have no idea who took it. But it's been in your dad's office for years."

"What did you tell him when he…well, talked about us?"

Stretching out his long legs, Hamilton settled back in the couch and took the picture from her, examining it in minute detail. "I told him the truth. That he'd soured you on the military."

Her mouth fell open. "You didn't."

"Not in so many words. But I explained that you weren't interested in an officer. I told him you wanted a regular nine-to-five kind of husband. One who came home every night instead of being gone months, sometimes years, at a time."

Fascinated, Liv prompted, "And he said…?"

"That you were just like your mother." He tore his attention from the photo and settled it on her instead. "He said that a lot, honey. Always with affection, never complaining. He loved her, just as he loved you."

That left Liv speechless.

Ham smiled. "And then he'd tell me I should damn well work harder at convincing you."

Before Liv could dwell on that too long, Hamilton drew out a variety of medals. "I figured you'd want these."

"They're all his?"

"All the ones I could locate before flying here. He might have more tucked away in his quarters. I'm sure he has more ribbons." Ham pulled out five Meritorious Service Medals, four Air Force Commendation Medals and a Bronze Star.

He gave her a long look. "In all my years in the air force, I've only known two Bronze Star recipients."

New emotions swelled inside her, crowding out the resentment. In a reverent whisper, she quoted, "Given for acts of heroism and meritorious achievement."

Holding up the medal, Ham said, "Weston was definitely a hero." He laid the small badge in Liv's hands, curled her fingers around it. He, too, dropped his tone to one of solemn respect. "Your dad did some pretty impressive things during wartime. He wasn't always there when you and your mother needed him, but a lot of soldiers relied on him and he never let them down."

Liv held the medal to her heart, overwhelmed, touched, forgiving.

Watching her, Ham flattened his mouth. "Plenty of men are willing to risk their necks to save the people they love. But Weston did it for people he didn't even know."

Liv absorbed the enormity of her father's contribution, how important he'd been to so many.

And Hamilton was no different.

He didn't think twice about the risks he took. Instead, he embraced them gladly, determined to serve the country he loved, the people who relied on him, without ever seeing himself as a hero.

Her heart expanded, and with it, her love. She put the medal back in the box and laid a hand on Hamilton's forearm. "I should have understood."

"Maybe," Ham said, "but Weston should have included you as one of his priorities. He didn't make it easy for others to get close to him. He was always reserved, very self-contained. Some men are that way, whether they're career military or not. Some women, too, I imagine."

Liv stared at him with new eyes. He was so selfless, so caring of others, that he didn't realize her new understanding extended to him. "You're right, of course."

"You knew my parents, Liv. They weren't very caring, but neither were they military. I keep telling you, one doesn't have anything to do with the other."

"No, it doesn't."

Her smiling agreement finally registered, and his brows pulled down with suspicion. "What did you say?"

Liv laughed, a little giddy, a lot in love, more at peace than she'd been in years. "I'm sorry. Now I've confused you, haven't I?"

His mouth opened, but then slowly closed. He surveyed her warily. "I would never deliberately hurt you, Liv. You have to believe that."

"I know."

Neck stiff, shoulders rigid and eyes direct, he added, "But I can't leave the air force."

Accepting, Liv nodded. "I know that, too." She lifted the box of medals and photos from his lap and set them on the table.

"Liv…"

Rather than hear whatever he planned to say, she rose to her knees, leaned into him and cupped his face—and kissed him silly. It wasn't often that she took the initiative, but for once, she wanted to put what Ham wanted, what he needed, first.

She'd been incredibly selfish, but no more.

At the prodding of her small tongue, he groaned and gave in. Gathering her across his lap, he returned her kiss with enthusiastic heat. Until she pulled his T-shirt out of his jeans.

Breathing hard, he rasped, "Hold up, Liv."

"No." Slipping both hands beneath the material, she stroked his hot, hard flesh, the crisp hair on his broad chest, over his impressive pecs. He felt *so* good, so much a man. *Her man.* Being with him felt right.

It always had. "Hamilton? What time is it?"

He went blank, a little dazed, then he glanced at his watch. After clearing his throat, he growled, "Nineteen hundred…"

Laughing, Liv caught his wrist and turned it so she could see the dial. "A little after seven o'clock. Hmm." Slanting him a coy look, she said, "Close enough to bedtime."

And truthfully, he had to be tired. God only knew how much running he'd done since the report of her father's death. Knowing Hamilton, he'd probably moved heaven and hell to arrange things to his satisfaction. The emotional toll was tough enough, but he had to be physically exhausted, too.

He held himself very still. "Bedtime?"

"Yes." Working up her nerve, Liv spoke straight from her heart. "Make love to me, Hamilton."

He squeezed his eyes shut—then caught her hands and held her still.

"Ham?"

"You don't know what you're doing to me, do you?"

"I know what I *want* to do to you."

He drew a breath, impaled her with his gaze. "I need everything, Liv."

Her heart beat so hard, it made her tremble. "Everything…meaning?" *Did he want to marry her?*

"Tell me you love me."

Emotions warred against one another, hope and tenderness, disappointment and desire. She wanted to tell him, she really did, but the words strangled in her throat.

"Admit it, Liv." And then, almost desperate he implored, *"Tell me."*

What did it matter? He obviously already knew. In the long run, it wouldn't change anything. As he'd said, he couldn't leave the air force, and she couldn't survive as a military wife, alone and lonely, always filled with worry.

But in the short run...?

They could make memories hot enough to carry them through the endless winter nights to come. At the moment, that's what she wanted most. Tomorrow, next week, next year—every long night that she spent without him—could be dealt with later.

Meeting his fierce gaze, Liv nodded. "Yes. I love you, Lieutenant Colonel Hamilton Wulf."

The change in him was astounding. One moment she was on his lap, and in the next, he'd blown out the candle and stood.

Holding her in his arms as if she weighed nothing at all, he asked, "What about Jack?"

The dog stared up at them anxiously.

Even now, with lust bright in his eyes, Ham had the consideration to think of her pet. Could there be a more big-hearted, strong, compassionate man anywhere?

Liv wanted to melt. She wanted to change the future so she could have him forever. She wanted him over her, inside her, loving her as much as she loved him.

"Jack often sleeps under my bed when it storms. Of course, I've never had a man sleeping with me while he was under there, but—"

Hamilton squeezed her for that admission, his expression wild with possessiveness. "C'mon Jack," he ordered in a voice rich with haste. "Time for bed."

The dog bounded up and loped after them as Ham strode for her bedroom. She'd had several years of buildup to this moment, which left her already primed and anxious and prepared.

Teasing Ham's neck with her fingertips, she asked, "What if he won't settle down with us doing... you know?"

Ham watched her with deep concentration while his long strides drew them nearer and nearer to her bed. "He might as well get used to me now." And then, after a firm kiss, "I'm not going anywhere."

Liv started to object, to explain that the dog didn't need to get used to him because he'd be heading back to the air force in two weeks—back to his duty, and out of her life.

But Ham took her mouth again, and didn't stop kissing her until he stood beside her bed. He laid her flat on her back, took precious seconds to rid himself of his boots and socks, and then his weight pressed her down and his hand slid inside her sweatshirt, boldly cupping a breast.

Liv forgot whatever she'd wanted to say.

PRESSED BY URGENCY, by the endless fantasy and unrelenting desire to make her his own, Ham covered her breast…and groaned. *God, she felt good.* His thumb found her nipple, already peaked, achingly tight, and he gently stroked, aware of the ripple of pleasure that ran through her. He felt almost violent in his need.

He deepened his kiss, savoring the taste of her on his mouth, the moist silky heat of her curious tongue. His hips pressed down and in and she gave a high, female moan of pleasure.

"Open your legs."

She did, anxiously spreading them wide so that his hips settled between and he could feel her heat cradling him. She lifted up, increasing the pressure, moving, stroking him.

"God almighty, it's too much." Eyes closed, he strained his upper body away from her, wedging his lower body closer.

"Ham," she said on a near wail, her fingers knotted in the coverlet, her head tipping back.

He loved seeing her like this. Hot for him. Nearly out of control. Rocking his hips in a rhythm that complemented her own, he watched her face and reveled in the heightened signs of desire and pleasure. Heat flushed her cheeks, and another moan broke past her parted lips.

He wanted to strip them both naked right now. But if he did, if he saw her bare and open to him, accepting him, he'd be inside her in seconds. She wasn't ready, no matter how far gone she looked. Their first time deserved special care.

Liv deserved special care.

Coming back down over her, he nibbled on her ear, kissed his way to where her neck met her shoulder. Sucking the delicate skin of her throat in against his teeth, he marked her with satisfaction, primal in his need to lay claim.

Her spicy scent—not perfume, but Liv, all woman and now all his—filled his head.

The storm outside abated, softening to a steady rain. Jack did indeed crawl beneath the bed and apparently, he slept, because he made no objection to Ham's presence.

Shifting his hold, Ham slid one arm beneath her, raising her back. With his other hand, he shoved up her sweatshirt. "I want to kiss you everywhere, Liv."

She held herself still, watching him, her breath suspended.

In the dim room, her pale breasts gleamed opalescent, shimmering with her nervousness and excitement. Seeing her taut nipples made his erection ache and throb. "I'll start here," he rasped, and closed his mouth around one small nipple.

The second his tongue touched her, Liv arched up, groaning raggedly. Ham sucked, not hard, but languid and easy, curling his tongue around her, suckling her with gentle deliberation.

Frustrated, she tried to pull off her sweatshirt

while panting and gasping. Ham jerked it up and over her head and tossed it to the foot of the bed.

When he started to return to her, she fended him off with both hands flattened to his chest. "Now you."

Blood thundered through his veins. His testicles were tight, his cock full and heavy. She wanted him. Finally. He nearly ripped his T-shirt getting it off. And still she held him back, her hands now moving over him, exploring him.

"I've dreamed of this," she murmured, her eyes a little dazed, her voice thick with need. "You have the most perfect body, and there've been so many nights when I've imagined getting to touch you, to kiss you."

She came up on one elbow, and put her soft, damp mouth to his shoulder. Her tongue came out, tasting his flesh. Her open mouth administered a soft, wet love bite.

"You taste—" her nose brushed up the side of his throat to his ear "—and smell even better than I'd ever imagined. All hot. All man." She licked his ear, along his jaw to his mouth. "Delicious."

The sexual connotation of that one word stole his breath. Hamilton prided himself on his control, on his iron resolve to do everything the very best that he could. He *would* make this good for Liv. But in order to ensure that, he had to take charge before she obliterated his already fractured patience.

The flannel pants she wore had a loose elastic waistband that made it easy for his hand to get underneath, onto her silken belly. "Let me enjoy you, honey."

Her eyes darkened. Stroking her skin, he teased his way lower and lower, and with a deep breath, she settled back onto the mattress.

"Are you wet yet, Liv?"

Her breathing stilled. Eyes wide with shock locked on his. Ham knew she'd be blushing, but he couldn't see it in the dim interior of the room.

"I—"

"Let me see." Touching her, sliding one long finger over her pubic curls, and farther down between her swollen lips, Ham whispered, "Yeah. You are."

As his finger moved, stroking, sliding, her eyelids grew heavy and she bit her bottom lip. Breathing fast and hard, she watched him, their gazes a connection beyond the physical. Ham felt it deep into his soul, just as he'd always known he would. He was the man who'd have Liv. Period.

"How's this feel, honey?" He pressed in, not far, just deep enough that her innermost muscles clamped around him.

"Ham…" she said raggedly, trying to lift her hips to take more of him, but he held back.

"Getting wetter, Liv. And hotter." He kissed her shoulder, her chest, and drew her other nipple into his mouth. Forcing himself to remain slow and steady, he suckled her, fingered her, licked and stroked, alternating his attention from her breasts to the slick, swollen flesh between her thighs, gradually gaining urgency, driving her closer to the edge.

When she cried out in dissatisfaction, Ham pulled out his finger, only to stroke two back in, fast and deep.

Her nails bit into his shoulders. Her head tipped back, her neck straining, her hips lifting.

"That's it," he encouraged against her wet nipple, feeling the start of her contractions, and so damn excited he wanted to shout. He found her clitoris with his thumb and carefully manipulated her, pressing, fondling in a steady rhythm, pushing her—and with a deep, raw groan her entire body bowed, damp in sweat and fragrant with lust, she came.

Ham wanted to savor the moment, to hold her and ease her, but he couldn't. Violent need shook his body. He'd wanted her too long—all his life it seemed. Waiting now would be impossible.

He knotted a hand in her hair, turning her toward him. Her mouth opened under the force of his. When he sank his tongue in, she sucked on it.

He needed out of his jeans—*now.*

Thrusting himself away, he went onto his back and raised his hips. Jerking open the snap of his jeans, easing the zipper down the bulge of his hardened cock, he freed himself.

Sated and limp beside him, Liv whispered, "Finally."

Damn it, she didn't help with her verbal prodding. It felt like he'd explode if he didn't get inside her soon. He had enough sense left to grab a condom out of his jeans pocket before tossing the pants, with his underwear, aside.

While he tried to ready himself, she kept touching him, and she said, "I wish the electricity hadn't gone out."

Hands shaking, Hamilton rolled on the rubber and turned to her. "Me, too. I want to see you."

"And I want to see you."

"We've got forever, baby. A million more nights, just like this one. I promise." He settled over her soft, warm body. She automatically adjusted her legs to allow the closeness, and put her arms around him.

"I love you, Ham." Her hips undulated under his, the slow, wanton movements firing his blood more, heating his flesh and causing all his muscles to clench.

He reached between their bodies, used his fingertips to spread her delicate vulva. She was very wet now, slick with her own orgasm, still tender and sensitive and he felt ready to shatter when he wedged the head of his cock against her.

Restraining himself, he rasped, "Tell me again."

"I love you."

A fine trembling invaded his limbs, making it

impossible to ease into her. Through his teeth, he said, "Again."

She hugged him fiercely. "I love you, Lieutenant Colonel Hamilton Wulf—"

Her words ended on a harsh gasp as he plunged into her, burying himself despite the tightness of her body, clamping his arms around her to keep her immobile.

He could feel her stretching to accommodate him, felt her small shivers as she tried to adjust.

He buried his face in her neck. Raw, unfamiliar emotions rose to the surface, bombarding him. He felt vulnerable. And he felt powerful.

In a voice unrecognizable to his own ears, he rasped, "You're mine, Liv."

"Yes." Her small hands moved over his back, both soothing and inciting him.

He drew back, pushed in again, deeper this time. *"Mine."*

Her warm tears tracked his shoulder; a small kiss seared his skin. She drew a shuddering breath. "I love you, Ham."

It was enough. It was too much. He began thrusting fast and hard, unmindful of anything but Liv and the fact that she'd finally accepted him, all of him. Their heavy breathing filled the room as they strained together. Her arms hugged him. Her legs hugged him. She gasped, writhed, clasped around him—and Ham felt himself ready to come.

Wanting to see her, he stiffened his arms to rise above her. Her face twisted with her pleasure. Her cries were sharp and throaty and *real*.

Looking at her, loving her, Ham let himself go. The turbulent release washed through him, wave after wave, each one stronger, more acute than the other. He groaned, kept himself pressed deep within her until finally, utterly drained, he lowered himself into her arms.

MINUTES WENT BY. His heartbeat slowed. His breathing evened out and his overheated skin began to cool. Ham decided that Liv was far too silent, almost withdrawn.

He didn't like it, but he felt so replete, so happy with her, so damned in love, he couldn't work up the energy for more than a smile. Rubbing his nose against her ear, he whispered, "Hey. What's wrong?"

With a deep sigh, she ran her fingers over his military haircut. "Nothing."

Why did women always say *nothing* when they meant *something?* "Tell me, Liv."

Her rounded shoulder lifted, nudged against him. She sighed again. "I just wish this moment could last forever."

Because he still had to do two years of study for his Ph.D., two years that'd keep him on active duty, which would involve compromise on her end, he didn't get into his plans yet.

Hoping for some middle ground that wouldn't spoil the moment or his mellow mood, he promised, "I'll make you happy, baby." He rose up to see her face. Her hair was wild, and he smoothed it, tucked it behind her ears. A slight whisker burn marred her smooth cheek, and he touched it with his thumb. Her breath caught.

Smiling into her smoldering eyes, aware of her nipples stiffening again, Ham continued to touch her softly and asked, "For now, can you just trust in that?"

"But—"

He put a finger to her mouth. "No buts, Liv. You love me. I love you. I'm not about to ruin that by doing anything that'll make you unhappy."

Still she hesitated, and Ham gave a partial admission. "I've made some plans, changed some things. It'll be all right, Liv. You have my word."

She searched his face, her eyes suddenly filled with hope. "I do trust you, Ham."

Thank God. She didn't yet know what his plans would be, but he knew she couldn't possibly get the wrong idea. He'd been too clear on his position in the air force. He wouldn't give it up. Her acceptance showed her willingness to compromise—just as he'd hoped.

He put a firm kiss on her mouth and left the bed to stand on shaky legs.

Their eyes had adjusted to the darkness, and she

visually devoured his naked body with interest. It was a good thing, to please the woman you loved, the woman who would be your partner for life.

Staring at his lap, she asked, "Just where are you going?"

Stifling his grin with an effort, Ham explained, "I have a box of rubbers in my bag upstairs."

"A whole box, huh?" Looking sassy and sweet, Liv raised herself onto one elbow. "You must have been feeling pretty hopeful when you came here."

"Honey, I've lived off hope since you turned twenty-one." He put a hand on her bare hip, trailed his fingers down to her knee, relishing her warmth, the silkiness of her bare skin. "Now I have you right where I want you, and I don't intend to let you sleep anytime soon."

Since she didn't object to that plan, Ham left to get the protection. And when he returned, she smiled and opened her arms to him. Finally, he had what he wanted.

He had it all.

CHAPTER FIVE

SOMETHING WOKE LIV, some strange pounding that barely penetrated her subconscious. Lethargy pulled at her, the results of a long, wonderful, sleepless night.

The pounding continued, and finally she stirred. Just as she'd done throughout the long humid night, she automatically smiled. Time and time again, Ham had curled her close, petting her, kissing her. They'd made love three times and each time had been as exciting as the first. After that third time, her mighty warrior had slept. Liv hadn't. She didn't want to waste a single second of their time together, so she'd watched him, listened to his breathing, and loved him more with each passing second.

The excess of pleasure threatened to burst her heart. She felt physically languorous and mentally relaxed, peaceful in a way that had eluded her until Lieutenant Colonel Hamilton Wulf had shown her how special lovemaking could be with the man of her heart.

And he had said he was changing things. *For her.*

Without opening her eyes, smiling in satisfaction, Liv stretched out an arm to the side of the bed he'd occupied.

Her hand encountered only cool rumpled sheets.

She bolted upright and surveyed the room. No sign of his clothes, but the drapes were open. The gray sky, still dark with storm clouds, gave no indication of the time, but it had stopped raining.

The humming of the house let her know the electricity was back on. Her battery-operated bedside clock told her she'd slept much later than usual. Her class would be on their first recess by now!

When Liv slid her naked legs out of the bed, she became aware of the chill in the air, and of all the places that now suffered a tantalizing ache. Another smile, sappier than the first, curled her mouth.

And then she heard the rapping of a hammer, the very sound that had awakened her.

Taking the sheet off the bed and going to her window, she looked out at the backyard. Jack ran along the side of the house, barking and looking up…at the roof.

It took Liv all of two minutes to pull on another pair of flannel pants and a sweatshirt. The loose, comfortable clothes were her favorite "at home" wear. She gave a brief glance in the mirror at her hair, finger-combed it back and secured it with a cloth-coated rubber band, then headed for the kitchen.

The scent of fresh coffee made her pause to pour a

cup. After two fortifying sips, she opened the kitchen door and stepped outside. The soggy ground froze her feet. Jack spotted her right off and came tearing toward her. Since his feet were muddy, she fended him off, and made do with a lot of petting on his scruff.

Going to the edge of the house, she looked up and found Ham on the roof, replacing her lost shingles. The chilly morning air cut through her sweatshirt, but Ham wore only a black T-shirt, jeans and boots. It was gloomy enough that he didn't need his sunglasses.

His squatting position showed off thick thigh muscles and the obvious strength in his back and upper arms.

She had experienced that strength firsthand.

With a rush of yearning, she called up, "Good morning."

He paused with his hammer raised, a few nails in his teeth. The moment he spied her, his gaze warmed and grew intimate. After removing the nails and scooting to the edge of the roof, he said, "Good morning yourself, sleepyhead."

Everything had changed, Liv realized. The way he smiled at her, the way he held himself in her presence. It was as if mammoth barriers had been ripped away. Even with him on the roof and her on the ground, a new closeness existed between them.

Her heart started thudding in fast, hard beats.

He'd said she would be happy with him, and since he knew her feelings on the military, that could only mean one thing.

Breathless, filled with hopefulness and expectation, she stared up at him.

"Liv? Yoo-hoo. Did you go into a trance?"

His smile touched her heart, encouraging her own smile. Because the previous night had been so wonderful, she didn't question the change, just accepted it as her dream coming true.

"You should have awakened me earlier."

"I thought about it. You looked so damned enticing, all warm and sleepy and...naked." He cocked one eyebrow, his expression wolfish. "Then the electricity came back on and I heard the weather report. More violent storms predicted." He indicated the pile of shingles with a tilt of his head. "As tempting as you are, I figured you'd appreciate a dry house."

Normally, she'd have been resistant to his assistance, but that, too, had changed. His promise to her had radically altered her outlook on life, because life now included Hamilton.

She smiled brightly, full of love. Sated with security. Content with their future.

Very softly, she said, "Thank you." Her gratitude visibly warmed him, made him appear more relaxed and more confident than ever. "How about I make some breakfast?"

"Perfect. I'm starved. I only need another twenty minutes to finish."

"Pancakes?"

"You know me too well."

Yes, she did. Better than she knew anyone else, especially after last night. She took great satisfaction in that fact. "You be careful up there. Everything is wet and slick."

Ham saluted her and returned to work.

Humming to herself, Liv went back inside and, while finishing her coffee and thinking pleasant thoughts, began breakfast preparations. Jack tired of watching the activity on the house and scratched at the door a few minutes later. Liv grabbed up an old towel to dry his feet before letting him in. When she started to fill his dish, she noted that Ham had already taken care of it.

So thoughtful.

He'd be great with kids, too, she mused. His attentiveness extended beyond his military duties; that was clear to her now. The community would love him as much as she did.

A few minutes later when Ham came in, she was at the table, setting out syrup and butter. Ham put his arms around her from behind and kissed the nape of her neck.

"I could just have you for breakfast," he murmured.

Oh, if only there were time. "I'm sure I'd love it,"

Liv admitted, leaning into him and sighing. Sadness intruded, and she pointed out, "But we need to eat, and I still need to shower and put on my makeup before I face the public."

Saying, "You don't need makeup," Hamilton effectively swept away her melancholy.

Liv rolled her eyes. "Don't overdo it, okay? There are mirrors in the house, and I've already seen one." She turned to kiss his chin.

His hand moved down her back to her bottom. Fingers spread, breath warm in her ear, Ham said, "I think you're beautiful."

The compliment, coupled with his touch, nearly took her knees out. "Well, thank you. But we still don't have much time, and I'm still going to put on my makeup."

Giving her backside a pat, he said, "Tonight, then."

Yes, tonight. And then she'd ask him about his intentions, when his obligation to the military ended and when they could marry. But that could wait until they finished the burial arrangements.

While Ham washed up at the sink, she said, "I want to swing by the school to pick up my car while we're out."

"Sure." He knelt down to pet Jack, who lifted his furry head with delight. "I was thinking—will Jack be okay here by himself while we're gone? If that storm hits again, is he going to be scared?"

"We're in Ohio. It storms here all the time, re-member? I just need to put him in the bathroom with a radio playing. It helps drown out the thunder and with no windows in there, he can't see the lightning. He'll probably sleep until we get home."

Ham continued to stroke the dog, who wallowed in the attention. "I had this awful image of him hid-ing under the bed, trembling in fear." Ham shook his head. "Not a pretty picture."

He never failed to please her with his consider-ation. "You're something else, you know that?"

His gaze met hers, warm with insinuation. "As long as I'm yours, that's all I care about."

The words were almost too wonderful to believe. "You're mine all right," she said with mock warn-ing. "And I'm never letting you go, so don't get any ideas."

He'd been teasing, but now he grew solemn, push-ing back to his feet, standing close to her. "That's something we need to talk about, isn't it? The future, how we're going to work this all out."

That sounded too serious by half. Liv bit her bot-tom lip, and nodded. "Yes."

He searched her face, glanced at his watch and scowled. "I suppose now isn't the time." He wrapped his hands around her upper arms, caressing. "How are you holding up? I know today isn't going to be easy."

Liv touched his face. "Actually, I'm fine. Sad, of

course. And a little hollow with the knowledge that I'll never see Dad again, that opportunities are lost. But thanks to you, I have good memories now, too, memories that had been buried beneath resentment. That was wrong of me, but from what you told me, Dad didn't have any grudges."

"No. Weston loved you a lot, he just wasn't a very demonstrative man."

"Unlike you, Howler?"

His crooked grin looked boyish and reeked of charm. "You've never called me that."

"But everyone else does." She turned to seat herself at the table, and Hamilton did the same. "I listened last night, you know."

Swallowing a mouthful of pancakes, Hamilton cocked an eyebrow.

"I kept thinking you'd…well, howl."

He almost choked on his food, then burst out laughing. "You're kidding, right?"

"Nope. What else would Howler mean? Howling during sex. Howling out your pleasure. I naturally assumed it was something like that."

"Well, smart-ass, for your information, I never howl."

"Not during sex, anyway." She carefully forked a bite of buttery pancake. "It's more like a growl. Or a groan."

He fought a grin. "What I do is roar. And only when I'm really pissed. But guys being guys, and pilots being bigger jackasses than most, they took a perfectly acceptable roar and starting labeling it a howl." He shrugged. "It stuck."

Liv let out an exasperated breath. "Well. I'm almost disappointed." Her lips twitched. "After all, it's something you and Jack could have had in common."

Displaying an enormous appetite, Hamilton shoveled down the last of his pancakes, then stood. "You wanna hear me howl, I can howl." He pulled out her chair and lifted her to her feet. "Let's shower together. If we hurry, we'll have enough time before we have to leave. Plenty of time for—"

"Howling?"

He lifted her into his arms. "Exactly."

IT TOOK HOURS BEFORE all the arrangements were complete. Watching Liv, how she dealt with it all while keeping her emotions in check, putting up a brave, proud front, made Hamilton want to burst with pride. He interjected where necessary, supplying information about the air force's contribution to the service, and by the time they left the funeral home, they had everything in order.

His arm around Liv's shoulders, his thoughts focused on her and her turmoil, Ham walked her outside to the rental car. As predicted, the storm loomed overhead again. Low-hanging clouds, bloated with rain, scuttled across the sky. Hamilton and Liv got into the car just as the sky opened up and the storm attacked with a vengeance, this time supplying large hail and tree-bending winds. Against the roof of the car, the hail sounded like gun shot. Debris rolled over the ground and already the streets were awash with runoff.

Wide-eyed, Liv snapped on her seat belt. "Talk about Mother Nature's fury."

Ham stared out the windshield. He didn't like the looks of this storm. Something about it, something beyond the obvious, put him on edge. Making up his mind, he said, "I'd wait for it to let up, but I hate the thought of Jack home alone." He started the car and eased out of the lot into the street. "The sooner we get home, the better."

Watching the storm through the passenger-door window, she said, "I'm sure Jack will appreciate your concern." Then she glanced at him and added, "Don't forget, I want to get my car."

Incredulous, Ham tightened his hold on the wheel. "In this downpour?" He gave a grunt of disbelief. "No, I don't think so, babe. Those hailstones are the size of marbles."

Slowly, her head turned toward him. "I'm not one of your men, Lieutenant Colonel. You don't dictate to me."

Uh-oh. Maybe he'd worded that wrong. Ham worked his jaw and tried for an olive branch. "We can go back later and get it."

"It might rain all day, Hamilton, so don't go caveman on me. I want to go now while we're already out, and with the school day over, I don't have to worry about running into anyone. Not that I don't appreciate their concern, but… I'd rather not face a lot of sympathy and condolences right now." Her hands laced together in her lap. "Not after just making the arrangements. I need some time."

"Liv…"

"I've driven in rainstorms before, and I'll drive in them again. Since I'm usually alone, I don't have much choice."

She sounded entirely reasonable—but it grated on him that she'd ever been alone, without backup or support. He was with her now, and if he had his way, she would spend very little time alone in the future. "I'll have Doc bring it over tonight."

"I don't want to impose on her."

"She's a friend. She won't mind."

"I mind." When Hamilton didn't reply, she rolled her eyes. "For heaven's sake, rain hasn't gotten the best of me yet. Besides, I think we've driven out of the worst of it."

Hamilton didn't want to, but he had to agree. The sky had suddenly calmed, the rain fading to a mere drizzle.

"All right. But my agreement is under duress."

Grinning, she quipped, "Duly noted."

Because it was on the way, they reached the school in a matter of minutes. By the time Ham pulled into the mostly deserted school lot, the rain had completely stopped.

"Look at that," Liv said, pointing out the sight of the clear, sunlit skies moving in behind the storm. "You were worried about nothing."

Hamilton narrowed his eyes at the calm, greenish sky. He couldn't recall ever seeing anything like it.

Since Liv got out of the rental car, he did the same. She circled the hood to reach him and twined her arms around him in a bear hug.

Pleased with her open show of affection, Ham returned her embrace. "I like this new side of you. Kissing me and hugging me. I can get used to it."

"You better." She hugged him again before stepping away. "I intend to do it a lot over the next fifty years or so."

With that awesome promise, Hamilton forgot all about the oddly colored sky and walked with her to her car. "You know, this'll sound corny, and don't take it wrong, but I was hoping that sex would put us on better terms. I wanted to wait until you admitted that you cared about me. I figured sex would help seal the bond between us." A bond she had denied until recently.

Liv faced him with chagrin. "That's why you held out so long? Why you wouldn't sleep with me before? You needed me to commit verbally first?"

He trailed his fingertips over her jaw and chin. "Hey, I'm only human."

Her eyes widened. "You're admitting it? And here I thought you considered yourself superhuman," she teased.

"Yeah, well, if I had realized that sex would have such a profound effect on you," he said with a grin, "you can bet I would have gotten you naked years ago."

Feigning disdain, Liv lifted her chin. "I'll have you know it wasn't your skill in bed that did the trick." She unlocked and opened her car door, then faced Ham.

She was so damn cute, Ham thought. "It wasn't, huh?"

"No, it wasn't." She smiled up at him. "It was your promise to leave the military."

Those words struck Ham with the force of a missile blast. He went rigid. "I'm not leaving the air force, Liv. I've been clear on that."

The color leeched from her face. "But you told me—"

He knew exactly what he'd told her, and apparently she hadn't been listening. "I said I'd make you happy. And I will." He caught her arms, feeling the tension vibrating from her. *With compromise.*

An awful expression stole over her features—disappointment, betrayal, pain. In a barely audible rasp, she said, "I told you I couldn't."

Damn it, he didn't want to have this conversation in an elementary school parking lot. He didn't want to have it at all. He'd thought, hoped, that they were already beyond it, well on their way to those fifty years she'd mentioned earlier. "We can make this work, Liv. Just hear me out."

She swung away, more wounded than she'd been over her father's death. Her stance, her expression, her tone, all reeked of accusation. "You told me to trust you. You said you loved me."

Jaw tight, eyes burning, Ham leaned his face down to hers and forced out the words he'd thought would save him. "You told me the same."

Liv flinched away from him, not denying her love, but not reaffirming it, either. Without looking at him, she whispered, "I…I need to think about this." She got into her car and started the ignition.

Ham leaned on her door. Fury, hurt and something more, something almost desperate, churned inside him. "Don't do this, Liv." He'd given her so many chances, and he'd made so many plans….

Big tears hung from her lashes. Her mouth moved, but nothing came out. Then compressing her lips, she closed her door, forcing Ham to step away.

And she drove out of the lot.

Without caring that he stood there, watching her go.

Christ, it hurt. His heart felt trampled. His lungs burned as he sucked in needed oxygen, trying to fend off the awful pain.

How could she claim to love him, and then not

even hear him out? So many emotions conflicted inside him, leaving him lost, furious and desolate.

Then he heard it.

A low roar that gained in cadence by the second. The hair on the back of his neck stood on end. A gust of wind blasted across the lot, buffeting his back, almost knocking him off his feet.

Ham jerked around, seeing that eerie green sky with new understanding. Tornado sirens began screeching throughout the small town of Denton. Off in the distance, roiling with fury, an enormous black cloud churned, spitting off spectacular shards of lightning, sucking at the ground. He stood transfixed as, a good distance from the school, the funnel scrambled from spot to spot, licking here and there with destructive negligence—hurtling toward the path Liv had taken.

No. Disagreements and disappointments ceased to exist. He had to get to Liv, had to protect her. The rental car tore out of the parking lot while Ham frantically searched the wet road for the taillights of Liv's car. As he drove into the path of the tornado, the roar grew, louder and louder. Fierce winds fought the vehicle. Debris lashed the windshield, diminishing visibility. Hamilton registered it all, but wasn't swayed from his purpose.

His heart beat in time to his panic, his hands locked on the steering wheel, his gaze unblinking.

Finally, he spied Liv's car, stopped in front of the

two-lane bridge. The river surged out of its banks, rising high, grabbing trees and rocks with the same ferocity as the tornado did.

His foot hard on the gas pedal, praying to reach her in time, Hamilton watched in horror as a gusting wind spun her car, throwing it hard against the guardrails. Metal ripped away, leaving a gaping hole on the side of the bridge. As if in slow motion, her car kept turning until finally, it dropped into the muddy, fast-churning water below.

Ham hit the brakes, bringing his car to a jarring halt. Too far away.

Too damn far away.

He exploded from the vehicle in a dead run. Fear drummed in his ears, louder and more insistent than the destructive force of nature. Prayers tripped silently from his mouth, adrenaline pumped through his veins.

With survival instincts honed by air-force training, he absorbed the destruction around him without letting it slow him down. Beyond the bridge, houses came apart, their roofs flying away, the walls pulling apart. Downed utility poles left live wires snapping and dancing.

Even as Ham pushed forward against the powerful wind, a huge elm split in half and crashed into the water close to where Liv should be.

He roared out his anger, refusing to believe she could be hurt. Something struck his face, knocking him back two steps, bringing him to his knees. He was back up in the same second, swiping away the warm trickle in his eyes, ignoring the sudden pain in his right arm and leg.

Jolting to a halt on the entrance to the bridge, he saw Liv's car stuck half in, half out of the fast-rising water, a few feet from the fallen tree.

There was no hesitation.

Gripping what remained of the guardrail, Ham bolted over the side, close to the shore, and landed hard in the slippery slope of muddy grass, sliding and stumbling to her car. He saw Liv's face, pale with fear, in her driver's door window.

She screamed, but Ham couldn't hear her words over the storm and sirens and his own clamoring terror.

Slogging in a rush through the water, he reached her in seconds. She pulled frantically at the door handle, but the car had buckled with the impact, jamming it shut. The trickling into his eyes threatened to blind him, but he again swiped it away.

Unwilling to wait seconds, much less any longer for rescue workers to reach her, Ham located a heavy rock. When Liv saw him lift it, she scampered back against the passenger's side door.

The window shattered into gravel-size pieces of glass. "Are you okay?" Ham yelled, and she nodded, crawling back toward him, her hands frantically brushing his face, her sobs loud and undisciplined, bordering on hysteria.

"It's okay," he yelled. "I've got you." And he hauled her out and into his arms.

For reasons Ham couldn't understand, Liv fought him, cursing and crying.

He tossed her over his shoulder, pinning her legs down with one arm, holding her backside still with the other. He plodded to the shore with difficulty, each step a strain as the air around them sucked and pushed and pulled.

The deafening roar seemed all around them, and the rain struck with bruising force.

Dropping with Liv in his arms, Ham covered her. He sunk his strong fingers deep into the soggy ground to anchor her. His lungs compressed, and he felt light-headed—but no way in hell would he ever let her go.

At the worst of it, he feared they'd both be torn away and his mind rebelled at such an awful thought. His muscles cramped and trembled with his efforts. Raw determination gripped him. He prayed.

And then the air calmed, the roar drifting away. Gasping for air, trying to protect her from harm with his body, Ham couldn't manage to loosen his hold. If anything happened to her...

"Shh." Liv touched him, stroking his hair, his neck, with shaking fingers. "It's over, Ham. It's okay. I'm okay."

Despite her reassurances, he couldn't unclench. Hell, he could barely draw air.

"Ham, it's okay. Let me see your head."

His head? Who gave a shit about his head? He found he couldn't speak so he just pressed in closer to her.

Her lips grazed his cheek. "Ham, please." Tears sounded in her voice. "You need to go to the doctor. Your head is bleeding."

By small degrees, with mammoth effort, he regained control of his body. The loud rushing of water mixed with the sirens—but the awful, animal roar of the tornado was gone. Hamilton pulled his face from her neck.

With his heart in his throat, he looked at her beautiful, bruised and dirty face. "You're really okay?"

Her lips were bluish with cold, trembling with an excess of emotion. She blinked hard, sobbed again, and said, "I love you so much." And then, with a surge of anger, "How could you *do that?* How could you go over that bridge—"

"You went over."

"And *risk yourself* and—"

Ham swallowed hard. "I love you."

Another sob, louder and more irate, and she said, "Damn you, *I love you, too!* I don't want you hurt."

His left eye twitched. "Then don't hurt me."

Gasping, she stared at him, touched him again, so gently. "Look at your head."

"That'd be a little hard for me to do."

And she smiled. "Look at what's happened to you. You're bleeding and you're going to need stitches and…and…" Openly sobbing again, she clutched at him. "Oh, God, Hamilton. I'm so sorry. I love you. All of you."

Finally, he could breathe again.

"Please," she whispered against his neck, "can you forgive me?"

"Yes." He didn't have any choice. He could never stay angry at her, not for anything. And then, with caution and a heavy heart, "Will you marry me?"

"Yes," she said, with an equal lack of hesitation, almost shouting that one, wonderful word. "Yes, yes, yes."

Ham heard the approach of a siren, not the tornado warning, but an emergency vehicle. Soon, they'd be rescued. He cupped her cheek, turned her face up to his.

His blood had gotten in her hair, mixed with mud and leaves. Her nose was red with cold, her lips pale. "I'm not going to let you change your mind."

"I'm not going to stop loving you."

"I'm still in the air force."

She gave a small nod. "I know."

"It's who I am, Liv."

"I know." She touched his lips. "I've been so afraid of losing you that I've wasted precious time."

"Yes." She needed to hear the truth. There could be no more misunderstandings.

"I'm so sorry."

He kissed her. The sirens drew nearer, then suddenly ceased, leaving a hushed vibration in the air. "Those plans I told you about? I can be a permanent professor at the academy in Colorado Springs. We can't live here, I'm sorry. But we wouldn't have to keep moving."

Her lips parted. "But…wouldn't that mean you'd have to give up the squadron commander position?"

"For you, yes."

A firefighter yelled down from the bridge. "Hey! You two okay?"

Ham turned and lifted one hand. "We're fine."

"Stay put and don't move. We'll come to you." The man moved away, shouting orders.

Ham turned back to Liv. "So. Will you marry me, Liv Amery? You'd be a colonel's wife, because the position comes with a promotion. And before you answer—"

"Yes."

"You should know that I'll be on active duty even longer—"

"Yes."

"And it'll take me two years to get my Ph.D. before we can move to the academy."

"Yes."

His heart lightened. "I'll still get full pay and—"

She pressed a hand to his mouth. "Yes, Ham. Yes to everything. Yes, no matter what you decide to do. Yes, because I love you. Yes, yes, yes."

That awesome emotion had him in its grip again. Then the firefighters were there, toting blankets and water and first-aid kits.

As Ham rolled off Liv, the man closest to him said, "That's a nasty gash you've got."

"I'm fine."

The firefighter gave him a dubious look. "Let me get a stretcher down here."

"No need. I can stand."

Frowning, the firefighter asked, "Are you sure?"

Ham turned to Liv. "Tell me again."

She smiled, paying little mind to the man who wrapped her in a blanket and began cleaning the mud from her face, checking for wounds. "I love you, Lieutenant Colonel Hamilton Wulf."

Hamilton smiled. "Yeah, I can stand." He pushed to his feet and offered Liv a hand.

"Lieutenant Colonel?" the firefighter repeated. "I'm impressed."

Liv laughed, wrapping her arms around Ham. "Yep, me, too."

The firefighter grinned. "Sir, if you'll come this way, we'll have you both checked out in no time."

And minutes later, they were on their way to the hospital—and on their way to a very bright future.

EPILOGUE

GIVEN THE DESTRUCTION caused by the tornado, the funeral for Liv's father took place later than planned. Parts of Denton were devastated, and Hamilton and Liv pitched in with the cleanup and repair. Luckily, despite the crippling damage to structures, there were no lives lost.

The sun brightened the clear blue sky the day they laid Colonel Weston Amery to rest. Several people spoke at the service, including Hamilton. Their words gave proof of the incredible man her father had been—not an overly loving dad, but a leader who had selflessly given to his nation.

With full military honors, the ceremony included a flag-draped casket, pallbearers in dress uniform and a highly impressive twenty-one gun salute. As the flag lowered to half-mast, "Taps" played, giving respect to a fallen comrade.

In military fashion, step by step, the pallbearers folded the flag into a neat triangle. Hamilton held Liv's hand, giving her his support, his love, during the very moving moment when the men knelt before her, their heads bowed.

They handed her the flag. "Our deepest regrets, with the thanks of a grateful nation."

Warm tears slid down her cheeks, and an invisible fist squeezed her heart. Yes, regret clouded her past. But her future was with Ham. He was her hero, and he was the hero for a vast number of unknown citizens, in America and around the world. They were the people he'd sworn to protect. The people for whom he'd willingly endangered his life.

No finer man existed, and she wouldn't regret one single second of being his wife, no matter what risks the future brought.

As he'd said, life was always uncertain.

But Hamilton's love and loyalty weren't. She had him, she loved him—and that meant she had it all.

* * * * *

COSMO RED-HOT READS
FROM HARLEQUIN
launches with
#1 *NEW YORK TIMES* BESTSELLING AUTHOR

SYLVIA DAY

A brand-new line of sexy, contemporary romance stories
for today's fun, fearless female, launched by
America's premier author of provocative fiction.

EBOOK ON SALE
AUGUST 15, 2013

EBOOK ON SALE
NOVEMBER 12, 2013

TRADE PAPERBACK ON SALE
NOVEMBER 12, 2013

A sizzling new miniseries about unexpected reunions,
bittersweet revenge and the fight for redemption!

Be sure to connect with us at:

Harlequin.com/Newsletters

Facebook.com/HarlequinBooks

Twitter.com/HarlequinBooks

H HARLEQUIN®
www.Harlequin.com

COSMOLAUSD

REQUEST YOUR FREE BOOKS!

2 FREE NOVELS
FROM THE ROMANCE COLLECTION
PLUS 2 FREE GIFTS!

YES! Please send me 2 FREE novels from the Romance Collection and my 2 FREE gifts (gifts are worth about $10). After receiving them, if I don't wish to receive any more books, I can return the shipping statement marked "cancel." If I don't cancel, I will receive 4 brand-new novels every month and be billed just $6.24 per book in the U.S. or $6.74 per book in Canada. That's a savings of at least 22% off the cover price. It's quite a bargain! Shipping and handling is just 50¢ per book in the U.S. and 75¢ per book in Canada.* I understand that accepting the 2 free books and gifts places me under no obligation to buy anything. I can always return a shipment and cancel at any time. Even if I never buy another book, the two free books and gifts are mine to keep forever.

194/394 MDN F4XY

Name _____ (PLEASE PRINT) _____

Address _____ Apt. # _____

City _____ State/Prov. _____ Zip/Postal Code _____

Signature (if under 18, a parent or guardian must sign)

Mail to the **Harlequin® Reader Service:**
IN U.S.A.: P.O. Box 1867, Buffalo, NY 14240-1867
IN CANADA: P.O. Box 609, Fort Erie, Ontario L2A 5X3

Want to try two free books from another line?
Call 1-800-873-8635 or visit www.ReaderService.com.

* Terms and prices subject to change without notice. Prices do not include applicable taxes. Sales tax applicable in N.Y. Canadian residents will be charged applicable taxes. Offer not valid in Quebec. This offer is limited to one order per household. Not valid for current subscribers to the Romance Collection or the Romance/Suspense Collection. All orders subject to credit approval. Credit or debit balances in a customer's account(s) may be offset by any other outstanding balance owed by or to the customer. Please allow 4 to 6 weeks for delivery. Offer available while quantities last.

Your Privacy—The Harlequin® Reader Service is committed to protecting your privacy. Our Privacy Policy is available online at www.ReaderService.com or upon request from the Harlequin Reader Service.

We make a portion of our mailing list available to reputable third parties that offer products we believe may interest you. If you prefer that we not exchange your name with third parties, or if you wish to clarify or modify your communication preferences, please visit us at www.ReaderService.com/consumerschoice or write to us at Harlequin Reader Service Preference Service, P.O. Box 9062, Buffalo, NY 14269. Include your complete name and address.

From *USA TODAY* bestselling author

B.J. DANIELS

Danger runs high and passions burn hot in Montana's wild country.

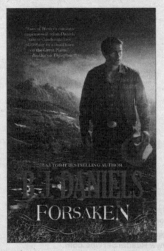

Big-city detective Bentley Jamison is a long way from home in the Beartooth wilderness when local rancher Maddie Conner's sheepherder goes missing. As the new deputy sheriff, Jamison is determined to protect every inch of this rough terrain—starting with unraveling a mystery that has left Maddie a wide-open target. But desire that flares hotter than their tempers only raises the stakes when a fierce storm traps them in the high mountains. Caught in a killer's sights, Jamison and Maddie must trust one another, because now survival…and love…are all that matter.

www.BJDaniels.com

Be sure to connect with us at:

Harlequin.com/Newsletters
Facebook.com/HarlequinBooks
Twitter.com/HarlequinBooks

LORI FOSTER

77806	ALL RILED UP	___ $7.99 U.S.	___ $9.99 CAN.
77779	GETTING ROWDY	___ $7.99 U.S.	___ $8.99 CAN.
77761	BARE IT ALL	___ $7.99 U.S.	___ $9.99 CAN.
77708	THE BUCKHORN LEGACY	___ $7.99 U.S.	___ $9.99 CAN.
77695	RUN THE RISK	___ $7.99 U.S.	___ $9.99 CAN.
77656	A PERFECT STORM	___ $7.99 U.S.	___ $9.99 CAN.
77647	FOREVER BUCKHORN	___ $7.99 U.S.	___ $9.99 CAN.
77612	BUCKHORN BEGINNINGS	___ $7.99 U.S.	___ $9.99 CAN.
77582	SAVOR THE DANGER	___ $7.99 U.S.	___ $9.99 CAN.
77575	TRACE OF FEVER	___ $7.99 U.S.	___ $9.99 CAN.
77571	WHEN YOU DARE	___ $7.99 U.S.	___ $9.99 CAN.
77491	UNBELIEVABLE	___ $7.99 U.S.	___ $9.99 CAN.
77444	TEMPTED	___ $7.99 U.S.	___ $9.99 CAN.

(limited quantities available)

TOTAL AMOUNT	$ _____
POSTAGE & HANDLING	$ _____
($1.00 FOR 1 BOOK, 50¢ for each additional)	
APPLICABLE TAXES*	$ _____
TOTAL PAYABLE	$ _____

(check or money order—please do not send cash)

To order, complete this form and send it, along with a check or money order for the total above, payable to Harlequin HQN, to: **In the U.S.:** 3010 Walden Avenue, P.O. Box 9077, Buffalo, NY 14269-9077; **In Canada:** P.O. Box 636, Fort Erie, Ontario, L2A 5X3.

Name: _____

Address: _____ City: _____

State/Prov.: _____ Zip/Postal Code: _____

Account Number (if applicable): _____

075 CSAS

*New York residents remit applicable sales taxes.
*Canadian residents remit applicable GST and provincial taxes.

HARLEQUIN® HQN™
™ www.Harlequin.com

PHLF1113BL